Dreaming *of* Flight

Also by Catherine Ryan Hyde

Boy Underground

Seven Perfect Things

My Name Is Anton

Brave Girl, Quiet Girl

Stay

Have You Seen Luis Velez?

Just After Midnight

Heaven Adjacent

The Wake Up

Allie and Bea

Say Goodbye for Now

Leaving Blythe River

Ask Him Why

Worthy

The Language of Hoofbeats

Pay It Forward: Young Readers Edition

Take Me with You

Paw It Forward

365 Days of Gratitude: Photos from a Beautiful World

Where We Belong

Subway Dancer and Other Stories

Walk Me Home

Always Chloe and Other Stories

The Long, Steep Path: Everyday Inspiration from the Author of Pay It Forward

How to Be a Writer in the E-Age: A Self-Help Guide

When You Were Older

Don't Let Me Go

Jumpstart the World

Second Hand Heart
When I Found You
Diary of a Witness
The Day I Killed James
Chasing Windmills
The Year of My Miraculous Reappearance
Love in the Present Tense
Becoming Chloe
Walter's Purple Heart
Electric God/The Hardest Part of Love
Pay It Forward
Earthquake Weather and Other Stories
Funerals for Horses

Dreaming
of Flight

A Novel

Catherine
Ryan Hyde

Published by Lake Union Publishing, Seattle

www.apub.com

Amazon, the Amazon logo, and Lake Union Publishing are trademarks of Amazon.com, Inc., or its affiliates.

ISBN-13: 9781542021586 (paperback)
ISBN-10: 1542021588 (paperback)

ISBN-13: 9781542033060 (hardcover)
ISBN-10: 1542033063 (hardcover)

Cover design by Shasti O'Leary Soudant

Printed in the United States of America

Dreaming
of Flight

Part One

Late Spring, Early Summer

Chapter One

Like the Mouse

Stewie

Stewie rolled his shoulders and pulled the collar of his shirt away from his sweaty neck. It bothered him when it clung there.

He had never gone down to that last house before, because he hadn't needed to. He had always sold out his wagon full of eggs without needing to walk so far.

There was a good quarter of a mile gap along the banks of the lake—an undeveloped spot with no houses. It was after six but still quite hot in an unseasonably summerlike spring. Four of his regular customers had not been home, or had not answered their doors.

If his sister, Stacey, had been there, she would have encouraged him to pack it up. She would have told him to put the leftover cartons in their fridge and try again the following day. But they wouldn't be as fresh the next day. Stewie prided himself on the freshness of his eggs. It was what set them apart—what made them more than worth what he charged for them. Maybe his customers didn't notice the difference. Maybe they didn't care. But Stewie cared. In fact, he was unable to *stop* caring.

He sighed slightly and trudged off in the direction of the last house.

It was located at the narrowest part of the lake. The shallows. The view from the deck was more mud and less water. The gray two-story house looked to be in poor repair and needed a good coat of paint, but it was clear that someone lived there. Stewie could see lights on in the windows.

It didn't seem feasible to haul his little red Radio Flyer wagon up the concrete steps, so he left it at their base. He carried with him one carton of eggs, cradled in his arms like a baby or something else of great value.

He rapped on the door.

Immediately he heard a shuffling of feet, and the door swung wide. In the open doorway stood a woman a little older than Stewie's much older sister. She had dirty-blonde hair, and looked tired. Her face gave Stewie the impression that all of life was simply too much for her. Hiding behind her legs was a shy little girl of about five or six.

"Fresh eggs, ma'am?"

"I don't need any eggs," she said, as if it was a thing he shouldn't have required her to say. "I get my eggs at the market like everybody else."

"Oh, but these are much better than what you get at the market. They're fresh. I gathered them myself just this morning. That's a big part of what makes them better. The ones at the market, if you knew how old they were, why, you'd never want to buy them again."

"It doesn't matter how good yours are," she said, swiping a stray lock of hair off her sweaty forehead as if in frustration. "What matters is that I already bought the ones I have, and so I don't need any more."

Stewie opened his mouth to thank her anyway, but he never got the chance.

A big voice bellowed out from the living room behind the woman and child. An older woman's voice.

"I might want some eggs," the voice said. "Did you ever stop to think about that?"

Stewie looked past the woman and girl, but saw no one.

Then the two people in front of him retreated, and an older woman filled the open doorway—filled his field of view. For a moment, Stewie got a little tingle of recognition down his spine, as though he were seeing a familiar person. But in the very back of his mind he knew *which* familiar person he felt he might be seeing, and it was someone it would have been plainly impossible for Stewie to see.

She was a small woman, and stooped. She had that curved upper spine his grandmother had used to have. Something about the size and shape of her struck him as deeply familiar. But then he looked closely at her face, and it was not his grandmother. Of course it wasn't. His grandmother had died.

Stewie didn't figure he understood death particularly well. In his eleven years of life—or more accurately, during the parts of it when he had been old enough to process and remember such things—death had never come near him or touched down close to him until the day Gam left the world. Still, he wasn't a baby, and he knew enough to know that after someone dies, you don't see them again. Not ever. They don't just open a door on the other side of the lake.

Anyway, she didn't look all that much like Gam. Her features had more of a pinched appearance, and her gray hair was cropped short.

But that profile. That silhouette.

And she was *a* grandmother. Not his, but still . . .

"Fresh eggs, ma'am?"

"How do I know they're fresh?"

"Oh, you can ask anybody, ma'am. I got happy customers all over town."

She narrowed her eyes at him. It struck him that she seemed not to like him, which was odd. They'd only just met, and he hadn't done anything especially controversial.

"Well, I'm not going to walk all over town asking everybody, now am I?"

"I just gathered these myself this morning. Slipped a hand right under the hens and pulled them out, and they were still warm." He gently undid the lid of the carton and extracted one big, brown-shelled treasure. Held it up for her to see. "I don't mind giving out a free sample," he said.

"I don't know that it's necessary. I guess I can buy a dozen. You can come back next week and I'll let you know what I think. If you were right, I'll say so and buy some more. If you were wrong, I'll tell you to your face. How much are they?"

"Four dollars a dozen, ma'am."

He watched her eyes fly open wide.

"*Four dollars?* That's a bit steep, don't you think? They're only two dollars a dozen at the market. Three if you get the fancy ones that're supposed to be from happier chickens."

"But these are much better eggs, though."

"Because they're fresh." It was not a question. She seemed to say it a bit derisively, as though making fun of him for saying it so many times.

"Not only because of that, though. I give the hens better feed, and that makes a big difference. Those giant egg factories, they just feed any old thing. The cheapest thing possible. And you can see the difference. See it with your own eyes. The yolks on those market eggs are all pale and sickly. Barely even yellow. Like when your blood is . . . what do you call it again when your blood is iron poor?"

"Anemic?"

"Yeah. That. You crack open one of *these* eggs and the yolks are bright orange. Bright. And it's not just all about looks, either. That shows they're more nutritious. And also, you said it like it's a joke, but it's no joke. Happier hens really do lay better eggs. When they're all stressed out, it hurts everything. All their body functions."

"Yeah, maybe. But *four dollars.*"

He held his sample high. His fingers were a little dirty, and he felt self-conscious about that. He hoped all her attention was going to the beautiful egg.

"You could take the sample," he said.

"No. That's okay. I'll try a carton. One week, like I said. Let me get my purse." She turned as if to walk away, then stopped. She peered at him over her shoulder. "Oh, but they're not fertilized, are they? I hate fertilized eggs. That nasty little spot of . . . well, anyway, it's disgusting."

"No, ma'am. They're not fertilized."

"You sound pretty sure."

"Oh, I'm very sure."

"How can you be that sure?"

"Because we don't have any roosters, ma'am. Not a one. My sister works nights at the county hospital. She's doing her internship as a nurse, and she can't abide any roosters at the crack of dawn. And when you don't have any roosters, then no eggs ever hatch, and so you never *get* any roosters. It's a foolproof way to do a thing like that."

She shook her head slightly, but then she went ahead and walked off to get her purse.

Stewie waited patiently on her stoop. He turned his head and watched the sun, which was beginning to set on a long slant over the lake. Then he looked back to the open doorway and carefully placed the sample egg back in its carton.

When he looked up, the older lady was standing at the door, counting money out of a change purse. All coins.

"I hope you don't mind change," she said.

"No, ma'am. I don't mind. It all spends the same."

She dropped the coins into his palm. He didn't count them out, because he didn't want to offend her by seeming suspicious. He simply closed his fist around it all and handed over the carton of eggs.

"Aren't you a little young to be selling door to door?" she asked him, that look of tight disapproval on her face.

Stewie shrugged. He got the question a lot.

"Not sure how old you need to be, ma'am."

"I guess I'm just wondering how the job fell to you. Why doesn't somebody else in your family do it?"

"Nobody else *to* do it, ma'am. My brother never could. It's just not something he could manage. And my sister works nights as a nurse, like I said. Besides, they're really my hens. I mean, they were my grandmother's, but now they're mine because I was the only one who wanted to keep them after she was gone. That pretty much makes them my project. But I don't mind. I like it. I like the hens and I like the people I meet going door to door."

"And your parents are okay with you doing it?"

"Oh, they died a long time ago, ma'am."

He watched the look in her eyes change. She looked softer now. More like she was sorry to be giving him a hard time. More like she was wishing she hadn't asked so many questions.

"Oh," she said. "Well, I'm awfully sorry to hear it."

"It's really okay," Stewie said. "I was just a baby, and I don't remember them at all. I figure you can't miss somebody you don't even remember."

He did not say that he remembered his grandmother, and missed her terribly. In fact, he had never said that out loud to anyone. He never tried to articulate how much her death felt like a burning loss that left scars on every one of his days. Maybe partly because he figured it went without saying. Maybe partly because he would have had no idea where to begin with a thing like that.

"What's your name, son?" she asked.

He thought that was nice, that she asked. Because if you don't care one way or another about somebody, you don't bother to ask.

"Stewart Little, ma'am. I go by Stewie."

"Oh! Like the mouse."

"Now, why do people keep saying that to me?"

"Nobody ever told you why?"

"Well, sort of, they do. One person said it was a book, and another said it was a movie. But I never read any book like that, and it's not like we have a movie theater anywhere around here. Besides, it doesn't make any sense. If he's a mouse, well . . . mice don't have first and last names."

"It's just a fictional story, though."

"Well, it shouldn't be *that* fictional. I mean, you can make up a thing that never happened for a story. That's all fine and good. But you have to stick at least a little bit to how things actually are. I mean, when the animals start talking and having first and last names, that just seems like going too far."

She offered a wry little smile, and he got the uncomfortable sense that she found him amusing, and not in any way he had intended. Then he started to blame himself for having said too much.

"I'll come back next week," he added. "Like you said."

"You do that."

And with that she stepped inside and closed the door.

Stewie stood on her stoop a moment, watching the sun hover over the watery horizon. Then he trotted back down the concrete steps to his wagon. He was happy to have sold one more dozen, but he was still bringing three cartons back unsold. They wouldn't be quite as perfectly fresh the next day, and that felt like a loss.

He trotted home as quickly as he could, the wagon rattling loudly behind him. There was no time to try again at the doors of the customers who hadn't been home before. Stacey would be awake, and she would worry about him if he was much later. And besides, she would be making something for dinner. His poor grumbly stomach needed dinner, and the sooner the better.

He counted out the change as he went along. The old woman hadn't cheated him. Every cent of the four dollars was there.

He wondered over the fact that she had asked his name and he had given it, but she had never told him hers. Grown-ups were like that, though. They figured every little thing about you was their business to know. Meanwhile they kept a tight hold on their own information, because, after all, you were just a kid.

It made Stewie feel that growing up couldn't come quickly enough.

———

When he got home, Stacey was standing in front of the stove, her back to him, her long blonde hair gathered into a ponytail. He came up behind her and rose up on his tiptoes to look over her shoulder. She was a petite young woman, but Stewie wasn't especially tall, either.

"What did you make?" he asked her.

"Tuna noodle casserole."

"My favorite!"

"That's why I made it."

She looked around at him, and seemed to notice the three cartons of eggs cradled in his arms.

"Oh, that's too bad," she said. "People not eating them as fast as they were?"

"More like some of my regular people just weren't home."

"Well, put them in the fridge and then go get Theo. Tell him dinner is on the table. Or it will be, anyway, by the time he gets out here."

Theo wasn't the fastest walker in the world, but Stewie didn't figure she meant it that way. Didn't think she meant anything special by it. More likely she just meant she was serving dinner immediately.

Stewie almost moved off in the direction of the fridge and ended the conversation, but something stopped him. Something that was on his mind and seemed to be tugging at him.

"I met a lady today," he said.

"Yeah?"

"I'm just saying."

"What was it about her?"

"What do you mean?"

"Well. There's got to be some reason why you're telling me about her."

"Oh. Right. I guess. She just sort of . . . she reminded me a little bit of Gam."

Stacey's head shot up and she looked straight at Stewie. Tried to look right into his eyes, but he averted his gaze to prevent it. In the split second before he did, he saw the look in her eyes. It was the one he had been trying to avoid causing. The one that said she hurt for him. Stewie figured you should never say anything that makes someone hurt for you, because that just seemed awfully close to hurting someone. Closer than he wanted to go, anyway.

"Aw, Stewie," she said, and her voice said the same thing as her eyes.

"I'm just saying."

"It's not her, though. You know that, right?"

"Of course I know that. I'm not a baby."

"I just don't want to see you get hurt."

It was the closest they had skated to discussing Stewie's feelings about the loss of Gam, and it reminded him that he had his reasons for not skating so close.

He opened the fridge door and stashed the leftover eggs inside.

"I'll go get Theo," he said.

Theo was in his room, staring at the screen of his laptop.

"Hey," Stewie said.

When Theo looked up and saw him standing there in the open doorway, he burst into a perfect Theo grin, all that dark shaggy hair hanging over his eyes. That went a long way toward healing the discomfort in Stewie's gut.

"Dinner," Stewie said.

"All right. Good."

Some people found Theo's words a little hard to understand, but Stewie was not one of those people.

He stood still in the doorway and watched his brother reach for his canes. Stewie called them canes, but some people called them crutches. They were the short metal kind with a brace that wrapped around Theo's arms, and a handle for him to grip. It would have been easy for Stewie to help by fetching them for his brother and handing them to him, but he had long ago learned that Theo didn't want the help.

"What'd she make?" Theo asked, slipping his arms into the metal braces.

"Tuna noodle casserole."

"Your favorite."

"I know, right? But you like it, too. Don't you?"

"Sure I do. What's not to like?"

They walked down the hall together, Stewie slowing his steps to match his brother's straining pace. Even though Theo didn't stand up very straight when he walked, he still towered over Stewie.

"Sell all your eggs today?"

"Nah. I had to bring three cartons home."

"They'll be just as good tomorrow."

"Not *just* as good."

"Good enough, though."

"I guess."

The truth was, they would be plenty good enough for everybody but Stewie, and they both knew it.

———

It was a little after five in the morning, and still pitch-dark. Stewie walked from nesting box to nesting box, feeling his way. There was no electricity in the henhouse.

He had been cooing to the hens from the moment he arrived at the door. That way they would know it was him.

"It's only Stewie," he sang, making up different sets of notes as he went along. "Not a fox. Not a coyote. Not a mean stray dog. Only your friend Stewie."

He spoke to each hen by name, though he knew it was possible to get their names wrong in the dark. They tended to go for the same nesting box day after day, but it was not an absolute. Then again, he wasn't sure they knew their names anyway. Mostly he figured they just liked it when you cooed and sang to them.

"Thank you, Bessie," he said when the tip of his fingers touched her egg, the back of his hand against the warmth of her feathery underside. "You did a good job today."

He wrapped his hand around the egg and gently slid it out from under her, placing it in the basket that hung over his left arm. It was growing heavy from all the eggs. It was a good morning for eggs.

That made Stewie furrow his brow, because he still had those three dozen left from the previous day. He would have to offer the day-old eggs at a discount. If that wasn't enough to move every carton, he would have to give them away. He would always have preferred to give them away over wasting them. They were something like a gift from the hens, something useful and good they gave in return for their feed and their safety from the outside world at night, and that wasn't a thing to be taken lightly.

"Thank you, Clara," he cooed. "You did a good job today."

"Thank you, Weezy. Let's see. Am I missing anybody?"

He would check again before he went out on his door-to-door rounds that afternoon, because in the light he would catch any he had missed. But first, a three-egg breakfast. And then school.

———

Stewie and Theo walked to the school bus stop together, as they did every weekday morning, Stewie slowing his pace to match his brother's stride. Now and then he glanced behind them, and side to side, to see if any of the other local kids were close by. Stewie always looked around for trouble, figuring it was best to be prepared. Theo always looked straight ahead, seeming to choose the focused approach.

Stewie heard a bark of laughter, and swiveled his head around.

Mark McMaster, Paul Sweet, and Jason Regalus had fallen in a few yards behind them. Jason was doing an exaggerated imitation of Theo's challenged stride.

"I'm a spaz," Jason squeaked in a high, girlish voice, his arms flailing like windmills, his steps drunken looking and awkward.

His friends laughed more enthusiastically.

Stewie felt his shoulders stiffen and rise up around his ears. His face felt hot, and he figured it was beet red. He spun around to confront them, but in the process his brother was able to catch his eye. Theo shook his head at Stewie, gravely, but almost imperceptibly.

Stewie faced forward again and marched along with his neck bent forward and his head down. But it was beginning to eat at his belly now. It flashed through his head that if this were a cartoon, he would have a dark cloud over his head, and maybe steam coming out of his ears.

"How does this look?" Jason asked his friends, imitating—exaggerating— Theo's inexact, slurred way of speaking.

Stewie could not stop himself from looking over his shoulder. Jason was combining his impression of a spastic person with an unrealistically effeminate one. Stewie looked forward again, his ears burning.

"Hell, you still look better than Theo," Paul Sweet said.

Stewie spun again to face them.

"Don't," Theo said, his voice calm. "Just let it go. If I can let it go, so can you."

"I'm sorry, Theo," Stewie said. "I just have to."

He launched himself at Jason, seeming to fly through the air. Or, anyway, that's how it felt to him. When he hit his target, he knocked

Jason off his feet and landed on top of him, raining blows around his head and neck. Jason was more Theo's age, fourteen or fifteen, so older and bigger. But Stewie had the advantage of surprise and sheer determination.

For a moment, Jason seemed unable to overcome those advantages. All he could seem to do was cover his head with both arms.

Then Stewie felt himself pulled away by the back of his shirt. The grasping hand pulled him to his feet, and roughly backward. The goal seemed to be to throw Stewie over onto his back on the sidewalk, but Stewie kept his balance and resisted falling.

A moment later Jason Regalus filled his line of vision. Filled up his world. And then the world was nothing but a fist racing in Stewie's direction. It hit him hard on the bone at the outside of his left eye socket, and sent him flying. He landed roughly on his back on the sidewalk, hitting his head.

He looked up at the flickering of sunlight between the tree leaves, trying to get his bearings. Trying to pull himself back together. A second or two later that pastoral scene was replaced by Jason's huge, sneering face.

"Loser," the face said. "Freak."

Then Jason stepped over him and the three boys walked on, talking and laughing.

Stewie squeezed his eyes closed and left them that way for a few seconds. When he opened them, he saw the familiar and welcome face of his brother leaning over him. Peering at him close up.

"You okay?"

"Sure."

"Why do you do it, Stewie? Why do you even bother with them? They're not worth it."

"I can't help it," Stewie said, gingerly touching the tender area near his eye. "Some things just won't let you not do them."

Chapter Two

That Egg Child

Marilyn

Marilyn was working on a jigsaw puzzle at the dining room table when she heard the doorbell ring. It briefly startled her, and made her think of trouble. But then she decided it was probably just someone to see the little girl. Lots of kids came by wanting to play with the girl.

Marilyn did not get up to get it. She let Sylvia answer the door. After all, it wasn't even her house.

The puzzle was a tableau of seventeen kittens in different patterns and colors. Marilyn was not especially fond of kittens, but it had been the only 1,000-piece puzzle the gift and drugstore had had left in stock. And besides, the price had been reduced. Marilyn had been counting that little stash of stolen money every day, and it wasn't getting any bigger.

She heard Sylvia, from the front door, say, "What the Sam Hill happened to *you?*"

She still did not get up. She was working on the outside border of the puzzle, and her eye had just landed on a corner piece. She placed her middle finger on it so she couldn't lose it again.

Sylvia stepped into the room.

"Someone here to see you," she said.

Her words hit Marilyn like a club to her belly. Like a truck crashing through her world. She had always known that sooner or later they would find her. That there would be a knock on the door and it would be for her.

And that would be the end of her freedom.

"Who?" she said, her voice trembling. Not moving a muscle.

"It's that egg child," Sylvia said.

The news filled Marilyn with a rush of anger. She had just had a good scare, and it was all that little boy's fault.

"Now what's he doing here? I told him to come back in a week, not a day."

"Tell *him*," Sylvia said. "Don't tell *me*."

And she hurried back into the kitchen.

Marilyn sighed, and rose, placing the corner piece in the pocket of her dress for safekeeping. She strode to the door, doing her best to keep her anger intact. But when she saw the poor little guy, everything flew away.

"Oh my goodness," she said. "What on earth happened to you?"

His left eye was a road map of purple and green bruising, and so swollen that he could barely hold it open. In his arms he held the predictable carton of eggs.

"Nothing much, ma'am," the boy said, averting his eyes toward the doormat.

"It doesn't look like nothing much. It looks like somebody hurt you. Does somebody hurt you at home? Your father?"

"No," the boy said. "I told you."

"What did you tell me? Oh, that's right. Never mind. You said your parents died when you were a baby. Who do you live with, then?"

"Just my sister, and my big brother. But they don't hit me."

"*Big* brother?"

"Yes, ma'am."

"I thought you said he was younger."

"I never said that."

"You said something. What was it? Something you said definitely made me think he was younger. Oh! I know! You said he wouldn't be able to sell eggs door to door like you do. That he just wouldn't be able to manage it."

"Oh, right. I did say that. But not because he's too young. He has trouble with . . . physical . . . things."

"Meaning what?"

"He has a disability."

"Oh. Why didn't you just say so? Is he the one who hit you?"

"No, ma'am! Never. Theo would never do a thing like that."

"Your sister?"

"No, ma'am. She's nice to me. It was one of the kids from school."

"You should report it to somebody."

"Well. No. Not exactly I shouldn't, ma'am. Because I . . . sort of . . . started it."

Marilyn put away her sympathy for him, and shut down her feelings. He had given her a reason to stop caring about his situation. It felt welcome.

"Well, then I have no sympathy for you at all. What kind of boy goes around starting fights? Why, I'm not even sure I want a boy like that coming to the door. And what are you doing here today, anyway? I told you to come back in a week, not a day. Do you honestly think I ate a whole carton of eggs since yesterday?"

"No, ma'am. I don't think that. If you don't want me here, I'll just go."

His eyes were still trained down to the mat, but Marilyn could see his face, and he looked so dejected that it made her hurt for him. It also made her feel guilty, and she didn't like it when people made her feel guilty. It always made her want to lash out at them even more harshly.

He turned and shuffled off the stoop, hanging his head.

"Wait," she said.

He did. He stopped, and waited to hear what she had to say, but he didn't turn around to face her.

"Tell me why you came again so soon if you knew I didn't need more eggs."

Still he stood with his back to her. But he turned his head slightly and answered the question.

"I had three cartons left over at the end of the day yesterday. I sold two just now by only asking two dollars for them. Because they were day old. I was going to give you the last one for free. If you wanted it."

"Turn around," Marilyn said.

The boy did as she had instructed. He kept his eyes down, as if memorizing something about his own shoes. He didn't seem inclined to say anything more.

"Day-old eggs aren't really a thing," she said. "Because eggs are not like baked goods. They last a lot longer than that."

"I know it, ma'am. There's not much you can tell me about eggs that I don't already know."

"Then why would you act like they're practically ruined after the first day you gather them?"

He shrugged. A bit helplessly, she thought.

"I just pride myself on the fresh part," he said. "It's sort of the . . . specialness of the whole thing."

"And here's another question. If you sold the other two cartons for two dollars each, why are you offering to give me that one for free?"

He shrugged again. He seemed heartbroken, and his heartbreak seemed to make him listless.

"I don't know. Just something I thought you might like."

Another shot of that unwanted guilt ran through her, and it made her want to push him away again. He was trying to reach out to her in some way, but she had no idea why. And whatever his reasons for trying, Marilyn didn't want anyone reaching out to her. The last thing she needed was anybody taking an interest in her situation. Coming around asking questions. Wanting to know her.

"That would be a lot of eggs to eat in one week," she said.

His face fell even further, if such a thing was possible.

"Did you even try them?"

"Yes. As a matter of fact, I did. I had two poached on toast this morning, and you were right. They're excellent. Much better than what Sylvia buys at the market."

That seemed to perk him up some. He reached the carton out to her, still not meeting her eyes.

"Well, you got nothing to lose by taking this, then. It's free."

But for the moment, she did not take it.

"You still never told me why it's free for me and two dollars for anybody else."

The boy only shrugged. Then he set the eggs gently on the stoop and retreated down the stairs.

"I hope you can use them," he called over his shoulder.

"Not the best thing for my cholesterol to double up on eggs."

"It's only just the one week."

He was almost down to road level, where his empty wagon sat waiting, so she had to call out quite loudly.

"Wait!"

He stopped and looked up at her.

"Yes, ma'am?"

"Thank you. That was thoughtful."

That caused his face to brighten considerably.

Marilyn walked three steps to the spot where the carton of eggs sat waiting on her stoop. She bent over with effort and picked it up.

"I told you my name," the boy called up the stairs. "But you never told me yours."

"That's right," she said. "I didn't."

And with that she walked back through the open doorway and into the house, closing the door behind her. She purposely did not look back to see how that statement had settled with him. She had been made to feel guilty quite enough for one day.

She walked into the kitchen and stashed the eggs in the fridge.

Sylvia was standing at the stove making macaroni and cheese from a box for her daughter, who was a picky eater.

Marilyn looked over her shoulder, not trying to hide her judgment and disdain. She was on edge now from her interaction with that boy, and feeling the need to let her irritation out somehow.

"Why don't you just insist that she eat what everybody else is eating?"

"We've been through this, Marilyn. Don't tell me how to raise my daughter. You barely know us."

"Fine. Whatever. It's just not how I was raised."

"I don't really care how you were raised," Sylvia said, in such a voice and tone as to end the conversation.

As Marilyn walked back into the dining room to finish her puzzle, she decided she should have told the boy her name was Marilyn. Since it actually wasn't. The adopted name would get him no closer to the truth, and nothing would be lost. She would tell him if he came back again. But he probably wouldn't, after the careless way she had treated him.

Too bad, because the eggs really were superior, and they were spoiling her for the supermarket variety, which would never taste as good to her again.

She sighed, and decided she was glad she at least had two dozen.

She sat back down in front of the puzzle, but she could no longer find that corner piece. She searched and searched, right up until dinner, and for almost an hour after dinner, but it never turned up.

It wasn't until bedtime, when she emptied out her dress pockets of tissues before putting the garment in the laundry hamper, that she found it.

She was surprised, to say the least, and though she searched her mind relentlessly, she was never able to recall having put it there.

Chapter Three

All Too Much

Stewie

"Stacey?" he called, hovering in the open kitchen doorway.

The poor failing bird held oddly still in his arms. He could feel her warmth. He could feel her heart beating.

"What is it, honey?" Stacey called back.

She was scrambling a skillet full of eggs at the stove, her back to him.

"I got a problem, Stacey."

"What kind of problem, hon?"

Still she did not turn to look. If she had turned to look, she would have immediately seen what kind of problem it was.

"It's Mabel. I think she's sick."

He took two steps into the kitchen as he said it, and his sister turned at the same moment. Stewie saw her face darken.

"Oh, honey, no. You can't bring her into the kitchen."

"But she's sick."

"Even so, though, Stewie. She's a barnyard animal. We don't bring barnyard animals into the kitchen."

"Okay, I'll take her into my room, then."

He tried to boldly march in that direction before she could argue.
It didn't work. She was quick to argue.

"Stewie, stop. Honey, I know you're upset. But we can't have any of
the chickens in your room. They're not . . . you know . . . housebroken."

"I could wrap her in an old towel, then."

"Still, what's wrong with the henhouse, Stew?"

"Nothing. Usually. But Mabel is sick."

Stacey wiped her hands on a kitchen towel and took a chance
by leaving the eggs unattended on the stove. She crossed the room
to him.

"What makes you think she's sick?" she asked, lightly stroking the
honey-brown feathers near the back of Mabel's small head.

"She's just . . . I don't know how to say it. Kind of . . . dull. She's
just not moving around very much. And her eyes aren't bright like they
should be."

He looked into Mabel's eye—that fine, perfectly round, black-
centered disk. The bird appeared to look back at him.

"Stewie. Honey. Mabel is old. I think she's just old."

"Well, whatever she is, I have to help her. I'm going to take her to
the vet."

"Oh, please, Stewie. I can barely afford all the expenses around this
place as it is."

"You don't have to pay. I'll take her with my egg money."

"That'll use up an awful lot of your egg money."

Stacey appeared to suddenly remember the scrambled eggs on the
stove. She raced back and stirred them with a wooden spatula.

"I still have to do it," he said. "I have to help her."

"I just hate to see you lose all those savings. Especially if the vet
tells you she's just old and there's nothing can be done about it. Then
it would just be a waste of all that money you worked so hard to save."

Stewie and his sister had a deal. He kept half of the money from
his egg sales and donated the other half to help out with the family

expenses. And he had saved quite a nice bundle over the past year. But it was all about to be gone, and he didn't care. Mabel needed him.

"Wait a minute," Stacey said. "You can't take her to the vet this morning. You have school."

Stewie took a deep breath and steeled himself for a fight. Not a literal one. But it was one he had to win. He felt as though his whole body had turned to stone. He would not be swayed or bested.

"I'm going to miss school. To take her to the vet. And you're going to write me a note."

He watched her furrow her brow and frown.

He quickly added, "Please."

For a minute or so, she did not answer. Just dished up the scrambled eggs onto plastic plates and set two pieces of toast on each plate.

Then she said, "Go get Theo. Tell him breakfast is ready."

It seemed she was ignoring the fact that Stewie would be going to get him with a chicken in his arms. But as he walked by her, she glanced over, and noticed. And Stewie knew she had just forgotten. She opened her mouth as if to speak, then seemed to think better of it. She closed her mouth again without saying a word.

When Stewie arrived back at the table, he sat down to eat with the hen on his lap. Mabel swiveled her head and looked around, seeming to notice the difference in her surroundings. Stewie just shoveled breakfast into his mouth, careful to avoid his sister's eyes.

He heard her sigh deeply.

"Okay," she said. "Okay. I know you're very emotional about the hens. If it means that much to you, I'll write a note. I'll say you have to stay home with a sick pet. But as long as that bird is in the house, I want her wrapped in an old towel. I mean, that's just basic sanitation, Stewie."

Stewie drew in a long, audible breath and then let it flow out of him again. It felt as though he were breathing for the first time in hours.

"Thanks, Stacey," he said.

Then he left the table to go fetch an old towel.

—

He sat in a hard chair in the vet's waiting room, Mabel wrapped in the same towel and held carefully on his lap.

The woman next to him had a huge cat. Looked to be maybe twenty pounds or more, that cat, with a long, matted coat. The cat was in a wire carrier, but it could see Mabel, and Mabel could see the cat. And the cat had begun making a strange hunting sound in its throat. And Mabel read that sound loud and clear. She began to fuss, and cluck, and Stewie could feel her stress. He held the hen more tightly to his chest. He could feel the woman staring at his bruised eye.

"I won't let anything bad happen to you," he whispered near Mabel's feathered head.

"I've never seen a chicken in a vet's office," the cat woman said to Stewie.

She was fiftyish, with carefully coiffed blonde hair, wearing a fussy-looking pantsuit with nylons at her ankles. And Stewie did not understand her. He understood what she had just said to him. But he did not understand *her*.

"I don't see anything strange about it. She's a small animal. This is a small animal vet."

"But that's a barnyard animal. Isn't there a different kind of vet for barnyard animals?"

In his head, Stewie began a litany. *Stop talking to me. Stop talking to me. Stop talking to me.*

He tried not answering her as an option. The cat continued to break the silence with that strange staccato hunting sound in its throat. Mabel continued to be stressed out by the sound.

"I'm only asking," the woman added.

"There are other kinds of vets who make farm calls," Stewie said. "But they come out to see horses and cows because it's easier to have the vet come see your horse or cow than it is to bring them in. But those are large animal vets. Mabel's not a large animal."

The young woman behind the counter, the vet's assistant, looked up from her computer monitor. She seemed to have been following the conversation in a distant way, but the stress in Stewie's voice had apparently drawn her attention.

"We don't mind seeing birds," she said. Loudly, into the waiting room in general. Then she smiled at Stewie.

He smiled back, and breathed a little easier.

"What's wrong with her?" the woman asked Stewie.

He couldn't tell if she asked out of genuine concern, or just wanted to pick at him further.

"I don't know, ma'am. If I knew, I wouldn't need to come to the vet. I come here because the vet knows what's wrong with an animal better than I do. She might be sick, or she might just be old. I'm not sure."

Stop talking to me. Stop talking to me. Stop talking to me.

"Does she lay?"

"No, ma'am. She hasn't laid for quite a while now. Years."

"Well, you just eat them when they stop laying."

Stewie felt his shoulders jerk up around his ears. His face felt hot. He jumped up, holding Mabel close against his belly, and stood with his back up against the wall in the far corner of the room.

"I don't want to talk to you anymore," he said, wishing he had said it much sooner.

He had been conditioned to be polite to grown-ups as long as was humanly possible. But now and then it came around to bite him, just as it had now.

"I'm only talking sense," the woman shouted over to him.

"He said he doesn't want to talk to you anymore," the vet assistant said.

Stewie shot her a grateful glance and she smiled at him again.

Amazingly, the terrible woman shut up. When a grown-up asked her to stop, even a young grown-up, there seemed to be no question that she would comply.

It made Stewie feel, as he so often felt, that growing up could not come soon enough.

The cat never once shut up.

———

The vet was a woman with a kind face and a gentle voice. Still, her voice bothered Stewie. She spoke to him as so many people did: as though he were made of glass. He had no idea if he was really as fragile as people seemed to think, but he got that tone a lot, and it made him uneasy.

She held a stethoscope to Mabel's chest, and looked into her eyes with a bright light that Mabel clearly didn't like. It made Stewie feel guilty for bringing her here. But he'd had to bring her. Life had given him no choice.

"How old is your hen?" she asked him, in that voice that made him squirm.

"Well now. I've been trying to think. Trying to figure that out. She was one of my Gam's first hens. The others from that first batch got taken by foxes. Oh, it was horrible. We've fixed up the henhouse a lot since then. I was only about one or two when she got the first hens, and I'm eleven now. And Gam passed away almost a year ago . . ."

"Oh," the vet said. In a more normal voice. "She's ten or older."

"Yes, ma'am. I guess so."

"That's old for a hen."

"I suppose it is, ma'am."

"I could do a blood test if you wanted me to, but I think you'd be spending your money for nothing." She straightened up and turned off the bright little light, and Mabel seemed to relax some. "Whether there's something we see in the tests or not, she's already lived longer than most hens do. Old age explains the listlessness you're seeing. If I were you, I'd just take her home and keep her comfortable. I can tell that you care a lot about her, but you seem to be a smart boy, and I think you're old enough to understand that none of us lives forever."

"Yes, ma'am," he said, wrapping his arms around Mabel. If he'd said more, he would have cried, and that would have been humiliating.

"She's lucky to live such a long life. Most chickens don't get to die of old age. Most people eat them when they stop laying."

Stewie yanked the hen off the table. As he did, she got her wings free and flapped wildly. He wrapped her wings in his arms again and headed for the door.

"I didn't mean you should have."

"Whatever, ma'am."

"I'm sorry I offended you. I wasn't speaking for it or against it. It's just a fact."

"Right. Got it. We have to go now. I'll just pay on the way out."

He reached into his shorts pocket and removed the massive lump of bills. It was all in ones and fives, with the very occasional ten, so the bulge in his pocket had been absurdly large. He wanted her to see that he could afford it. Although he did feel the visit had been a waste, just as Stacey had warned him it might be.

"There's no charge for that," the vet said. "Good luck with your hen. I hope she lives a while longer. And I'm sorry if I upset you. You're not the only young person raising animals that they think of as pets and other people think of as food, and I know that's a hard thing."

"Thank you, ma'am," Stewie said. "I appreciate getting your time for no charge."

And he carried the ailing hen in the direction of home.

As soon as he got clear of the vet's parking lot, the tears got out, and he didn't try to stop them. You can only hold back tears for just so long.

—

He was crying in a corner of his room when Stacey stuck her head in. It was much later that evening, and he and Mabel had been curled up together that way for quite a long time.

"I'm about to leave for work, and . . . Oh. You still have the hen in the house."

"I have to," he said, holding her more closely. "I have to have her in because I don't know how much time she has left, and if I leave her in the henhouse, then she might . . . you know . . . might . . . run out of time. And then she would be alone. You know. *Then*. And nobody should have to be alone at a time like that. But if it really bothers you, I'll sleep in the henhouse with her tonight."

He clearly heard Stacey sigh.

He was facing the corner, not looking at his sister, because he didn't want her to see him crying. Even though she probably knew anyway. Even though she could undoubtedly hear it in his voice.

A moment later he felt her sit on the floor behind him. He felt her warm hand on his shoulder.

"Oh, Stewie," she said, and it was in that awful voice people used. The one that let on that they were afraid of breaking him. "Don't sleep in the henhouse. I guess it's okay so long as you keep her wrapped in that towel. I just wish . . ."

He didn't want to ask her what she just wished. If he asked, she would tell him.

A moment later she restarted herself, and told him anyway.

"I just wish you didn't take everything so hard. For your own sake, I mean. Sometimes I wish I could wave a magic wand over you and fix it so you didn't have to care about everything so deeply."

"What's wrong with caring?"

"Nothing's wrong with it. The thing about caring is you want to have *some*. You want to care, but in the right measure. Not too little and not too much. If you care too much, then something like this happens and it just makes you so sad."

"But then good things happen and they make me extra happy. Besides. If you waved a magic wand over me and made me different, then I wouldn't be me."

She gave his shoulder a little squeeze. "Well, I wouldn't want *that*," she said. "I have to go to work now."

"'Kay," Stewie said, a light sob bending the word.

She left his room, and he expected to hear the front door click open and then closed. But he waited, and things didn't seem to go that way. Instead it sounded as though she was talking on the phone.

Still pressing Mabel to his belly, Stewie stood, walked to his bedroom door, opened it a crack, and eavesdropped.

"It would have to be on a sliding scale. Definitely. Jeez, Fred, I can barely afford to keep this family going as it is. Actually, free would be ideal, but I know that might be hard to come by. Maybe a free clinic or something? Do free clinics even do counseling?"

A pause, during which she did not talk, and Stewie pictured her listening. Just for a split second he imagined he could supercharge his ears and hear what was being said on the other end of the line, but of course that was only a foolish imagining.

"Oh, no, not *that* brother," she said suddenly. "No. Theo is the one with the disability, but emotionally he's really balanced and strong. He's quite amazing, actually. Everybody thinks so. No, this is Stewart. He looks perfect on the outside and he's the nicest little guy, but he just takes everything so hard, and it's scaring me. He's been really fragile since our grandmother died. He's taking care of her chickens now because he couldn't bear to have them sold off. He just couldn't bear to part with them. Now he never talks about her, but he's just completely obsessive about her chickens, and I think it has more to do with losing Gam, but I'm afraid to even bring it up because he just seems so fragile. But I guess I said that already. Maybe I *should* bring it up, but I'm not a professional. I just thought maybe this is a job for a professional. I'm not sure if you know that his parents—our parents . . . well, our father and his mother, my stepmother, died in an accident when he was just a few months old. And I've never really known how to deal with that original loss with him. I used to try to talk about it, and he said it didn't matter to him, because he doesn't remember them, and you can't miss what you don't remember. But I'm not sure that's true. I think kids do miss having parents, even if they didn't know them at all. And I think his grandmother had to fill that outsized role and now she's gone and . . . oh, I don't know, Fred. It's too much for me. It's just all too much."

Another pause, during which Stewie noticed that his ears were burning with shame.

"No, I checked with our insurance. It's pretty bare-bones. They just don't cover mental, not even with a diagnosis. And I don't think there *is* a diagnosis in there, Fred. I think Stewie just is who he is."

Pause.

"Okay. Thanks. Give me a minute. Let me get a pen and I'll write that down."

Stewie shrank back into his bedroom and eased the door closed. He settled back in the corner with Mabel and tried to think about something else, but the words he had overheard stuck with him. They stuck *into* him, from the feel of it, like the scratchy tag you forgot to take off a brand-new shirt. They bothered him the way it bothered him when his sweaty collar stuck to his neck. And no matter how hard he tried to leave them behind, they clung.

And there was nothing he could do against them.

He couldn't even fail to care.

Chapter Four

You Just Have to Know Stewie

Marilyn

The knock on the door made Marilyn jolt upright. Her heart immediately began to hammer.

She had heard that egg boy knock twice, and this wasn't his knock. This was much harder and louder. More sure of itself.

She had been lounging on the couch, reading a magazine. Or perhaps it would be more accurate to say she had been looking at the magazine. Half a dozen times she'd begun an article about baby sea turtles, even though she didn't find the subject especially interesting. But each time, her mind wandered within the first paragraph and she'd had to begin again, grudgingly acknowledging that she had absorbed nothing.

She set the magazine down and froze there a moment, hoping Sylvia would answer the door. But she heard no movement or sound.

After a time she stood, carefully and silently, and crept around the house in hopes of finding Sylvia and getting her to answer the door. Even the little girl would do at a moment such as this.

No one seemed to be home.

Marilyn ransacked her brain in search of some memory of where they had gone or why, but found nothing. Maybe she had not been told. Or maybe she had, but the information surrounding it was no longer there to be accessed.

A second hard knock jolted her out of those thoughts.

She tiptoed quietly into the front room and over to a window she knew could not be seen from the front stoop. She drew back the curtain an inch or two, hoping to see what kind of car was parked in front of the house. Would it be a police or sheriff's patrol car? Or one of those vans from Eastbridge? Or would they send a dark, unmarked vehicle for that exact reason? So she would not know to fear it from the window?

There was no car. No vehicle in front of the house at all.

Would they have parked around back on purpose, to fool her into opening the door?

But as she watched the deserted scene in front of the house, she noticed the wagon. The little red Radio Flyer wagon, like the kind kids used to have when she was a child. They hadn't changed much in all these years, those red wagons. Sitting inside it were half a dozen egg cartons.

She sighed in relief. And moved to the door.

She had thought he would not come again, because she hadn't been all that friendly or nice. But she had been aware that this was the day he *would* come, if he was still so inclined. And she had hoped he would over-look her rudeness, because the eggs were very good, and she had finished both cartons.

She threw the door open, ready to compliment him on his new, bolder knock.

On the stoop stood a boy she'd never seen before. He was older than the egg boy, whose name she could not recall. He could have been as old as fifteen or sixteen, but it was hard to tell. He could also have been thirteen or fourteen. He was lanky and tall, even though he didn't hold himself up very straight on his brace-type crutches. He needed a haircut. His masses of curly dark hair fell well over his eyes. But those eyes. Those dark-brown eyes of his. There was something very clear and knowing in them.

He was wearing an olive-green T-shirt, untucked, hanging down over his jeans, but with a belt on the outside of it. That seemed odd.

"Stewie specifically asked me to come to your house today," the boy said. "To ask if you're ready for another dozen."

He had a way of speaking that clearly marked his disability as some type of palsy. Marilyn knew many people would find his speech hard to understand. She did not find it hard. Not at all. She'd had a roommate at Eastbridge who had been the survivor of a fairly serious stroke. Marilyn had become an expert in following words not clearly enunciated.

She missed that woman as the thought ran through her head, which struck her as strange, because she hadn't realized she'd been particularly attached to her old roommate. She hadn't thought of herself as being attached to much of anyone anymore.

"That was thoughtful of him," she said, still not remembering his name, though she knew she'd just been told it. "I was hoping to get another carton."

"You'll have to come down the stairs to the wagon," he said. "I'd be afraid I'd break some if I tried to bring them up."

As she walked down the stairs with him, slowing her pace to match his, it hit her who this was.

"You're his brother," she said.

"Yes, ma'am."

"He told me about you."

"Oh? What did he say?"

"Just that it would be too hard for you to do the route with the eggs. No offense intended. On his part, I'm sure, and definitely not on mine."

"No offense taken, ma'am. It did require some figuring."

They had both reached the wagon now, and they stood staring down at it, as though it might have something relevant to add to the conversation.

Marilyn was aware of a warm breeze on her face. It blew the leaves in the trees over her head. She could hear that pleasant rustling. The sun had dipped to a long slant behind the lake, low enough that she could glance at it briefly without hurting her eyes. It struck her that she did not go outside nearly often enough, and that she had missed it sorely.

"How are you able to pull the wagon and use your crutches all at the same time? That is, if you don't mind my asking."

"We figured out how to hook the handle to my belt in the back. And people can come get their own eggs, and there's a coffee can in the corner of the wagon so they can put the money in themselves."

"Still, it must be hard going up and down all those stairs."

"Not at all, ma'am. I'm very good at stairs, just so long as I don't have to carry anything at the same time."

She lifted the lid of a carton, checking to be sure that none of its eggs were broken. It was perfect. The eggs were mostly brown with a few green, all smooth and fairly large. They looked appealing. She replaced the lid and cradled the carton in the crook of one arm.

"I'll have to go back upstairs and get the four dollars."

But for some reason, maybe just out of sheer instinct, she drove her free hand into her skirt pocket and felt some bills there. She scanned her mind for a memory of having put bills in her skirt pocket. Usually she didn't carry money in her pockets, feeling it was safer in her purse. Had she done it in anticipation of a delivery of eggs?

She pulled the money out, unfolded it, and spread it out to count. It was four singles. That must have been what had happened.

"Wait, never mind. Turns out I have the egg money right here."

She dropped it through a slot cut into the plastic lid of the coffee can. She watched the boy attach the wagon handle to the back of his belt with a makeshift hook. It seemed to have been fashioned from a wire coat hanger, like the kind they still used at the dry cleaners.

A thought struck her. As soon as it did, she realized it should have struck her much sooner.

"Is your brother sick?"

He had just begun to move away, trailing the noisy wagon behind him on the cracked and broken sidewalk. He stopped in response to the question, and glanced at her over his shoulder.

"Not exactly," he said.

That seemed curious.

"What do you mean, not exactly? I don't really know what that means. He strikes me as a boy quite dedicated to his egg route."

The boy smiled. It was a broad grin, toothy, and with an infectious quality.

"Oh, Stewie is all of that and then some, ma'am."

She made a mental effort to retain the name this time. *Stewie,* she repeated in her head. *Stewie. Stewie. Stewie.*

"I'm guessing it must be something pretty major, if it has you out doing his route for him."

She watched his eyes. His gaze seemed to cut down toward the pavement, and his forehead furrowed just a bit.

"It's major *to him,*" the boy said after a pause. "I don't know if it would seem major to anybody else."

Marilyn felt her patience straining. Though, truthfully, she was not at all sure why she felt so concerned about any of it.

"You're talking in riddles. What's going on with . . ." But the name was gone again. ". . . your brother?"

"One of the hens is sick. She's old. We think she's dying."

"Oh. Well. That's too bad. I'm sorry to hear it, but I guess you're right. I'm not sure why that would be something that would keep him away from his route. He seems to love it so."

"You'd just have to know Stewie."

Stewie, she repeated in her head. *Stewie. Stewie. Stewie.*

The young man looked more than ready to walk away from her, and from the conversation, but he was polite enough to stay and answer her questions if she wanted him to.

At least the boys in that house were well raised, she thought. *The way people used to raise their children in my day.*

You didn't see that much anymore.

"I'll bite," she said. "Tell me what I don't know about Stewie."

"I'm not really sure if it's something you can *tell,* ma'am. It's not like a story. It's just something you'd understand if you knew him better. He's just very . . . I guess *intense* would be a good word. He just feels everything real strongly. Takes things hard."

"I see." But she wasn't at all sure she did see. "When does he go back to selling the eggs himself? He's bound to get over this eventually."

"Not really, ma'am. I doubt he'll ever get over losing the first of Gam's original hens. He still hasn't nearly gotten over losing Gam, and that might be part of the problem here. But he can grieve a loss and deliver eggs at the same time. It's not that. It's that the hen is alive, but it seems like she doesn't have a lot of time. And Stewie doesn't want her to die all alone. Now he won't leave her side. After . . . you know, after that situation wraps up . . . I expect he'll go back to living his life no matter how he feels."

Marilyn tried to process that assessment in her mind, but it wouldn't add up to anything that made sense.

"That's ridiculous. He can't just stay with a hen every minute. What about school?"

The boy shifted his gaze down to the broken pavement again.

"He hasn't been going."

"Well, that's just silly. And wrong! A boy his age has to go to school. Why, there's an actual law to that effect. Isn't there? There must be someone in that house who can insist he go to school."

Marilyn could feel a sense that she was overstepping her boundaries. Inserting her opinion where it might have had no business going. But she felt so strongly about the subject that she did not feel inclined to stop.

"There's our sister. And she tried. But again, ma'am, you just have to know Stewie. You can insist all you want, but he's not leaving that hen's side. We did get his schoolwork from his teachers and we brought it home, and he's been doing it in his room or in the henhouse."

"Don't tell me the hen is allowed in his room!"

"Okay, ma'am. If you don't want to know, I won't tell you."

That should have been enough to satisfy her on the subject. Or so a voice in her head told her. He was keeping up with his schoolwork. What more did she need to hear? But it still left her feeling irritated. Regardless, she decided to go no further down that conversational road.

"Give your brother a message for me, please. Tell him I said thank you for making sure I got fresh eggs this week. I did want them. But I was worried that he wouldn't want to come back. I was a little . . . well. I'm not quite sure how to say it. If I had it to do over again, I might speak to him a bit more kindly."

She had been glancing up at the rattling leaves as she spoke. Possibly because it wasn't the easiest confession in the world to make. When she stole a glance down at the boy, he had an odd, knowing look on his face. Which was not at all what Marilyn had expected.

"Why are you looking at me like that?" she asked him.

"Oh, nothing. Just something I was thinking. Just, my sister and me . . . Well, I was just saying to her the other day . . . what am I trying to say here? We think maybe that's why he likes you so much."

Marilyn felt bowled off her feet in a way that felt unfamiliar. And unwelcome.

"He likes me? Why does he like me? I haven't been all that kind to him. As I was just saying."

"Here's the thing, though. That's just how our gam was. Not all that kind. I'm not saying she was mean. She wasn't a bad person at all. Just, whatever she was thinking, she'd just level you with it. She didn't waste any time trying to think of the nicest way to say a thing. She'd just spit it out. He's used to that. And he misses her, even though he won't say so. But I might've mentioned that already."

"Oh," Marilyn said.

Then she could not think what to say next. The conversation had taken a very odd turn, and she had not quite caught up to how she should feel about it. For that reason, she said nothing more.

The boy had apparently grown impatient, and he began to walk off again.

"I'll give Stewie your message," he said over his shoulder.

"Wait. Maybe you shouldn't. Maybe he'll like me better if I'm not sorry." She was half kidding, but she didn't much like the joke once she heard it outside her head.

The boy stopped walking. Turned back. It was hard for him to turn around completely, though, because of that hook attaching the wagon handle to his belt.

"What do you want me to tell him, then?"

"Tell him my name is Marilyn. He asked me my name last time he was here, and I wouldn't tell him. Which was rude."

"Okay, will do. I'll tell him your name is Marilyn and you specifically wanted him to know it. He'll like that."

"And your name is?"

"I'm Theo," he said.

He turned and pulled the wagon away. And she stood in the dappled shade and watched him go.

Stewie and Theo, Marilyn repeated in her head. *The boys' names are Stewie and Theo. Stewie and Theo. Stewie and Theo. Stewie and Theo.*

Then she realized it was probably an unnecessary risk to stand outdoors in plain view for so long. She carried the eggs back up the stairs and into the kitchen, where she stashed them in the refrigerator.

She sat back down on the couch and picked up her magazine, pleased because she had memorized the boys' names. That proved that her children were exaggerating when they criticized her memory. Didn't it?

The boys' names are . . .

But the boys' names were gone.

Chapter Five

We're All Tired

Stewie

Stacey came into his room after dinner, at about seven o'clock in the evening.

He was curled on his bedroom rug, wrapped around the small cardboard carton that contained the ailing Mabel. He had fixed it up with newspaper on the bottom, which made it easy to keep it—and his room—clean.

She sat down behind him on the floor and put one warm hand on his shoulder. Stewie wished she would go away, because he could feel her energy. She had that "I'm going to gently argue with what you're doing" energy.

"We need to talk," she said. It was the bad pity voice, only it was getting worse.

"What about?"

"About what we'll do if this goes on a lot longer."

"It won't."

That seemed to surprise her. For a moment, she had no comeback. Stewie lay still, enjoying the silence. Watching the way the evening breeze through his open window twirled the thin white curtain around.

"How do you know that?"

"Mabel told me."

Another silence, this one more strained. For as long as it lasted, Stewie couldn't enjoy anything.

"Honey? You don't think . . . you don't hear Mabel saying anything to you, do you?"

It hurt Stewie, that she would allow for the possibility that he was crazy. He felt it as a burning in his belly while he answered.

"Of course not. What do you think about me, anyway?"

"Don't take offense. Just something about the way you said it. You said she told you it wouldn't be much longer."

"Well, she did. And I can't explain how. You just have to understand animals. You don't spend very much time with them, so you don't know. You just have to let them know you're listening. That you want to hear what they want to say. If they know somebody cares how they feel, they'll let you know. I can't explain it. You just pay attention, and you know."

"Okay. That sounds reasonable, I guess. So she told you . . ."

"She's tired."

"Well, honey. We're all tired."

"She's different tired. Her lungs are old. She can't breathe with them as well as she used to. Pretty soon she just won't want to do it anymore. It's too hard."

His sister didn't answer right away, so he went back to watching the curtain blow. The breeze through the window had begun to feel cool, and it felt good to him. But he wasn't sure if the draft would be good for Mabel, so he pulled a thin, threadbare blanket over most of her box. He left open the part where her head was. He didn't want to make things harder for her poor old lungs.

"You said something a minute ago," Stacey began. "It was something about knowing someone's listening and wants to know how you feel. Is that something that would help you as much as it helps the animals?"

He chewed that over for a minute, but wasn't sure how to get it to take on a recognizable shape in his brain.

"What would that be like?"

"Like I would take you to an appointment. With a new person. And you would tell this person how you feel and what your problems are."

"Why a new person? Why not an old one like you or Theo?"

"Because . . . this person . . . it would be someone whose job it is to know how to solve people's problems."

"I don't have problems," Stewie said.

"Really? Are you sure?"

"I have *sad*. But that's not the same as problems. Problems are something you have to figure out a way to solve. You can't solve sad."

"Maybe . . . ," she began. For a moment it struck Stewie that she was listening to him, but with more than just her ears. Listening more the way he listened to the hens. ". . . maybe *not knowing how to deal* with sad is a problem. And maybe there's somebody who could help you solve that, by learning to deal better with your feelings."

Truthfully, Stewie wasn't sure how he felt about that. What he was able to sense didn't seem very positive. But apparently it was important to Stacey, and she didn't ask much of him. It was rare for her to push him in any direction.

"Could I bring Mabel?"

"I was thinking maybe we'd do this later. After she's gone and doesn't need you anymore. You said yourself it won't be very long."

"I guess I could try it," Stewie said, though he knew he would regret having said so as the time drew nearer.

"You're a very fine little guy," Stacey said. "And I appreciate you."

That made everything worthwhile. That replaced the burning in his belly with a warm buzz that seemed to have a vibration to it.

"In the meantime," she said, "is there anybody it would help you to see? Somebody you might want to have come here for a visit? Maybe a friend from school? You haven't been getting out much."

"No," Stewie said. And he did not feel inclined to elaborate.

"You have friends at school, right?"

"Yeah. Sort of. But nobody who'd be any help with a thing like this."

"Okay. Well, if there's anybody else you can think of . . ."

She began the process of pulling to her feet as she spoke.

"Maybe Marilyn," he said.

"Who's Marilyn?"

She was towering over him now. He did not look up.

"That lady I told you about."

"The one you said reminds you of Gam?"

"Yeah. That one."

"Stewie. Honey. We hardly know that lady. She's just somebody you sold eggs to a couple of times. I'd feel funny asking her to come here for a visit."

"It's okay. You don't have to, then. You just asked if there was anybody . . ."

"I would just feel . . ."

"Theo knows her. Maybe Theo could ask her."

Stewie heard his sister sigh. She sounded tired. Mabel-tired.

"Let me think about that," she said.

And she left his room and left him alone. Left him to wonder if his family was really brave enough to do a thing like that for him or not.

———

Stewie clutched Mabel more tightly to his belly and dug into his spaghetti.

He looked up—a bit guiltily, though he hadn't meant it that way—at Stacey and then Theo. They both returned his gaze evenly.

"I know what you're thinking," Stewie said.

"Oh?" Stacey sounded far away in her own head, as though she barely heard herself saying it. "What am I thinking?"

"That I told you six days ago it wouldn't be much longer. That Mabel told me it wouldn't. And it was true. That was all true. All about how her lungs are getting weak and it's just too much trouble. And how pretty soon she just won't want to do it anymore. It just won't be worth it. But . . ."

He found it hard to finish that thought.

"But what?" Stacey asked.

When she asked it, Stewie realized she was tired and exasperated. It came through in her voice.

Theo's head was up, and he was staring at Stewie. Waiting, apparently. But he did not choose to jump into the conversation.

"It's hard to think how to say it."

"Try. I'm having a little trouble understanding."

"It's her life."

"Yeah. I know it's her life, honey."

"No, I mean *it's her life*. Her one life. People want their lives. Right? Everybody wants their life. Right?"

"Not everybody," Theo said, in that deep bass voice he had developed. "People commit suicide."

"Theo!" Stacey barked. "That's hardly appropriate at the dinner table."

"Well, they *do*." He looked down at his plate of spaghetti, his face flaming red. "I'm just saying."

Stacey sighed deeply and turned her face back to Stewie. "We'll give it a little more time, honey. But we can't do this forever."

———

Stewie was convinced—and would forever feel—that his beloved hen had understood Stacey's final proclamation at the dinner table earlier that evening. He knew she hadn't understood the words, because chickens don't understand much English. Still, he felt she must have picked up on the overall feelings surrounding the situation.

Because she woke him that night and told him it was time for her to go.

How she woke him he would never know. He couldn't have felt any movement from her, because she was in her box. And he didn't think she had made a sound. But he was bumped out of a dream just as surely as he would have been if someone had shaken his shoulder.

He had been curled up on the rug, around her box, but he sat up and turned on the soft light beside his bed. He looked into her eyes and she looked back.

"Okay," he said, and started to cry. "If that's the way it's got to be."

He carefully scooped her up into his arms and held her softly to his chest. She made a quiet sound in her throat. Then she pulled in a huge, deep breath. For a moment Stewie's heart soared, thinking she was telling him she could breathe again. But as she let the breath out, he could feel what was happening. He could feel that it was her last one.

It just kept going. As though she had hung on to a certain amount of oxygen at the end of every other breath she had exhaled, all her life, but this time she was letting the last of it go. Her body softened, and her feathers contracted until they were flat against her body.

Then her head drooped and she was gone.

Stewie held her for another minute or two, just absorbing the situation. There were no more breaths from her.

He rose after a time, and slipped into his shoes.

He carried the limp and abandoned body of the bird out to the barn, where he flipped on the light and found a suitable box for her. He was buoyed by what he was able to find. It was fitting. It was good enough. It was a crate made of thin wood, a little bigger than a cigar box and much deeper. It had a flat lid that slid on using a groove system.

He arranged her respectfully inside, slid the lid into place, and fetched a shovel.

Still in his pajamas, he dug a grave for her under the big oak tree. It was a strangely warm night, and the moon lit up his work from behind and above him, as though it were looking over his shoulder.

Other than that moon, there was no one there to see him cry.

———

In the morning Stacey stuck her head into his room.

It was after eight, according to the clock beside his bed. Stewie never slept that late. But he had only just wakened up as the door opened.

She looked at him, seeming surprised to see him in his bed. He hadn't slept in his bed for many days. Then her eyes shifted to the newspaper-lined box on the floor. He was able to watch the changes on her face as she registered that it was empty.

"Oh," she said. "That's too bad. Are you okay?"

Stewie didn't want to tackle that question. So he just said, "I'll go to school today. I don't want to. But I promised."

"It's Saturday."

"Oh. Is it? Good."

She walked to the bed, leaned down, and stroked the hair off his forehead. But ultimately she said nothing. Maybe there was nothing to say.

She let herself out of the room and he fell back asleep.

———

When he woke again, Marilyn was sitting on the edge of his bed.

At first he was positive it was a dream. But he sat up, rubbed his eyes, and looked around, and she was still there.

"You came," he said.

"It's nearly eleven o'clock" was all she said in reply. She seemed to be chastising him for sleeping so late.

"I'm surprised you came."

"Your sister asked me to. She said you were in a bad way because of that hen. She gave me a ride and everything. At first I wasn't sure—to put it mildly. But she asked so politely and she seemed to feel it was important."

"It was nice of you," he said. He noticed his hands were dirty. He had forgotten to wash them after the previous night's digging. He shot them under the covers and under his pajamaed seat, where they could not embarrass him. "I know we don't know each other very well."

He was about to say it was nice of Stacey, too, especially since this was her sleeping time. But she spoke up before he could say more.

"I remind you of your grandmother," she said. It was a flat statement. It was not a question.

She was wearing slacks and a sweatshirt in a matching cheery yellow. Her short gray hair was carefully combed. Stewie thought he could still see the comb marks.

"Yes," he said.

"But I'm not your grandmother."

He felt his heart fall. He knew in that moment why people say their heart fell. Because that really was the way it felt.

"Yes, ma'am. I know it."

"Good. Because that's more than I could take on right now. But that's really not the inspirational message your sister was hoping I would have for you. Is it now?"

"No, ma'am. I wouldn't say so."

"Let's see then. What can I say to make you feel better? I know it hurts when you love someone and they die."

"Yes, ma'am."

For a moment, nobody said anything. It felt awkward.

Then he asked, "Did you ever love anybody and then they died?"

"Oh, yes. My husband died eleven years ago next month."

"I'm sorry to hear that, ma'am."

"It was a little like this situation, in that it was a long time coming, and I had to put my life on hold to be with him. And then when he was gone, that was hard. But at least I got my life back. At least the situation was behind me and I could go on. I guess I'm saying, sad as you are this morning, at least you're free of that situation and can go on."

"But she's dead."

"Yes," Marilyn said. "Both of those things are true at the same time. Let me tell you something about life, young man. It's always like that. People are forever feeling like everything in their life is wrong, but somehow in a minute they'll turn a corner and everything will be right. But it's never that way. Life is never all good or all bad. It's always a trade-off deal. It's always 'something is lost, but something else is gained.'"

Stewie sat quietly for a minute, taking that in. Blinking too much. He was still a little sleepy, and the sunlight streaming through his bedroom window hurt his eyes. He wasn't quite sure he understood what she was trying to tell him, though he got the general drift.

"Where is she now?" the lady asked.

It confused him.

"Who? The hen?"

"Yes."

"I thought you knew. She died."

"Yes, I do know *that*. I'm asking where she is now."

"Oh, gosh. That's a hard question, ma'am. I have no idea where people go when they die. I like to think she's with Gam now, but I'm not the one to say."

She gave off a laugh that sounded half like a sneeze. "That's not what I meant. I meant what did you do with her body? Did you bury it?"

"Yes, ma'am."

"Show me where."

He got out of bed, doing his best to keep his dirty hands out of view, and slipped into his shoes.

Still in his pajamas, he walked with her out to the big old oak tree.

They stood in its shade for a time, staring down at the mound of freshly dug dirt. Stewie had his hands in his pajama pockets. He felt lucky because he just happened to be wearing the ones with pockets.

It was already a baking-hot, windless day, and the leaves over their heads held perfectly still. A breeze would have been nice, he was thinking. Also he was thinking he would have to come up with a simple marker for the grave.

"Well, it's a lovely spot to spend eternity," she said. She sounded distant, and a little distracted, as if only saying the very least she felt it was decent to say.

"I thought so, ma'am."

"I should probably get your sister to drive me back home now. Get on with my day."

"It was nice of you to come. Seeing as we don't know each other all that well and so forth."

"Right. Well. What can I say? One-time thing. Just so long as you're clear on the fact that I'm not your grandmother. Because that's more than I could take on at this point in my life."

"Yes, ma'am. I'm clear."

And it was true. He was. But behind that simple fact, Stewie had a problem. Because the more firmly she drew lines in the sand and pushed him to the far side of them, the more familiar she felt, and the more she reminded him of Gam.

Chapter Six

Where There's Smoke

Marilyn

It would make a convenient story, she later decided, to say that the knock on the door had distracted her. Maybe she could even adopt that into her thinking. But the truth of the matter was a different thing. She had already wandered out of the kitchen several minutes earlier, leaving the bacon frying in a cast-iron skillet on a gas burner of the stove.

The little girl was lying on her belly on the rug, watching cartoons, and the volume was too loud. Marilyn had gone out into the living room to turn it down.

"Hey," the little girl said. "I'm watching this."

"I know you're watching it," Marilyn said. "And you can watch it just as well with the sound a little lower. And you can hear it just fine that way. I know you can. I have old ears, and I can hear it perfectly well all the way in the kitchen. You have young ears, and you're sitting right in front of it."

The girl sighed, and mumbled something unintelligible under her breath. Marilyn assumed it was some sort of quiet sass, and that the little girl was testing the concept of old ears.

"Don't be like that," Marilyn said firmly, though in truth she didn't know what had been said.

"Well, your ears aren't *that* old, then."

It irked Marilyn to be tested in that manner, and she opened her mouth to say something about it. But at that moment the knock came at the door.

She walked quickly to answer it, hoping it was eggs. Sylvia and the girl had taken to eating Marilyn's eggs, because they were better. Even though she had asked them not to. And now her carton was gone, leaving only a few stray eggs of the supermarket variety, which no longer sounded like anything Marilyn wanted to eat. And besides, they had been sitting in the fridge for weeks.

She had been spoiled by freshness.

She threw the door wide and was pleased to see Stewie standing on the landing with a carton cradled lovingly in his arms.

"There you are," she said.

She sounded even more pleased to her own ears than she had realized she felt. For a moment she questioned herself as to why she would feel that much emotion around the subject. Because she was glad to see him up and around again? Because she enjoyed his little visits?

The last one seemed like a bridge too far, so she dismissed it and chose to believe she was only hungry for those superior eggs.

"Yes, ma'am," he said. "People always say you can set your clock by me. But I think really they should say calendar, not clock. Because I don't always come at exactly the same *time*. I just always come on the *day* they're expecting me."

"How have you been feeling since I last saw you?"

He cut his eyes down to the brick of the door stoop. He clearly was not a fan of talking about his emotions.

"I don't know," he said.

She thought it was interesting, and possibly significant, that he didn't add the usual "ma'am" at the end.

"How can you not know?" she asked, half standing outside herself and wondering why she was pushing him. "You're you. You're inside yourself. You must know what it's like in there."

For a moment he only shuffled his feet, continuing to look away from her face.

Then, hesitantly, and in a voice quieter than usual, he said, "I know what people want me to say when they ask that. They want to hear it's all better now, but I don't like to lie, and they don't really want to hear what I want to say, so I just say I don't know."

"I wanted to hear whatever is the truth," she said.

He raised his eyes to hers. Fleetingly. Hopefully. Then he quickly looked away again.

"You sure? Because nobody else does."

"I'm positive. I know all about grief. I know it takes longer than most people want to believe. I know you'll still be feeling it after everybody else has decided it's time to move on. It's not a straight line."

"I didn't understand that last part, ma'am. I didn't think it was any kind of a line."

"What I meant to say . . ." She looked past him to the sun beating down on the lake, causing the surface of the still, sluggish water to sparkle like scattered gems. ". . . is that people think it gets a little better every day. But it doesn't. It doesn't go in only one direction like that. You'll go along for a couple of days thinking you feel better. Thinking you're able to cope a bit more. And then some little thing happens, or maybe nothing at all, and it comes back around. And you get dropped right down into a big pit of it again, maybe without even knowing why. It seems to go in cycles instead of in one straight line. Now do you know what I mean?"

"Yes, ma'am. I think I do. And I think you're—"

But he never finished the sentence.

Much to her alarm, he flew past her, bumping her roughly, and ran into the house. It brought a flare of anger in her, because she had just grown to trust him. She had come to think of him as polite and predictable. But this was simply outrageous.

"How dare you?" she called after him, her voice a bellow of rage. "I did *not* say you could—"

But by then she had spun around to watch him go. And she never finished the sentence, because by then she saw the smoke.

A thick cloud of it had drifted toward the living room, just visible outside the doorway into the kitchen. It smelled acrid and dangerous, and she wondered why the smell hadn't alerted her sooner. Must have been because she had been standing mostly outside, breathing outdoor air. But she only entertained such thoughts in a distant, disconnected way as she ran into the kitchen.

The boy had the flaming cast-iron skillet by the handle, and was running with it.

He dropped it hard into the empty sink.

In her panic, Marilyn opened her mouth to shout, "Don't run water on it!" Water on a grease fire would only cause a near explosion. And there were curtains on the window above the sink. Filmy, flammable curtains.

But somehow her voice wasn't working.

The boy didn't run water on it. He grabbed a pan lid from the dish rack beside the sink. It was a lid for a bigger pan, which was good. He wouldn't have to hold it there, his poor small bare hands in the flames, to center it just right. He dropped it over the flaming pan, and jumped back.

Everything went silent and still for a moment.

It was over.

Marilyn breathed deeply.

"I could have burned the whole house down," she said on a rush of breath.

"No, it was my fault," Stewie said.

He turned to face her, his hands slightly extended. One, his right hand, had already begun to blister.

"How can you say that? It was my fire, and you put it out."

"But I made you forget you had something on the stove. I came to the door and then I was talking too much, and I made you forget."

Marilyn only stood still, feeling slightly dizzy. Exploring the weight and the scope of the bullet she had dodged. Even a small fire might have caused Sylvia to deem her an unsafe and unsuitable babysitter for the girl. And babysitting was the only reason she was allowed to live here. She would have lost the roof over her head.

A big fire might have brought the police. Some kind of investigation, anyway.

She looked at the boy, who was staring at his burned right hand.

It was a good story. Someone came to the door, and that's why she forgot the frying bacon. That's what she would say if anyone asked. Maybe she could even rewrite history in her own head. Erase the fact that by the time he had knocked on the door, she had already forgotten she had something on the stove.

She unstuck her feet and raced to the refrigerator, which had a dispenser in its door for water and ice. She pressed in on the lever and allowed three or four ice cubes to drop into her hands.

Marilyn placed them in the boy's right hand, wrapping her two hands around his smaller one and just holding it that way for a moment.

She stood breathing for a time, trying to settle her heart.

"It wasn't your fault," she said.

"But I knocked on the door."

"Yes. But it was still my responsibility to remember. Now hold that ice for a minute. I have to open all the windows and air out the kitchen before the smoke detectors go off. Stand right here while I do that. Then we'll do some first aid on your poor hand."

But still she stood a minute, holding his hand around the ice. Not really wanting to let him go. In her peripheral vision she was barely aware of the little girl standing in the kitchen doorway, watching. But she paid that situation no direct attention.

"I think I broke those eggs I brought you," he said.

She realized, as he said it, that she had lost track of what had happened to those eggs when he ran into the house. Had he simply dropped them? And why hadn't she noticed?

"That doesn't matter now," she said. "You're burned, and we need to take care of that first. It's more important."

"I just want you to know I won't make you buy the carton I dropped. I'll go down to my wagon and get you a nice fresh carton. I have one left."

She wanted to tell him she would buy both. He had dropped them to prevent her entire world from falling apart. He had already suffered burns for his heroism. She would not also force him to suffer financial losses. And she *would* tell him that. Later, when the world straightened out. When her voice worked again. When her brain worked again.

In that moment his concern for her four dollars, while he gingerly held ice in his small, burned hand, was almost more than she could bear.

———

They stood together in the small bathroom, feeling cramped. Or, at least, Marilyn was feeling cramped. That space was small enough without having to share it with another living human. But she wasn't thinking about any of that directly.

She was slathering ointment, thickly, onto his burned hand.

She briefly looked over her shoulder at the open bathroom doorway. She didn't know where the little girl was. She wasn't sure if she was out of earshot—if her prying ears were safely far away. Seeing no one, she reached behind herself and swung the bathroom door closed.

Then she spoke to the boy in a low voice. Just above a whisper.

"You mustn't repeat this to anyone."

"Repeat what?" he asked, turning his big eyes up to hers.

"What I'm about to say."

"Oh. Okay."

"Can you keep a secret?"

"Oh, yes, ma'am. I'm very good at secrets. It's a trust thing. When people trust me, I'd just about die before I let them down. You can tell me anything."

"It wasn't your fault." He opened his mouth to argue, but she cut him off. "I know what you think, but it wasn't. And I'm about to tell you why not." She reached into the medicine cabinet and brought down a paper-wrapped gauze pad and a roll of gauze bandage. The boy only stood like a statue, offering his hand in a state of utter surrender. Allowing her to do whatever she saw fit to treat it. "I had already forgotten I had something on the stove, before you knocked. So I don't want you to blame yourself for this. But I also don't want you to say anything in front of Izzy."

"Who's Izzy?"

"The little girl. Information is not safe with her. She has big ears and a big mouth, and she'll blab to her mom in a heartbeat. And then I won't be able to live here anymore."

She gently pressed the pad of gauze onto his hand and began wrapping a bandage around it to hold it in place.

He was still looking up at her with those huge, piercing eyes. For a brief moment she got a flash of an image. That those eyes were a battering ram, attempting to roughly take down her front door and gain access to everything she wanted to keep hidden.

"But they can't throw you out. You're the grandmother. You're *family.*"

Marilyn kept her eyes on her work while not answering him. She used two short strips of white medical adhesive tape to hold the bandage in place.

"Just don't say anything," she said when she was done. "Please."

"Yes, ma'am. Your secret is safe with me."

"Come on. I'll walk you home."

"That's very nice of you to offer, ma'am, but you don't have to—"

Before he could finish the sentence, she had swung the bathroom door open. On the other side of it stood Sylvia. She had one hand raised, poised to knock. Predictably, she did not look pleased.

"Well," Sylvia said. "There's a carton of broken eggs on the stoop, and the whole house smells like a fire sale. I figured there must be some kind of story behind that. Why don't you go ahead and tell me that story?"

Marilyn opened her mouth to speak, but the boy beat her to it.

"It was my fault," he said. "Both those things were my fault."

"You started a fire in my house?"

"No, ma'am. But Marilyn had something on the stove, and I came to the door and talked her ear off."

"It was still her job to remember," Sylvia told the boy, her voice firm with anger.

"Yes," Marilyn said. "You're right. It was. I'm not putting it off on anybody else, but I'm only going to say it was an unusual situation, and one not likely to happen again."

"You sure?" she asked, drilling her gaze right into Marilyn's face, one eyebrow arched. "Because it seems to me a lot of these 'unusual situations' have been happening lately."

"Not at all. I just let myself get a little distracted. I promise I'll be more careful from now on. Now, if you'll excuse me, I want to make sure the little egg boy gets home okay."

She hurried past Sylvia, towing the boy by one narrow forearm. Hoping Sylvia would let the thing drop. Though letting things drop was hardly her strong suit.

Surprisingly, nothing more was said.

———

"It's kind of a long walk," Stewie said.

It pleased her that she remembered his name, finally. It was Stewie. That proved her memory certainly was not as bad a situation as people were making it out to be.

"I don't mind."

"It's all the way around on the other side of the lake."

She did not reply directly to that. Instead she said, "Thank you for saying what you said."

"What did I say?"

"That the fire was your fault."

"Oh. That. Well. I told you I'd keep your secret."

"And I appreciate it."

He was towing his empty wagon behind him with his left hand. It rattled and bumped over the broken pavement. She had bought the last carton from that wagon. She had paid him for both.

"It's nice of you to walk me home . . . ," he began.

He was trying to say something. She could tell. She already knew he was not the best at pushing out what he needed to say. Depending on what kind of thing it was.

He pushed harder, and it came out. ". . . I'm just not really sure why."

"You burned your hand."

"That doesn't make it any harder to walk."

"No, I suppose not. But I was worried about what your sister would think. You come to my house and come home hurt. I don't want her to think I put you in harm's way."

"What would that mean," he asked, turning his huge eyes up to hers, "to put somebody in harm's way?"

"Well. Let's say there had been a fire and I had told *you* to put it out. Because I didn't want to take the risk myself. That would be putting you in harm's way."

"I don't think she'd think that."

"Well. Regardless. I'd like to talk to her myself. If you don't mind."

"Oh, I never mind if you want to come along, or visit. I like your company."

That stopped the conversation in its tracks, because it was a candid admission of affection that she was in no way prepared to meet.

They walked in silence for a time. Half a mile, maybe. The flat water of the lake was still. The air was still. The sun was nearly down on the other side of the lake, yet it was still hot. Marilyn felt as though it had been hot as long as she could remember. That it always had been and always would be, even though she knew in her mind that such a thing was not objectively true, or even possible.

She had never gotten to eat that bacon sandwich, and her hunger was getting the best of her now. She felt it as painful pangs in her belly.

"If I'm being honest . . . ," she said, surprising herself. She hadn't really planned on saying it out loud. ". . . I also wanted to get out of the house for a while, to give Sylvia a chance to cool down."

He looked up at her again with those eyes. Those gigantic, needy eyes. They were beginning to feel like a weapon. Something he could use against her. Something against which she could not properly defend herself.

"I can understand that, all right. Nobody likes to be around some-body who's mad. But . . . she's your daughter. She can't stay mad forever."

Marilyn struggled within herself for a moment. Should she flat-out lie to him? Claim Sylvia was indeed her daughter? Or could she answer the question in a more roundabout way? "Oh, but she does have a temper." Something vague like that, just short of a lie.

Instead she took the conversation in an entirely different direction.

"I was glad to see you up and around again. And just a handful of days after you suffered that big loss. It reminded me of a story. Kind of a parable, I guess you'd call it. I'm not sure where it's from, but someone told it to me once. About a man whose son was sick in bed, and he wouldn't leave the boy's side. He was very distraught, and wouldn't do anything else but tend his son. And everybody thought if the boy died, that would just about be the end of the man. That he'd just fall apart. And then one day the son died. And the man got up and washed his hands and went back to work."

They walked in silence for most of a block, save for the rattle of his wagon wheels.

"That's a sad story," he said after a time.

"I suppose it is."

"I'm not sure . . . I'm not sure how to say what I'm not sure about."

"You don't know what I meant for you to take away from the story."

"Yes, ma'am. That."

"I suppose . . . that it's more appropriate to put that kind of caring in with someone while they're alive. After they're gone you might feel devastated, but if you don't get back to your own life, you're doing that for yourself, not for them. They're gone. It's too late to show you care. Do you understand what I mean by that?"

"I think so," he said. But he sounded a little confused. "I just mostly figured people needed their fresh eggs."

———

The boy's sister was in the kitchen, setting the table for dinner. Marilyn did not remember her name. But she didn't know if she had forgotten it, or had never been told.

The young woman looked up at them standing in the kitchen door-way. She looked first at Marilyn with mild surprise, then at her little brother's bandaged hand. Her eyes filled with alarm.

"Stewie! What happened to you?"

"I burned my hand."

"On what?"

"I can explain," Marilyn said. "That's why I came here uninvited. I wanted to explain."

Her eyes came up to Marilyn's face again. She looked . . . Marilyn wasn't quite sure how to describe what she saw. A bit . . . skeptical? Impatient? It struck her that Stewie's sister was not her biggest fan, which hurt more than she would have imagined. More than she likely would ever want to admit.

"Stewie," the sister said, her eyes still locked with Marilyn's. "Go wash your hands."

"Now how am I supposed to—"

"Okay. Fine. Got it. Go wash your *hand*. And then after dinner I want to take a look at that burn."

The boy shuffled out of the room, leaving the two women standing on opposite sides of the table, considering each other.

"I put ice on it," Marilyn said. "And ointment. And that's sterile gauze."

"I'm sure you did a good job. It's just that I'm a nurse, and I want to see it with my own eyes."

"Understood," Marilyn said.

An awkward silence fell. Marilyn knew it was her turn to speak. She knew what it was she needed to explain. It seemed clear that they both knew.

"There was a small cooking fire at my house," Marilyn said. "He took it upon himself to put it out. He had the pan in his hand before I even knew what was going on. Before I'd even gotten into the kitchen to see. He was too fast for me. I would never want you to think that I would tell him to do a thing so dangerous."

For a second or two, Stewie's sister only continued to consider Marilyn. As if weighing something. As if deciding how much of Marilyn she wanted to buy.

"Oh, I wouldn't have thought *that*," she said, cutting her eyes away.

She went back to setting three places at the table. Forks, knives, spoons.

Marilyn wasn't sure if she had just been given a vote of confidence. And she wasn't sure she was prepared to ask.

"You wouldn't?"

"I've *met* Stewie," she said, still looking at her work. "When you know Stewie like I do, a thing like that isn't very surprising. He wants to fix everything. He doesn't want there to be any disasters in the world, so he tries to single-handedly prevent them."

Marilyn had no idea what to say in response to that, so she said nothing at all. She only stood there, watching the sister step over toward the hallway and call for Theo and Stewie to come to dinner. Marilyn thought about the long walk home. Her empty stomach ached and burned.

Stewie's sister turned back and considered her again. "As long as you're here, would you like to stay for dinner? We're having homemade macaroni and cheese."

"Homemade?" she breathed, almost unable to believe her good luck. "Why, I haven't had homemade macaroni and cheese in as long as I can remember. I used to make it for my husband, but that's been a very long time ago now. Thank you. That's a kind offer and I believe I'll take you up on it. I'm very hungry, because I never got to have that bacon sandwich I was making for myself."

"I'll set another place."

Stewie and Theo spilled into the kitchen and took their places at the table. Stewie held his burned hand aloft, as though he didn't dare touch it to anything. Based on the look on his face, Marilyn imagined that even the air that touched it seemed to worry him.

"Bacon sandwich?" the sister asked from the far side of the kitchen, where she was taking more flatware out of a drawer. She asked as if the concept confused her.

"Yes," Marilyn said, and sat at the head of the table. It was the only spot that did not seem to be expecting someone else.

"Is that like a BLT?"

"Something like it, yes."

"What's the difference?"

"I didn't have any lettuce or tomato in the house."

"Oh. I see."

She handed Marilyn a plastic plate, and the three pieces of flatware with a paper napkin wrapped around them, and Marilyn placed them on the table herself.

Then Stewie's sister put on hot mitts and brought the casserole to the table.

Marilyn could only stare at it in admiration. It had been baked golden brown with buttered bread crumbs on top. It was the most beautiful dinner she had seen in as long as her memory served to remember.

The boys held their plates out anxiously, but their sister shot them a stern look. First one boy, then the other.

"Who gets served first?" she asked in a grave voice.

"The guest," they both said. Dejectedly, and nearly at the same time.

Marilyn held her plate out and watched a mountain of the golden cheesy heaven being served onto it. She pulled the plate back, and set it in front of her. And fidgeted, wishing she could begin eating.

"Don't let it get cold," Stewie's sister said. "Eat."

Marilyn shoveled in a huge bite, and it tasted even better than it looked.

They ate in silence for a time. It wasn't an awkward silence. The food was just good, and nobody seemed to want to stop eating it long enough to chat.

Marilyn watched the dusk set through the kitchen window, nursing an unfamiliar feeling. After a time she decided what it was. What it must have been. She felt safe and content.

No wonder it felt so unfamiliar.

Chapter Seven

Flight Limitations

Stewie

It was the following Sunday, and Stewie's burns had improved enough that he was wearing only two extra-large adhesive bandages on his palm. He was walking down the hall past Theo's room when he heard his brother speak to him. He couldn't make out the words, though.

He stopped. Backed up two steps.

"What'd you say, Theo?"

"I asked if you'd ever heard of a chicken flying contest."

Stewie felt a tingling that started in his scalp and moved down around his ears. Even without knowing more, it was an inherently exciting idea.

"Where do they have those? How did you even hear about it?"

Theo was hunched over his laptop computer, staring at the screen. Stewie moved closer, imagining there was something about chicken flying contests up for viewing. With pictures, he was hoping. But it was just a page of search results that didn't seem to contain the word *chicken*. At least, not that Stewie could see.

"It was weird," Theo said. "I wasn't looking for it at all. I was doing this thing for school, and I pulled up this news story about a state fair. And it was the headline of another story on the same website. It was about a chicken flying contest."

"You're saying they have them at state fairs?"

He leaned closer to the laptop's display as he asked, staring. As though something chicken related would appear, responding to his sheer will.

"I guess."

"We don't have a state fair anywhere near here."

"We have the county fair in July."

"Think they'll have that contest at our county fair?"

"Dunno," Theo said. "Worth finding out, I guess."

Stewie hovered over him for a moment without speaking. The tingle of excitement had morphed into a sort of electrified trembling all over.

"Know who'd be perfect for that contest?" Stewie asked.

Both brothers answered the question at the same time. Near-perfect unison.

"Elsie," they both said.

———

Stewie would have been the first to admit that chickens were notoriously poor fliers. In fact, he noticed that people tended to be confused regarding whether they flew at all. Well, they did. And Stewie knew it as well as anybody. They just didn't fly very far, or very high.

Elsie was a potential exception to that rule. Granted, Elsie also did not fly far or high. But, on the grading curve of the flight limitations of chickens, she did surprisingly well.

Stewie had discovered this talent in her more than a year earlier.

He had been walking through their outside pen with a tray of dried corn, which was Elsie's favorite treat, when he realized he was just about to step on poor old Mabel. He had allowed his attention to be distracted by a bright bird in a nearby tree, and when he looked back, his foot was just about to land on her. He jerked backward so suddenly that he fell over onto his back, flipping the tray wildly. As he fell, he watched the bulk of the dried corn fly up onto the corrugated tin roof of the henhouse.

He lay there a minute, scanning his body to be sure he was unhurt.

Then he heard a wild flapping, and turned his head to see who it was, and why. That was when he saw her. Elsie was gaining a surprising amount of altitude. The effort on her part looked enormous, but she was doing it. He watched in wonder as she landed on the tin roof and began pecking up the spilled corn.

He'd gotten up carefully and walked to the edge of the henhouse, his eyes more or less level with the talented bird.

"That was amazing," he'd said.

But Elsie had been too busy eating to pay him any attention.

Now he walked into the yard to get her, his pockets filled with dried corn, to begin the training that would make her the star she so deserved to be.

"Come on," he said, scooping her up and pinning her gently to his torso with his left arm. "We've got a lot of work to do."

———

Stewie set Elsie carefully in the dirt of the henhouse yard and reached into the pocket of his shorts for a handful of dried corn. He had been putting things in his left pocket—money, interesting rocks, loose change—because that way it hurt less to go digging around to fetch them again.

He showed the hen the contents of his left hand, then stretched up on tiptoes and reached up to scatter the corn on the henhouse roof. It made a rattling sound, like heavy drops of rain on the tin.

Elsie launched into the air immediately, flapping wildly against the sheer force of gravity. For a moment it seemed as though gravity would win. But the hen mustered something within herself, and lifted up boldly toward the low roof.

Her talons scrambled for purchase against its edge.

They did not find what they were looking for.

She tumbled backward and began to fall. Upside down, which made it very hard for her wings to help her.

And there was so much flapping. Oh, the panicky sound of the flapping!

Later Stewie would realize that it wasn't outwardly different from the flapping of her rise to the roof. Or, at very least, it shouldn't have been different. But it was. He heard it the way he would hear a scream.

In those split-second impressions one tends to have in the midst of panic—the ones that seem as though they shouldn't fit into the time frame—it struck Stewie that he had been around the hens long enough to read and understand their wingbeats the way other people read in a second language. Certainly not in those words, maybe not in any words at all, but it struck him.

His heart seeming to sail up into his throat, Stewie dove in to catch Elsie. He winced as he did, because he knew it would hurt his burned hand. It all happened very fast, almost faster than Stewie could move. He was almost too late. But, amazingly—and probably because he was not prepared for things to end any other way—he managed to dive in and get his hands under her in time.

He did not literally succeed in catching her. His burned right hand resisted much movement, and she tumbled off into the dirt. But he had sufficiently broken her fall.

And yes, it hurt his hand.

He dropped into a sitting position in the dirt and sat with his arms around the hen, his forehead against her feathered back. His heart pounded so wildly that he thought it might kill him, and there was a deep, disturbing trembling in the cores of his arms and legs.

Granted, the hen would have survived such a fall. But if she had landed wrong, she could have broken a wing or a leg. And then what would Stewie have done? Everybody would say she should be put down. Stacey had told him that people didn't do a lot of advanced veterinary medicine on their hens. The world viewed them as easily expendable.

He pushed those dark thoughts away again.

He would have to build something safer for them to use in their training. A raised platform, lower to the ground. With something she could really grab onto, like a nice thick perch. And he would have to get something to put on the ground to cushion any future falls. A mat, or a thin mattress. Or maybe even folded blankets would do the trick, though he couldn't help feeling that more padding could only be better. If not for Elsie, then for his own poor heart.

Stewie raised his head to see the hen looking into his eyes, as though aware of something in him.

"That's enough flying practice for today," he told her. He couldn't help noticing that his voice was trembling. He wondered if hens noticed things like that, too. "That was scary, but, anyway, you're okay."

He pulled to his feet and reached as high as he possibly could, gathering the corn off the henhouse roof. He gave half of it to Elsie and scattered the balance in the dirt of the yard to give the other hens something to do while she ate.

Then he left them in the yard and walked into the house. But he didn't go inside feeling as though it had all turned out for the best and Elsie was okay. He moved like a person rattled to his very core. His heart seemed to work unevenly now, and there was a trembling in the very deepest parts of him.

He lay on his bed and waited for the dreadful feeling to subside.

It never entirely did.

He literally ran through his egg route after school the following day, jogging down the sidewalks. Jumping over the cracks.

When he had sold the last dozen, he sprinted to Marilyn's house, where he stood on her landing, panting desperately.

He knocked, still panting.

He leaned his hands on his own knees and gasped, and gasped, and gasped.

When he looked up, she was looking down on him.

"Oh," she said. "Well, this is odd."

He wanted to answer, but he couldn't speak yet.

She looked past him and down the concrete stairs, probably to the spot where his empty wagon sat. He didn't bother to look around to be sure what she was seeing. He was too busy breathing.

"Well, I know you didn't come to sell me eggs," she said.

He shook his head, still not ready to speak.

"It hasn't been a week, and besides, you're all out."

Stewie opened his mouth, but no words came through. Only noisy, raspy breathing.

"I'll just wait here until you're ready to explain yourself," she said.

She leaned one shoulder against the frame of the open door. Then she reached into her skirt pocket and absentmindedly pulled out a peppermint candy. It was the kind with the swirls of red in an otherwise white disk. She unwrapped the cellophane and popped the candy into her mouth. Then, as though suddenly remembering something she had forgotten, she reached again into the same pocket and produced another candy, which she held in his direction.

"Thank you, ma'am," he said, and took it from her. His words, though breathy, sounded intelligible.

"Now how about you tell me to what I owe this visit?"

"Pardon, ma'am?"

"It means 'What brings you here?'"

"Oh. That. I thought you might . . ."

But he couldn't quite force out the ending of the thought. Because she might not like it. It might even make her mad. He wanted to do what he was doing, but he didn't want to present the idea to her in words. It made him feel afraid.

And he had been extra afraid since Mabel's death and Elsie's near accident. It had left him feeling as though something terrible was hiding around every corner, waiting to surprise him at any time. Waiting to leap into his life and rip something away.

"What?" Marilyn asked when she seemed to grow tired of waiting. She wasn't looking at him, which helped. She was staring past him and out over the lake. Stewie could see the slight lump of the peppermint candy in her cheek. He could hear the way it interfered with the clarity of her speech. "What did you think I might?"

"I thought you might need . . ."

But again, he could not bring himself to finish.

He briefly closed his eyes and tried to will himself away. It made no difference to where. Just elsewhere. Then he opened his eyes, and he was still on her stoop.

"What did you think I might need?" she asked. Her voice was even, and he couldn't tell if she was already mad or not.

Stewie took a big, deep breath and forced out the word.

"Help."

At first, no reply. He didn't dare look at her face.

"Why would you think I need help? Help with what?"

"You know."

"If I knew, I wouldn't ask."

"You know. Babysitting. For the little girl."

"Oh," she said. "I see now." She definitely sounded as though she'd moved closer to being mad, but he couldn't tell if she had arrived yet. "You think I'm going to burn the place down."

"Not necessarily that again."

"But something."

"Maybe," he said. He sounded desperate to his own ears. "Maybe something."

"I'm not going to forget to turn off the stove again."

Stewie thought that was interesting, because she seemed to have purposely avoided the fact that there were other somethings that could go wrong.

"If you say so, ma'am. If you say you won't, I'll believe you. I just figure we don't know what we're gonna forget. Why, if we knew, then we could just be sure we didn't forget it. Couldn't we? I bet when you were cooking that bacon last time, if anybody had asked you, you'd have said you wouldn't forget to turn off the burner. I shouldn't say for a fact, because I don't know things about other people for sure. It's just that I never met anybody who figured they were about to forget something."

He allowed a pause. A silence. In case he had made her mad. In which case, he figured it was better to find out as soon as possible, rather than keep talking and chance making her any madder.

While he waited, he untwisted the cellophane ends of his candy wrapper.

She did not fill his pause.

"I just wouldn't want to see you get in trouble," he said.

"When I said that, I was just worrying out loud. I didn't mean for you to take that on as your own problem."

"No, ma'am. I know you didn't. Nobody ever does."

"But you always take it on anyway."

"Yes, ma'am. That seems to be what I do."

"I see," she said. "Well, then, I guess you'd best come in."

Stewie let out a long breath, popped the candy into his mouth, and stepped inside.

"I'm going to enter Elsie in a chicken flying contest," he said.

"Who's Elsie?"

"She's a chicken."

"Well, I might've seen that coming. I thought chickens couldn't fly."

"Most people think that. But they do fly. Some. Well. A little. They just have . . . what do you call it when you have things holding you back?"

"Limitations?"

"Yeah. That's it. They have limitations."

"Don't we all," Marilyn said.

He wanted to tell her more, but he had promised to help her baby-sit. And he had to stay true to his word about that.

Chapter Eight

The Anti-Disaster Patrols

Marilyn

Marilyn finished applying polish to the fingernails of her right hand, then sat back against the couch cushions and gently blew on the wet polish. She could hear the kids playing in the next room.

A voice in her head said she should go in and check on them again. After all, Izzy was her responsibility. And that little egg boy, why, he was just a child himself.

Then again, she hated to smudge the wet nail polish by moving around too much, especially near unpredictable children.

One of her soap operas was playing on the television, but she had turned the volume down low so she could hear how things were going in the den.

Before she felt confident that her nails were dry, the boy burst into the living room again on one of his patrols.

It was almost humorous the way he moved, though she would have felt guilty laughing at him, even silently on the inside of her head. Still, there was something almost . . . bustling about it. A tense bustling. That was the only word she could find to describe it.

He kept his arms to his sides, as if nervousness had him tied around the waist. His legs moved very fast but not very far. They stayed mostly under him, which forced many quick, small steps in the place of more-normal large ones. His eyebrows seemed to knit down and together with worry.

He had been reminding her of something all afternoon, with that odd way of bustling about the house, but she hadn't quite been able to pin it down. Now it struck her that he moved like one of those chickens he so revered.

He stuck his head into the kitchen first, then shuffled off to the bathroom. Why, Marilyn didn't know, and hadn't asked. Maybe he thought she had drawn a bath and carelessly left it running. She certainly hoped he hadn't made it his business to check that she had remembered to flush the toilet.

He sped by her again on the way back to the den to rejoin Izzy.

"I could take offense to this, you know," she called as he bustled past.

"I hope you don't, though," he said, and kept bustling.

A minute or two later she sat up, blew on her nails again, and walked to the den doorway to look in on the children.

They were sitting on the rug, playing with Izzy's interlocking plastic blocks. Building something Marilyn could not identify, but that seemed wildly ambitious in its scope. Maybe a sprawling ranch, or some kind of military complex.

They did not look up.

She gazed down on them for a minute or so, feeling grateful for her good fortune. It was almost ridiculously luxurious, having this time to herself and not even needing to look after the troublesome girl.

Her better angels commented that it might be unfair to ask the boy to do her job for her. After all, he was receiving nothing in return. She quickly reminded them that he had chosen to do it. She hadn't asked.

Just as she turned to go back to the couch and her TV stories, Izzy spoke up in protest. Marilyn was surprised that the girl hadn't complained sooner. Complaints were not merely in Izzy's wheelhouse, her wheelhouse had been more or less constructed from them.

"I'm *tired* of Legos," she whined. "I want to do something *else*."

"Like what?" the boy asked her.

"Like *anything*."

"We could play with your dinosaurs."

Izzy had a fair collection of molded plastic dinosaurs.

"You can't play with them," Izzy whined.

"Why can't you?"

"Because they're just *plastic*," Izzy whined in that nasal tone that Marilyn found so deeply irritating. "They don't *do* anything."

"You make different characters out of them and act stuff out."

"That sounds really stupid," Izzy said.

Still they did not seem aware of Marilyn standing in the doorway observing their play. Or their argument, as the case might be. With children it was often hard to tell the difference, if indeed there *was* a difference.

"Fine," Stewie said, though he was clearly exasperated and it was clearly not fine. "What do *you* want to play?"

Izzy answered without hesitation. "Barbies," she said.

The boy threw his head back and rolled his eyes expansively. Izzy noticed.

"What's wrong with Barbies?" she asked, her tone defensive.

"Well, first of all, they're just like dinosaurs. They're plastic, and if dinosaurs don't do anything, then neither do Barbies."

"Right, but they're *Barbies*," Izzy said. As if the very fact of being what they were sufficiently redeemed them.

"But I'm a boy."

"So? Boys can play Barbies."

"Maybe they can, but they don't want to."

"Some boys would want to."

"Well, this boy doesn't."

Both children fell silent a moment, as if examining the depth and breadth of their impasse.

Then Stewie said, "You be a Barbie, I'll be a dinosaur."

And they dove for their respective toys of choice.

Marilyn smiled inwardly and turned back for the living room.

Before she could even reach the couch, she heard a high scream. She ran back to the den, her heart in her throat. But it was only Izzy voicing the screams of her Barbie as she ran for her life from Stewie's dinosaur.

She shook her head and turned back to the living room again, where she ran into Sylvia. Almost literally. She had to jump back a step to avoid a collision. It startled her.

"Oh," she said, letting off that jolt of fear. "It's you. When did you get home? I didn't even know you were home."

"I just got here." She craned her neck and looked past Marilyn and into the den. "What's that little egg boy doing here?"

"Playing with Izzy."

"That doesn't seem right."

"What's wrong about it?"

"He's so much older than she is. Like, five or six years older."

"I assure you he's a lovely young man and it's perfectly appropriate play."

"I wasn't suggesting otherwise. I'm just not sure why he'd want to."

Marilyn raised her arms and spread them wide. "Who knows why anyone wants anything?"

Sylvia narrowed her eyes and stared in the direction of one of Marilyn's hands. "Had time to do your nails, I see."

"The children seemed nicely occupied on their own."

"That's convenient." She turned her gaze to Marilyn's face, her eyes still narrow and searching. "Don't you think it's taking advantage of his good nature?"

"I didn't ask him to do it. It was his own idea."

Sylvia sighed. "Whatever. Anyway, I'm home. And it's time for him to go home now." Another shriek rang out, and Sylvia turned her attention to the children again. "Why is he chasing her?"

"He's not chasing her."

"I'm standing here watching him chase her."

"His dinosaur is chasing her Barbie."

"Oh," Sylvia said. But she sounded less than convinced. "Izzy," she called sharply.

Both children stopped running and turned their attention to the grown-ups standing in the doorway.

"What?" Izzy said sternly. "We're playing."

"Are you okay?"

"I *was*. Until you messed everything up."

Sylvia sighed, and turned to Marilyn.

"Tell your little friend to go home now," she said.

"Are you sure? It's nice for Izzy to have someone to play games with her. Nice for us, too."

"I just want dinner. I just want quiet."

Marilyn opened her mouth to call the boy by name. But she no longer remembered his name. It was frustrating and troubling, because she had been so sure she'd memorized it once and for all.

"Kids!" she said loudly. As though they had never stopped running. As though they were not already frozen in their tracks and listening. "You," she said, pointing at Izzy. "Time to wash up for dinner. And you. Time to get home for dinner at your own house."

"Yes, ma'am," the boy said.

"He's polite," Sylvia half whispered in her ear. "I have to give him that."

—

It was a couple of hours after dinner. Marilyn had given Izzy her bath and tucked her into bed, and the girl had blessedly—and unexpectedly—gone to sleep straightaway.

She was sitting on the couch with Sylvia, watching a police drama. It wasn't very good.

Sylvia had long since lost interest and was staring at her notebook computer, which she had open on her lap.

Marilyn craned her neck as inconspicuously as possible to see what she was viewing. It appeared to be a selection of blouses.

"What are you doing?" she asked, though she could already see that Sylvia was shopping.

"Shopping," Sylvia said.

"Is that a clothing company website? Or is that one of those sites where they sell everything?"

"They sell everything." Sylvia sounded distracted, as though she wished Marilyn would stop talking to her.

"So they have books."

"Yes. They have books. That's more or less what they started out to sell."

"Order something for me, too. Will you?"

Sylvia's attention broke. She shifted her eyes away from the laptop's display and frowned into Marilyn's face. "Why would I order something for you?"

"I'll pay you back for it."

"Oh. Well, that's okay, then, I guess. What do you want?"

"A book."

"Right. I knew that much."

"*Stuart Little*. E. B. White is the author."

Then she realized that by remembering the name of the book she wanted, she was also remembering the name of the boy.

Sylvia typed that into the website's search bar.

"Finish your own shopping first," Marilyn said.

"It doesn't matter. I wasn't finding anything anyway. My goodness," she added as the detail page for the book came up. "That's a very old book. Did you know how old it was? It says right here on the cover that it's seventy-five years old. They say it like it's a good thing. This gold sticker saying 'celebrating' seventy-five years. But it doesn't seem like much cause for celebration to me. It's just a very old book."

"That's a newer edition, though," Marilyn said, leaning in to better see the computer screen. "See if they have any of the originals."

"What difference does it make?"

"Just look, please. See if they're very expensive."

Sylvia sighed. Her fingers clattered on the keyboard. A moment later Marilyn was staring at a page with an image of a clearly ancient hardcover book. On it, a mouse in some kind of flowing outfit seemed to be tugging on a hanging rope. The title of the text on the book's detail page read, "By E. B. White Stuart Little Hardcover—May 13, 1905."

"That's the one!" she cried out. "That's what I want. Is it expensive?"

"Hardly. They have used copies as cheap as . . . well, less than seven dollars. No, wait. After they add the tax, it'll be over seven dollars."

"That's fine. What about shipping?"

"I get free shipping on this site. What do you want this old book for, anyway?"

"It's for the little boy."

That just sat on the couch with them for a moment. Sylvia did not seem to know what to do with it.

So Marilyn said more.

"I didn't think he'd want to take money from me for being over here playing with Izzy. It's just something he wants to do. But it does make my job ever so much easier. That's why I thought a little gift might be in order."

"What makes you think he wants an old book?"

"Because it's his namesake. Or he's its namesake. Anyway, that's his name. Stuart Little. Though I'm not sure if he spells Stuart the same way. In any case, when he tells people his name for the first time, they always say, 'Oh, like the mouse.' And he's really not quite sure what they're on about with that."

Sylvia's face did not look convinced.

"Well," she said. "It's your seven dollars. Should I hit the 'Buy' button?"

"Yes," Marilyn said. "Please do hit the 'Buy' button."

Then she sat back and turned her attention again to the not-very-good police drama. And felt satisfied.

She had no idea how long the book would take to arrive. She had no idea how the boy would feel about reading it. But it had struck her as an appropriate gift for him. Almost . . . thoughtful.

There was no doubt in her mind that the boy was trying in his own way to be a good friend to her, and this gesture made her feel as though she was being a less terrible friend in return.

Chapter Nine

His Psychology

Stewie

Stewie sat in the doctor-person's plush-looking office, glancing around and feeling uneasy. There were diplomas on the walls, but their words remained indecipherable to him. The chairs were covered with baby-soft burgundy-colored leather. It stuck to the backs of his bare legs. The skin that his shorts didn't cover felt sweaty. And his face felt sweaty. Which seemed odd to Stewie, because the office was only vaguely warm.

He wondered how things were going over at Marilyn's house while he was stuck here. He thought about how he would feel if there was a disaster at her house and he wasn't there to prevent it. Then he forced himself to stop thinking about it, because it made him feel too panicky inside his lower belly.

"Tell me again what kind of doctor you are?" he asked.

As he asked, he peeled his attention away from the room and its furnishings and looked directly at the man. Even though he had generally been avoiding doing so as much as possible.

The doctor was surprisingly old. Surprising to Stewie, at least, in that Stewie tended to think that people stopped working and stayed home when they got so old. He had gray-white hair that seemed untamed and unruly. It billowed out from his head, reminding Stewie of the photograph of Albert Einstein in his science textbook.

The doctor had an almost pasted-on kindness and patience on his face. Well, maybe not pasted on, but . . . it felt like too much. Like overdoing the kindliness to the point of looking down on Stewie. It gave Stewie an uneasy sensation inside.

"I'm a psychologist," the man said, and his voice was overly kind as well. "I'm a doctor of psychology."

"I'm not absolutely sure I know what that is."

"Psychology? It's the study of the mind, and behavior."

"Is there something wrong with my psychology?" he asked, squirming in his chair. Or at least, he attempted to squirm. But his sweaty legs stuck to the soft leather.

"No, of course not," the doctor said. "That's a common misconception." Then he stopped himself, and backed up. "A misconception is a wrong idea. People tend to have a false idea that if you see a psychologist it means there's something wrong with you. But in most cases it just means a person is under some kind of pressure. That they're dealing with grief, or stress, or confusion, and they need some help with it."

"I don't think I'm under pressure," Stewie said. "I mean . . . I sort of am. Now. Because I'm here. But before I got here, I didn't feel that way."

"I hope you'll relax and think of me more as a friend," the doctor said. He sat back in his soft leather chair.

He had a pad of paper and a pen in his hand. That made Stewie even more uneasy—if such a thing were possible—because it made him feel as though he was expected to say something important. Something worth writing down.

"What do we do here?" Stewie asked.

"Just talk."

"Really? That seems easy."

He settled a bit as he spoke, sinking more deeply into his chair.

"It *is* easy."

"What good does that do, though?"

"Just give it a try with me. You might be surprised. Tell me something about yourself."

Stewie felt his gut tighten again. Because it felt like a test. It felt hard.

"I don't know what to say." The words came out sounding breathy. They seemed to betray his panic.

"Anything you want."

"But that's too hard. I mean, there's so much about me. Eleven years of somethings, and I don't know where to start. You have to help me know where to start."

"All right. Tell me about your parents. Your sister tells me they died in a motorcycle accident when you were just a baby."

"Then you already know," Stewie said, more convinced than ever that this was confusing and hard.

"I thought you could tell me more about that situation."

"But I was just a baby, so I don't really know. I only know the things people told me about them later. I know the stories Stacey and Gam told me, but I didn't really know *them*."

"Well, on some level you did. But let's come back to that when we know each other better. Maybe just tell me how it made you feel."

"It didn't make me feel anything. I was too young to know it even happened."

"But you know now."

"Right."

"How do you feel about it now?"

"I don't know. I don't feel anything about it. It was just a story I was told. If somebody tells you a story about people who died . . . if you didn't know them, then you don't feel much of anything. Right? I mean, that's how it is for me. I don't know how it is for other people."

"She also told me your grandmother died less than a year ago."

Stewie held very still in his chair and felt all the inside parts of him go empty and still, like a house must feel when nobody is home. He squeezed his eyes shut and thought about willing himself away. But he was not a baby, and he knew it probably wouldn't work, especially since he'd tried it before. Then he thought about getting away in the more dependable sense. Getting up and walking through the office door. But Stacey had asked him to do this. "For me," she had said. And he had said he would.

He opened his eyes again and pinned his gaze to the gray carpeting. He was careful to avoid the doctor's face.

"But I don't want to talk about that," he said.

"I hope we can eventually," the doctor said. "But it's a first session, and there's no need to push you too fast. Let's talk about something happier. Tell me something from your life that's good."

"Hmm," Stewie said. He straightened his back and sat up in his best classroom posture, as though it would help him think, and perform the task well. "Stacey and Theo are good."

At the corner of his eye he saw the doctor writing that down. It seemed odd to Stewie, because a brother and sister shouldn't have been hard to remember.

"What else?"

"The hens are good. I really love the hens. And one of them is even a good flier. For a chicken, I mean. Usually chickens aren't very good fliers. I'm going to enter her in a chicken flying contest. So that's very good. Don't you think?"

"Your sister told me they were your grandmother's hens."

"But I said I don't want to talk about that."

"That's true. You did. I'm sorry. What else? Anything else in your life feel like a good thing?"

"Marilyn."

Stewie braced himself, thinking the doctor was about to say, "Oh yes, your sister told me about her. She told me Marilyn is this lady who reminds you of your grandmother." It occurred to him that if the doctor did that, he really might get up and leave. Even though it would be breaking a promise to Stacey. It made his face feel hot just to think about it.

"Tell me about Marilyn," the doctor said.

Stewie waited a beat or two, but the doctor said no more.

He sat back, breathed deeply a few times, then said everything he could possibly think to say about his new friend. But nothing that would lead back to the topic of Gam.

———

They drove toward home in silence for a time. Stacey was driving with her window open, her elbow on the edge of the door. The hot wind whipped in and blew her hair around. Stewie mostly watched his own bare legs dangling over the edge of the car seat and bouncing.

"Did you like Dr. Briggs?" she asked suddenly.

"Oh, is that his name?"

Stewie figured he had been told the doctor's name. But it hadn't stuck in his head. Maybe because he'd never particularly wanted it to.

She seemed to be waiting for him to say more. To answer the question. He didn't.

"So did you like him?"

"Not very much, I don't guess."

"What didn't you like about him?"

"He just kept asking me all these questions. He asked me about Mom and Dad. That wasn't too bad. But then he asked about Gam. Not even just about who she was and what I liked about her and stuff like that, but about her *dying*. And he brought it up more than once. I don't see what good it does to talk about things like that. I know he said to give it a try. And I know he's the doctor, and I'm not the doctor, and he probably knows more about it than I do. Probably everybody knows more about everything than I do. But I don't like to talk about Gam dying, and if I don't want to, I don't see why anybody would want to make me do it. It only makes me feel bad, and he said he wanted me to think about him as my friend, so I know he doesn't want me to feel bad. And I know you don't, either." Then he paused. And, suddenly unsure, he added, "*Do* you?"

"No," Stacey said. "Of course not. I want you to be happy."

"I'm happy," Stewie said. But it sounded more, to his own ear, like arguing a point, or defending it. Less like simply stating a fact.

"*Are* you?"

"I think so. Don't you think so?"

"No. Actually, Stewie . . . no. I think you could be a whole lot happier than you are. I think you've been a little sad for almost all the time you've been alive, and so maybe now you don't even know it's sad. Maybe you're just used to it and it feels normal to you. But it looks sad to everybody else."

Stewie felt his eyes go wide.

"*Everybody* thinks I'm sad?"

"Well. I don't know. I don't know what everybody thinks, so I shouldn't say. I guess I should just say what *I* think."

Outside the window, Stewie watched the Olsen place flash by, a big ranch with lots of black-and-white cattle. Stewie had always liked those cows and steers, at least from a distance. They made him feel a little better just by being there, chewing.

"I'm happier when I'm not talking about Gam dying," he told Stacey, careful not to look over at her. "Why even do it, then?"

"Because things hurt us even when we're not talking about them. Even when we're not paying attention to them. We think we're getting away with not feeling it. And we think that when something feels painful, it's better not to feel it at all. But it's almost like . . . if you had drunk poison, or eaten something that was spoiled. You might want to resist throwing it up, because that's such an icky process. And because maybe we associate throwing up with being sick. But why hold on to something if it's hurting you? Especially if you could feel better by getting it up and out. It's better for you in the long run. More likely to lead to your being happier."

"That's gross, Stacey."

"Okay, I'm sorry. It might not have been the best way to say it. But I think you probably know what I mean." She allowed a pause, in case there was something Stewie wanted to say. But there wasn't. "*Do* you understand what I mean by all that, Stewie?"

"Yeah. I think so."

"Good."

"But I still don't want to do it, though."

Stacey only sighed, and they drove on in silence for a time.

"You need to take me by Marilyn's," he said suddenly. Then, realizing he had sounded rude, he added, "Please?"

"Why do you need to go by there?"

"I worry that she burned the house down because I wasn't there to help."

"Stewie . . ."

It made him wince, the way she said it. He thought it was interesting how neither one of them really needed to say more. The whole comment was contained neatly in the way she said his name.

"Please, Stacey? Please? You said you wanted me to be happy."

Stacey only sighed again, but that was how he knew he had prevailed, and that she would take him.

—

Stewie knocked on the door, then glanced over his shoulder at Stacey waiting in the car. She didn't seem to notice. She was staring out over the lake as if lost in thought.

A second or two later the door swung open and Marilyn looked down on him.

"Oh," she said. "There you are. I actually thought I'd see you earlier."

"Yeah, sorry," he said, shifting his weight from foot to foot. "I had something I had to do."

"You don't have to be sorry. You're not required to be here. It's not your job. But I'm beginning to know you a little, so I was just surprised is all."

They both just stood a moment, neither looking at the other. An awkwardness had seized the conversation, and Stewie wasn't quite sure how to defeat it.

He could hear Izzy's voice in a far-off room. A kind of droning narration, tons of words all run together into one long sentence, as if she was lecturing one of her dolls.

"Everything okay in there?" he asked after a time.

"Yes, I haven't burned the place to the ground yet today."

"I didn't mean any offense by it, ma'am."

Stewie wasn't looking at her, but he heard her sigh.

"Oh, none taken, I suppose. I know you're only trying to help. But your sister is waiting for you in the car, and Sylvia will be home any minute. You should go now and have dinner with your family. If you want to come by tomorrow or the day after that, I'll have a small gift for you."

Stewie stood a moment, unsure what to say. He wanted to be elated about what she'd said, but he felt strangely sure that he must have heard her wrong, or somehow misunderstood.

"A gift?"

"Yes. A small one. I don't mean to oversell it."

"You bought me a gift?"

"I ordered one. It hasn't arrived in the mail yet."

"But you bought a gift, and it's for me?"

"Are we just going to keep going around like this?"

"Sorry. Why did you buy me a gift?"

"I'm not sure I need a special reason. People buy little gifts for each other all the time. But I suppose it's because you put out my cooking fire, and then came over and helped me babysit for Izzy."

"I would've done that for nothing, ma'am."

"I realize that. That's why I thought a small gift was in order. But I really think this is getting built up too big, because it's just a little token and wasn't very expensive, and I'm not even sure if you'll like it."

"Oh, I know I'll like it," Stewie said, "because no matter what it is, you got it for me."

As soon as he said it, Stewie could sense that he had pushed the matter of his affection a step too far. She seemed to retreat slightly, as though closing a door Stewie couldn't see.

"Well, we'll see," she said. "Run along now and don't keep your sister waiting. Sylvia will be home any minute and I'll be fine in the meantime."

And with that she took a step back into the house and closed the actual door. The one Stewie could see.

He trotted down the concrete steps, barely feeling his feet touch down.

When he opened the door of Stacey's car, it seemed to startle her, as if he had brought her up from a deep sleep.

She looked at him long and hard as he climbed in, and he squirmed slightly under her gaze.

"Huh," she said.

"What?"

"It's just . . . *now* all of a sudden you look happy. And I guess I'm just not used to that."

Then, to his surprise, she drove them home without giving him the third degree about why.

Chapter Ten

Returns

Marilyn

When she opened the mailbox, Marilyn was gratified to see a small flat package that was almost certainly a book.

But that little elation did not last long.

The mail had been coming late. Nearly scandalously late, it seemed to her. She couldn't help thinking, as she often did, that all her husband's and her tax dollars over all their years should have bought better service.

The sun was nearly setting behind the lake as she carried the wrapped book up the stairs and into the house.

Sylvia was home, on the couch with her notebook computer open on her lap, as always. The younger woman looked up as Marilyn walked into the living room.

"That was fast," Sylvia said, her eyes on the package.

She watched with only mild interest as Marilyn ripped the padded paper envelope away from the book.

"Anything for me?" Sylvia added.

"No, just this and the usual junk."

She pulled the book free and held it in her hands, and her heart fell. It was the edition with the little mouse rowing a canoe down a river. It was not the one she had ordered.

"But this isn't what I wanted at all."

"What do you mean?" Sylvia said. "Let me see."

Marilyn turned the book around to show her.

"That's *Stuart Little*."

"But it's not the original edition. Remember how you showed me the page when you ordered it? And it was the edition with the mouse pulling down on some sort of rope. It was from 1905."

"Well, now that I think about it," Sylvia said, "I was making fun of the fact that a seventy-five-year-old book was being advertised as a good thing . . ."

"And?"

"Do the math," Sylvia said.

While Marilyn struggled with those numbers in her head, Sylvia's fingers clattered over her keyboard.

"The book was published in 1945," Sylvia said. "Not 1905."

"But it said 1905 on the page you showed me. I saw it with my own eyes."

More clattering. It seemed odd to Marilyn that someone could be so utterly comfortable on one of those infernal devices. As if the real world could only be seen through the portal of its monitor, and everything around it was simply a distraction.

"You're right," she said. "There's an error on the listing page."

"Well, how dare they?" Marilyn walked a few steps to the couch and flopped down beside Sylvia, leaning over to see the page in question. "Now look at that cover. That's not the same as what they sent me at all. You should be able to return a purchase over a thing like that."

"You can. You can return it for just about anything, especially if there's a mistake in the way they listed it. But are you sure you want me to? I really doubt that little egg boy will care."

"*I* care. It's the principle of the thing."

Sylvia sighed. Then she tapped keys for quite an extended time.

"Well, good news," she said, two minutes or so later. "They'll issue a refund, but they don't even need you to return the book."

"That seems odd."

"It was only seven dollars. They'll do that sometimes with cheaper items. Not worth it to them to pay the return shipping. You just got yourself a free book."

"Well, that's nice, I suppose. But now I still need a gift for the boy."

"Give him that one. He won't know or care."

"I really wanted to give him that original edition. Only . . . I really don't know enough about the internet to find one. I can only do that if you'll help me."

Sylvia sighed again.

The little girl came into the room, purposely stomping her feet too loudly. She stood in front of her mother, hands on hips, arms akimbo, and frowned. As if she owned and operated the household, Marilyn thought. If not the world.

"I'm hungry," Izzy said. "Why aren't you making dinner?"

"It's in the oven," Sylvia said. "Twenty minutes." Then, to Marilyn, "There are a bunch for sale online, but you won't like the prices."

"I suppose I should have known that an original edition wouldn't be seven dollars. How much?"

"Well, this one is two hundred ninety-nine dollars."

Marilyn felt her eyes go wide.

"That's out of the question, then," she said, nursing a surprisingly sharp sense of disappointment.

"Wait. Don't give up just yet. The prices vary a lot. One forty-seven. Here's one for only forty-nine ninety-nine."

"Still too much."

"Let me keep looking."

While she looked, the little girl, who had not given up and gone away, stamped her foot dramatically. Neither adult paid her any mind.

"Cheapest one I can find," Sylvia said, "is just under twenty dollars. Used, in good condition. What do you think?"

The little girl stamped again.

"Izzy!" Marilyn shouted. "Go play until dinner!"

The girl sulked away, clearly shocked to have been spoken to in such a tone.

"Don't yell at my daughter," Sylvia said.

"Well, someone needs to."

"I was just about to say the exact same thing to her."

"Then what's the problem?"

"*I* can talk to her that way. She's *my* daughter. Now, do you want the book or not?"

Marilyn opened her mouth, but found herself undecided and did not speak.

"I guess you have to figure out how much that little egg boy means to you."

"He doesn't mean anything to me," Marilyn said. "He just did me a couple of favors is all. Yes. Get the book, please. I'll pay you back. I really want to get him that first edition."

"Okay, done," Sylvia said. "But I think you're lying to yourself. Either that or you're lying to me. You actually care about that troublesome little boy."

"He's not troublesome," Marilyn said, her voice hard.

"See? You're only proving my point."

The oven timer went off, and Sylvia jumped up to go check the roast chicken, leaving her computer open on the couch. It displayed a copy of the book Marilyn had just ordered.

She rose and followed Sylvia into the kitchen.

"I think you're wrong," Marilyn said as she walked. "But what if you're not? It's not a bad thing to care about someone, and I don't know why you say it as though it is."

Sylvia shot a withering look over her shoulder before opening the oven door.

"You don't care a whit about my daughter, and you've known her much longer."

"That's because your daughter is . . ."

But Marilyn caught herself in time.

"What?" Sylvia asked. She had turned back to Marilyn and was standing with her hands on her hips, almost exactly the way her daughter had. Except her hands were covered with bright yellow oven mitts. "My daughter is what?"

"Nothing. Never mind. I shouldn't have brought it up."

"But you did bring it up. And now I want to hear it."

"I'm just not a fan of raising children too permissively."

To her surprise, Sylvia turned away. Turned back toward the stove, seeming to drop the whole subject. But Marilyn heard her mutter under her breath. Something along the lines of "Like you haven't told me *that* a hundred times."

Marilyn pretended she hadn't heard.

Thankfully, no more was said on the matter.

———

The boy showed up the following day after school.

He stood on the concrete stoop, panting desperately, his empty wagon abandoned at the bottom of the stairs.

"You're earlier today," she said.

"Yes, ma'am," he said, breathlessly. "I got here as soon as I could."

"You finished your egg route already?"

"Yes, ma'am. I ran all the way."

"Well, that was kind of you. But I really don't need help babysitting today. Because the little girl isn't here."

Marilyn watched his face fall. He had absolutely zero talent at assuming a poker face, that sad little child. Everything he felt played out right across his face for all to see. And, in truth, Marilyn did more than just watch his emotion. She actually felt the letdown right along with him—a heavy, sinking feeling in her gut—though she could not have explained why.

"But if you want to come in," she added, "you may."

He perked up at that, and walked past her into the living room.

She watched him walk around touching the edges of everything, as if he had lost his sight. He ran one finger over all the knickknacks, and the tops of picture frames.

"Why isn't Izzy here?" he asked aimlessly. He sounded distracted. "Where did she go?"

"Her mother left work early and took her to the doctor."

The boy stopped suddenly. Stopped moving, stopped touching. He gave Marilyn his full attention, his eyes wide with alarm.

"Oh no. What's wrong with her?"

"Nothing. There's not a darned thing wrong with her. That girl is a classic hypochondriac." She watched the alarm in his eyes turn to confusion. She explained without his having to ask. "A hypochondriac is a person who's always thinking they're sick when they're not."

"Like . . . they just make up being sick?"

"More like they keep convincing themselves that they really are."

"That seems strange," he said.

And with that he resumed walking and touching.

"I know you were hoping I had that little gift for you."

Again he froze in place, dropping his arms to his sides.

"Do you?"

"Yes and no. It did come in the mail, what I ordered. But they sent me the wrong thing."

"Really? That seems strange. Like, you ordered one thing, and they sent you a whole entirely different thing?"

"Not exactly," she said. She decided to tip him to the fact that it was a book. In case he would find that disappointing. She had begun to worry that her small gift had been built up too big in his mind. "It's a book I wanted to give you." She watched his eyes as the word "book" landed. She expected him to look let down. Instead he looked . . . well, almost . . . alarmed. "And they sent me the wrong edition of the right book."

"I don't know what that means," he said.

"I wanted the original one. From the year it was first published. But they sent me a newer one, which is not worth as much, and I just don't think it's as nice a gift."

"Can I see it anyway?"

"I suppose," she said.

She walked off into the bedroom to get the book.

"I guess I'll just keep this one for myself," she said as she carried it out to him. "And give you the nicer one when it comes."

"That's very kind of you, ma'am."

He took the book into his hands when she offered it to him, but hesitantly. As if books might bite, or prove otherwise unpredictable. He held it in his partially healed right hand and ran the fingers of his left hand over the title.

"That's my name," he said. "I'd know my name anywhere."

"I know. That's why I got it for you."

He ran his fingers over the illustration of the mouse in the canoe. "So this is that mouse everybody talks about when I tell them my name."

"Exactly."

"I see why you would get this for me, then."

"I thought you'd want to have it, for that reason."

"He spells his first name different from mine. He spells his last name the same."

"There's only one way to spell *Little*. I thought we could read a chapter at a time, and then discuss it. Especially since we'll each have a copy."

His eyes flooded with an emotion she could only imagine labeling *relief*.

"Oh, good. You can read it to me."

"That's not what I was thinking."

"Oh."

"I was thinking we'd each read a chapter a day, and then we'd get together and discuss what we read."

She watched his relief turn to panic.

"Are they very long chapters?" he asked, flipping through the pages.

"No, not very long at all. It's written for children about your age, so it shouldn't be longer or more difficult than you can handle."

"Okay, I should go, then," he said.

He bustled over to the door in that tight and nervous way of his—arms clamped to his sides, legs flashing in short, quick steps.

"You don't have to go if you don't want."

"I just figured I should get started on this. If we're going to do what you said. Oh, wait. You won't have a book here at your house if I take this home. Here. I should leave you this one."

He bustled back before she could argue, and held it out to her. She did not take it.

"No, that's all right. You take it. Bring it with you when you come tomorrow and I'll read the chapter while you're playing with Izzy."

"Oh," the boy said. "Okay."

But he didn't sound as though he thought it was okay.

On his expressive face—and in his very telling, unguarded eyes—Marilyn saw something that looked downright intimidated. As if he had just agreed to climb Mount Everest and then report back to her to tell her how it had gone.

Chapter Eleven

Different

Stewie

Stewie stood in the open doorway of his brother's room, the book clutched in his left hand, shifting from foot to foot. He was hoping Theo would notice him without his having to speak up. It felt rude somehow to disturb Theo, who was peering closely at his laptop. He didn't seem to be looking at anything fun on the internet, either. He was staring at a dense page of text and seemed to be taking notes.

Schoolwork, Stewie figured. Homework.

Stewie should have been doing his own homework. In fact, he had tried. But he couldn't seem to pry his attention away from the problem of the book he'd been given. Not long enough to make anything work, anyway.

He coughed lightly into his hand to get Theo to realize he was there. It worked.

"Hey, Stewie," Theo said, without looking away from his laptop screen. "What's up?"

"I was hoping you could do me a favor."

Theo made a grumbly noise in his throat. It didn't sound like the kind of noise a person makes when the answer is yes.

"What kind of favor? And does it have to be right now? I'm kind of stuck working on this report. It's due tomorrow. And yeah, before you say it, I know. I shouldn't have put it off till the last minute."

"I wasn't going to say anything."

"No," Theo said. "I guess you weren't. I guess that's Stacey's department. So what did you want?"

"I was hoping you'd read me a chapter of this book."

Theo looked away from his screen for the first time. Looked right into Stewie's eyes. Or tried to, anyway. Stewie quickly averted his eyes to hide his shame.

"Read it to you?"

"That's what I was hoping. Yeah."

"I'm kind of busy, buddy. Can't you just read it to yourself?"

"It seems hard," Stewie said, careful not to meet his brother's eyes.

Theo sighed deeply.

"All right. Whatever. Bring it over here."

Stewie felt a great lifting in his chest—a sort of elation caused by the weight of a problem being taken away.

It didn't last.

"I'm not going to read it to you," Theo added. "I just want to look at it and see why you think it's so hard. Do you have to read it for school? They're supposed to give you things that aren't too hard for your grade level."

"No," Stewie said, handing him the book. "Not for school."

"Well, why do you need to read it, then, if it's so hard?"

"Marilyn gave it to me."

"Oh," Theo said. "Marilyn." He didn't say her name like he thought she was a good thing. Just as Stewie was trying to convince himself he was wrong about that, Theo added, "Why do you like her, anyway?"

Theo wasn't looking at the cover of the book. He was looking at the side of Stewie's face. Stewie could see his brother staring in his peripheral vision, so he carefully gazed out the window at the chicken coop in the backyard.

"I don't know," Stewie said. "Why not?"

"She's not really all that nice."

"Gam wasn't all that nice."

"But she was our gam."

Stewie didn't answer. Just continued to stare out the window.

A moment later Theo's gaze shifted away from him. Dropped down to the cover of the book.

"Never mind," Theo said. "Forget I brought it up. I guess you can like who you want to like. Oh. This is that book people always bring up when you tell them your name."

"Yeah."

"I guess that was pretty nice of her to give you this, then. I guess I take back what I said."

Theo flipped the cover of the book back and began reading.

The first chapter was only about six pages, and they weren't even full pages. Stewie had counted them carefully, noticing that the drawings took up nearly half the page. On some of the pages, anyway. Except page four, which was all words. It had made his heart sink to look at page four.

An uncomfortable minute or two passed. Theo just kept reading. It struck Stewie that it might have taken no more time for his brother to just read the chapter to him out loud, which felt frustrating.

"This doesn't seem very hard," Theo said, still reading.

"Seems hard to me."

"Maybe Stacey will read it to you."

"I hate to bother Stacey."

Which was a true enough thing. But there was another, deeper truth, and Stewie wished to skate over the top of it. Stacey was more likely to ask questions about why he found the reading hard. There was a small chance of the same problem with Theo, but small enough that Stewie had felt inclined to risk it. Theo was not a deeply curious sort, and never acted like Stewie's boss or teacher or parent.

Theo closed up the book and handed it back, seeming to want to end the discussion and get back to his schoolwork.

"Maybe save it for a year," he said.

"But she wants us to talk about it."

"Oh. Well, tell her it's hard for you. Maybe *she'll* read it to you."

"Maybe," Stewie said. But he knew he could never bring himself to admit to her that he couldn't read it on his own. "Did you read the whole chapter?"

"Pretty much. I skimmed toward the end."

"Can't you just sort of tell me what happened in it?"

Theo sighed deeply, and tore his attention away from his schoolwork again.

"Okay. Let's see. These two people had a baby, but he was really small and looked like a mouse. And then I guess when all was said and done, it turned out he *was* a mouse."

"Wait," Stewie said. "His parents were *people*?"

"Seems that way."

"*People* had a baby that was a mouse?"

"What part of that couldn't you understand the first time I said it?"

"All of it, I guess. It's just weird. People don't have mice babies."

"It's just a pretend story," Theo said.

"I know. But still. And I thought the mouse having a first and a last name was going too far. Even for a made-up story. So, was that it? For the whole chapter? They just had him and then noticed that he was a mouse?"

"No, there was more. The mother dropped her ring down the drain and couldn't fish it out, so they put the mouse on a string and sent him down the drain after it."

"That doesn't seem very nice."

"Well, nobody else was small enough to do it."

"Still. What did Stuart Little think about that?"

"He wasn't too thrilled about it. He said it made him feel slimy. But he didn't say it out loud, though. He didn't tell his parents he minded. He just took a shower and put on some kind of perfume or something. He never complained."

It made Stewie squirm slightly to hear this about the fictional mouse, though he could not have put his finger on exactly why.

"Okay, thanks," Stewie said.

He was halfway to Theo's bedroom door with his book when his brother's voice stopped him.

"Stewie. Wait."

He stopped. Turned back.

"What?"

"I've been trying to decide whether to show you this or not."

"What?"

"You're not going to like it very much."

"What is it, Theo?"

"I never want to be that person who steps all over your dreams or anything. Especially since I was the one who got you going on it in the first place."

"Theo!" Stewie shouted. He hadn't meant to shout. It filled him with a pang of guilt, but he had no time to stop and process it. "This is making me really nervous!"

"Sorry," Theo said. He sounded ashamed. "Come over here and I'll show you."

By the time Stewie had crossed the room and leaned his shoulder against his brother's chair, Theo had a video up and playing. It was some kind of clip from a local news show. But it didn't seem to be local to *them*. He heard the news anchor say they were going to go live to the fair.

A moment later a news reporter was talking to a girl. She was about Stewie's age, and she was holding a hen. She told the reporter the hen's name, which was Brown Sugar. Stewie didn't think that was a very good name for a hen.

"Oh, it's a chicken flying contest!" he said, his chest and voice all full of excitement.

"Just wait, though," Theo said.

Only in that moment did Stewie remember that this was supposed to be a bad thing, something he had been told he wasn't going to like.

Meanwhile the girl had handed her hen to a man who held the poor bird with her wings pinned to her sides.

"I wouldn't want to have to give Elsie to somebody else to hold," Stewie said. "I don't think she would like that. She doesn't even know that man. I'd want to get her flying myself."

"Just wait," Theo said again.

The man lifted the hen and placed her inside what was clearly a mailbox. The flap door was down in the front, allowing him to put the hen inside. But it had no back to it. Then the man picked up a plunger. Just a regular rubber plunger on a stick, like the kind you use when your toilet stops up.

"No!" Stewie shouted. "Don't push her out! Let her go in her own time."

The man pushed the hen out with the plunger.

The poor bird flapped wildly in the air, falling fast. Stewie hadn't realized the mailbox had been up on a high platform, but the way the camera followed the hen made it clear. It was a long way down.

The bird hit the ground with a sickening thump. A crowd of kids raced in and tried to catch the poor frightened thing, who ran like her life depended on it. But she got picked up anyway.

Then the news cut back to the anchors sitting inside, in the regular news studio. They were smiling broadly.

Stewie was not smiling. He just stood a moment, feeling all the blood drain out of his face.

"Sorry," Theo said. "But I figured it was better if you found out now."

"Maybe that's just one chicken flying contest. Maybe there are others that are better for the chickens."

"'Fraid not, kiddo. I looked at, like, three or four of them."

Through his horror, as he stood there feeling it move through him, Stewie found another emotion. Relief. He still had that awful picture in his head of Elsie falling as he tried to practice with her—of racing in to catch her and almost missing. Now they didn't need to practice anymore. It felt like a great weight had been lifted away.

"It's okay," he said. "Elsie can just be a laying hen. She doesn't have to be a star. She doesn't have to do anything special to get me to love her."

When he was done talking, he just stood for a moment, letting the shock of the violence he had just witnessed move through him. Then he noticed his brother was staring at his face.

"What?" Stewie said.

"Nothing."

"Why are you looking at me like that?"

"I don't know. I guess I was just thinking that you're different from most people in a certain way. But I can't quite put my finger on what way it is."

"Different good or different bad?"

"Neither, I guess," Theo said. "Just different."

—

Stewie sat outside, cross-legged, in the dirt of the hens' yard, holding Elsie on his lap. The other hens wanted to cluster around, in case he had treats for them. Stewie didn't want to be rude to them, but he had wanted a moment to talk to Elsie more or less alone.

In time he gave up and decided he would just have to share the moment with all the girls.

"I just want to make sure you know you didn't disappoint me and it wasn't your fault," Stewie said quietly.

He looked around the yard as he spoke. He had made her a perch to flap up to, and a soft stack of packing blankets to break any possible tumble Elsie might have taken. He would have to take all that apart now and put it back in the barn.

It made his stomach sore to think about it.

"*I* know you're the best flier around," he told her, his voice a little stronger now. "It doesn't matter if anybody else knows."

But it made him feel ashamed to say it, because it wasn't entirely true. He felt it *shouldn't* have mattered. But it did. He had wanted everyone to see his talented hen. He had wanted to fill to bursting with pride while everyone watched.

But it didn't matter. He was not going to mistreat his hen for the sake of pride.

"I'm still proud of you," he said.

But there was no way to slice it that did not feel like a loss. He would simply have to file it away with all the other things—both small and large—that should not have been asking too much from life, but which life had taken from him all the same.

Chapter Twelve

Stress

Marilyn

Marilyn was crossing the living room on her way to the kitchen when a movement outside the window caught her eye.

She stopped dead, frozen in fear, and craned her neck to see. But just that quickly the person—what she'd seen had struck her as about the right size and shape to be a person—was gone.

Would the police creep around the house, looking in windows to see if she was home? It seemed strange. Wouldn't they just rap on the door?

With an additional jolt to her gut, her mind filled with an image of the door exploding inward, demolished by a battering ram.

But that made no sense, she told herself. There probably was a warrant out for her arrest, but she wasn't a dangerous criminal. She couldn't physically hurt them. She was just a frail older woman. Surely they knew that.

Still hearing the pounding of blood in her ears, she hurried to the window, but could see nothing.

She hovered there a moment, trying to decide if she dared go out to investigate.

It was probably only a meter reader. And even if her time had come, and her freedom was over, it was over just as surely if she did not go out. She was only buying herself a very few minutes by waiting until they knocked on the door.

She drew a huge, bracing breath, strode to the door, and threw it wide.

In her peripheral vision she saw a carton of eggs on the doormat.

Her momentum was already carrying her forward onto the stoop. It was too late to stop, so she extended her right leg to step onto the other side of the carton. It came down hard, twisting her knee and ankle slightly. She nearly lost her balance. She windmilled her arms wildly to try to stay upright, and, fortunately, regained her balance. But by the time she did, between the fear and the pain, she found her temper strained.

Knowing now that it was probably only that egg boy, she walked around the side of the house.

He was standing under the kitchen window, looking down at the ground. She could only see the top half of him because of a group of bushes.

"You there!" she barked. Because, embarrassingly, she had forgotten his name again.

He looked over at her.

It was clear by the look on his face that he knew she was mad. Yet he didn't seem as though he was intimidated by it, as she would have expected. He seemed determined. As if he knew something difficult lay ahead but he had every intention of barging bravely through that danger.

He didn't answer, so she said more.

"What on earth are you doing skulking around the side of the house?"

"What's skulking?" he called back.

"It's what you're doing now. And it scared me to death to see somebody outside the window."

"Why?"

"*Why?* That's an odd question. Everybody is scared when they see someone skulking outside their windows."

"Did you think I was a burglar? It's not night. I think they always come at night. And I'm still not sure about that 'skulking' thing. You said it's what I'm doing right now, but I'm not doing anything right now. I'm just standing here talking to you."

Marilyn sighed loudly, feeling her patience strain even further. That is, if such a thing were possible.

"Let's not focus on what exactly you're doing," she said. "Instead, tell me why you're doing it."

"Just checking," the boy said.

"For what?"

"To make sure everything's okay out here."

"What could possibly go wrong under the kitchen window?"

"I was worried you might've left the hose on."

"I don't even use that hose," she said.

"Oh. I didn't know that."

They stood awkwardly for a moment.

Marilyn was trying to hold on to her anger because it had a safe, clean feel to it. It seemed to tell her it could keep her well protected, though she suspected that might have been a lie. In any case, it was hard to stay mad at that well-intentioned but pesky child.

"Even if I had left the hose on," she began, "that's not really in the category of a disaster."

"Oh, I wouldn't say that, ma'am. My gam forgot and left the hose on once. Toward the end, when she was starting to forget things. Then, when she got the water bill, she screamed. Just stood right there by the mailbox and screamed bloody murder. It was so loud the neighbor came running, thinking somebody was robbing her or killing her or something. But it was all about that bill."

Marilyn felt herself sigh. With the sigh, she gave up and let go of the anger.

"Come in the house at least," she said.

He dared to walk in her direction then.

"I brought you a carton of eggs," he said when he was close enough to talk at a normal volume.

"I saw that. I nearly broke my neck trying not to step on them."

"Oh. Sorry. I figured I'd be back at your door to pick them up again before you came outside."

"I'm not sure why you brought me more. It hasn't been a week."

"They're free," he said. "I just brought them for you for free."

They began to walk, side by side, around to her front door.

"Oh. Well, that's very kind of you. I guess I can let Sylvia and Izzy have some. Usually I keep them all for myself."

The front door had been left standing open. Marilyn bent down to pick up the eggs, aware of the volume of Izzy's cartoon program.

They stepped inside together.

The boy walked straight to the couch, where Izzy sat slumped, watching. He was partly blocking her view of the TV, so she leaned over and craned her neck to see around him.

"Hi, Izzy."

"Whatever."

"Want to play something?"

"I'm watching this."

Marilyn could see the side of the boy's face. She could watch it fall.

"Come in the kitchen," she said. "I was just about to make some tea, and we'll talk about the book."

He walked with her, looking as though he were marching up to the front of a firing squad. Marilyn had no idea why his face showed so much stress.

She put the eggs away in the refrigerator. He flopped into a chair and rested his elbows on the kitchen table.

"You probably don't drink tea," she said. "I could pour you some milk."

"Gam used to make me tea with honey."

"Oh. All right. I could do that."

"But it can't have any of that . . . what do you call it when it has that stuff in it that makes you jittery?"

"Caffeine."

"Right. None of that. Stacey does *not* like it if I have any of that. She says I get too wound up and then it's hard to be around me."

"I'll see if I have anything herbal," she said.

She dug around in the cupboards for tea, and spread what she found onto the kitchen counter. She filled the whistling kettle with water. Sylvia didn't have a microwave, because she didn't believe in them. It seemed silly to Marilyn.

Now and then she glanced over her shoulder at the boy, who still seemed inordinately stressed.

"Did you get your feelings hurt because Izzy was rude to you?"

"No, ma'am. Well . . . maybe a little. Yeah."

"If it helps any to know, she's more or less rude to everybody."

"I'm not sure if that helps or not," he said.

She set three boxes of herbal tea bags on the table in front of him. Strawberry, chamomile with lemon, and mint. He pointed at the mint.

"Did you read the first chapter?" she asked, turning back to the stove.

"Oh, I'm definitely ready to talk about that, ma'am."

It struck her as an odd way to phrase his answer. Possibly even evasive. But she wasn't quite sure how to find a door into her curiosity about that, so she left it alone.

"Did you like it?"

"I thought it was a little weird," he said.

"How so?"

"Well. Like . . . when two people have a baby, it always turns out to be a baby. It never turns out to be a mouse."

"In real life. Yes. But this is just a story."

"I know. It just seemed weird."

"You have trouble with things like that, don't you?"

"Things like what?"

"Never mind. It's too hard to put into words. Tell me what you *did* like about the chapter."

"Um . . ."

Then he stalled for a long time.

She looked over her shoulder at him. His eyes looked downright panicky.

"And another thing I thought was weird," he said after a time, veering in an entirely different direction. His voice sounded breathy with fear. Or with something. She wasn't quite sure if she was reading his reactions properly. "The part when they made him go down the sink drain."

"What about it?"

"It didn't seem very nice."

"He was the only one in the house small enough to do it."

"That's what my brother said. Still, though. Why didn't they just call a plumber? Didn't they have plumbers back in those days?"

"Of course they did. But, again, it's just a story. A ring goes down the drain and the family calls the plumber. That doesn't make for a very interesting story. Wasn't there anything you liked about it?"

Another stony, panicky silence.

"I guess I'd have to read it again," he said.

"You do that. And we'll talk again tomorrow."

She fixed their tea without speaking for a few minutes.

She patiently waited for the water to boil and placed honey and sugar on the table, with spoons. She got down little saucers to hold the discarded tea bags when the tea was brewed strong enough.

When she set his tea on the table in front of him, he leaned forward and took a long sniff, his face in the rising steam.

"That smells like mint," he said. He sounded mildly disappointed.

"Of course it smells like mint. It *is* mint. Because you *chose* mint."

"Oh" was all he said.

"Didn't you know what you were choosing? I put the boxes in front of you so you could see what your choices were."

"Yes, ma'am. I guess I just . . . just . . . pointed at something. Like . . . like when you just want it to be a surprise. You know?"

It seemed strange to her, but it wouldn't click into any boxes in her head, so in time she let it go.

They sipped their tea in silence for the longest time. It wasn't like the boy to allow long silences to fall, and Marilyn wasn't sure how to read that.

He spoke up suddenly, startling her.

"I was hoping you could read it to me," he said, his voice breathy.

"Why would I read it to you? You already read it to yourself."

"Well. You know. Just because . . . it's nice. It's a nice thing when somebody reads a book to you. Don't you think so?"

"Yes," she said. "I like it, too. Maybe I'll have *you* read it to *me*. Did you bring it?"

"No, ma'am. I didn't think to bring it." He sounded oddly relieved to have forgotten.

"Well, then how did you think I was going to read it to you?"

"Oh. Duh. I guess I didn't think of that."

"Bring it next time. We can read parts of it to each other."

He nodded vaguely. But he seemed uneasy. And Marilyn had a sense that he likely would not bring it next time, though she could not have clearly articulated why she thought so. It was more a set of feelings about the situation, gathering inside her.

Chapter Thirteen

I Can So

Stewie

Stewie was cleaning out the henhouse when she surprised him by coming over—and coming in. It had been six days since he had gone to see her. Six, exactly. He had been keeping track in his head.

He was sweeping up the dropped bits of straw from the nesting boxes, along with the dried droppings. He had a shovel to sweep it all onto—the way you would use a dustpan—and a wheelbarrow to drop it in, and then he had planned to take it outside and add it to a pile that Stacey had used to use to fertilize her garden. Back when she'd had time for a garden. Nobody talked about the fact that the pile only grew taller now, or that nobody fertilized with it anymore.

Before he could even move it all out into the yard, he looked up and she was there.

She was wearing that same yellow sweatshirt and standing in the open doorway, her shoulder leaned against the frame. He wasn't ready to talk to her—if he had been, he'd have gone to her house long ago—so he continued to sweep. Or rather, he pretended to sweep. Really there was nothing left that needed sweeping up.

She seemed to know Stewie had seen her there, and she waited quite a while, maybe thinking he would start talking on his own. If so, it was a sign that she didn't know him nearly as well as she thought she did.

In time she seemed to realize that if she didn't start a conversation, there would never be one.

"You haven't come to my house in six days," she said.

Stewie thought that was interesting, because it seemed to mean that *she* had been keeping track in *her* head, too. Almost as though the visits were as important to her as they were to him.

He had to speak then, because he had not been raised to ignore an adult who addressed him directly. It would have been rude.

"I know it," he said.

"Today would have been my egg day."

"I know that, too."

"I figured it was up to you whether you wanted to come around and help me babysit, but I was shocked that you didn't come sell me eggs. It was my day."

Stewie sighed deeply, and paused the pretense of sweeping. She was staring at him as he worked, and surely she had seen that there was nothing left to sweep. He leaned on the end of his broom and gazed out the open window to the yard, where the hens scratched and pecked. It seemed to offer him some feeling of solidity to watch them.

"I gave you that extra carton, though," he said, still looking at the distant hens and not the lady.

"I still thought you'd give me the option to buy a carton on my day. This is *my day*," she said again.

She said it stridently, as though it was something Stewie were required by law to do. As though she could repeat that sentence to a judge and he would be shocked at Stewie's negligence.

But Stewie always reached a point where he regretted owing any responsibility to anyone. And this was one of those times.

They stood in silence for what he guessed might be a minute or more. She wanted something from him. And the more he could feel her wanting it, the more opposed he felt to offering it up.

"Why are there no hens?" she asked after a time.

"They're out in the yard."

"I didn't see them when I came through."

"The yard is on the other side."

"Oh."

She paused for a moment. Opened her mouth. Closed it again. She seemed to be trying to decide about something. But what? Stewie couldn't imagine.

"I brought you something," she said, and reached into her purse.

That got Stewie's attention, and softened his resistance. Because he always liked it when someone brought him something. Who wouldn't?

But then it was out of her purse and in her hand in the light, and it was another book. The feeling of it sank down into his belly. It was a sensation as though he had swallowed something heavy and dense. He looked away and said nothing.

"This is the one I really wanted to give you. It's the original one."

He moved a step or two closer and looked at the cover. It had his name on it, just like the one she had given him. It must have been the same book. He remembered, but only vaguely, that he was supposed to trade her for a better copy when it arrived.

It looked much more old-fashioned.

The mouse—who Stewie seemed to recall was a boy mouse—was wearing what looked like a dress, or a long dressing gown, and appeared to be trying to climb a rope. Or pull one down. The cover was made with some kind of tan fabric on it, and it had a couple of light spots, as though somebody had accidentally dropped bleach on it over the years.

"Why is this one supposed to be better?" he asked her.

As he spoke, he realized he had gotten closer to her than he'd meant to go.

"It's an original edition. The original editions are always more sought after."

"I don't know what that means."

"It means people want them more."

"Well, not this person. I like the one with the mouse rowing a canoe down the river. It looks nicer to me."

"You're welcome to keep that one if you like it better."

"Thank you," he said.

Then, owing to his embarrassment and his sudden inability to hold still, he went back to sweeping nothing.

She watched for a moment in silence. Then she said, "It all looks pretty well swept to me."

Stewie held still and leaned on the end of his broom again, feeling his face flame red. He did not answer.

"I think I know why you've been upset," she said. "Why you've been avoiding me."

He glanced at her for a split second, but only at the very edge of his vision, where he hoped she wouldn't see. Again, he didn't answer. He didn't dare.

"I think you can't read."

"That's just not true!" he shouted. "Why would you say a thing like that? I can so read! I just can't read *everything*. Nobody my age can read everything. Right? It was just hard, that book. It's not my fault if it was hard. You shouldn't come around here accusing me of being bad at a thing like that."

"You do it to me all the time."

"How do I do that to you?"

"You come around all the time and remind me that I can't be trusted to look after a little girl. That I'll forget something. Flood the house or burn it down or cause some other tragic accident."

"I was only trying to help! I didn't want anything terrible to happen to you. This is different. Nothing terrible happens if you can't read."

She said nothing. Absolutely nothing. For the longest time. When he could stand no more silence, he braved a look at her face. Then he immediately wished he hadn't. She pitied him. It was right there in her eyes. And there was nothing worse than pity aimed in your direction. Stewie had always thought so.

"Do you really think that? Oh, son. *Everything* bad happens if you can't read. It follows you and holds you back your whole life. You want to get a job, so you go in to apply and they hand you a long application to fill out. How will you fill it out? How can you answer questions when you can't even read them to know what questions they are? Or you learn to drive, but then you're trying to find your way around in a world of street signs. Why, I can't think of anything much more terrible than that."

"It was just a hard book," he said. Quietly.

While he waited for her to answer, he toyed with the idea that she really did mean to help him. That maybe her intentions were as pure as his had been when he checked her bathtub and her hose and her stove burners. It caused a funny buzz in his chest to think she might care. Still, he couldn't help thinking she could help him more by leaving this sore subject alone.

"I looked it up," she said. "The age recommendations for the book. Not before I bought it, I'm ashamed to say, but before I came over here. It's supposed to be a good book for kids as young as eight."

Stewie leaned his broom against the wall and sank down onto the floor with a thump.

"I'm sorry," she said. "It wasn't my intention to embarrass you."

"Well, you did anyway," he said, and set his face in his open hands. Even though they were dirty from cleaning out the henhouse.

"I'm sorry. I just can't help wondering why your teachers didn't notice."

"Oh, they notice."

"And then why they don't pass their observations on to your pa—" She stopped herself before the word came fully out of her mouth. "Sister."

"They ask her to come in for conferences, but she works nights and sleeps during the day. She doesn't have time for that."

"And then they move you up from grade to grade without basic reading proficiency skills? That's unconscionable."

"You just used a lot of big words," he said, his voice sounding despondent to his own ears. "And I didn't understand half of them. But if you're saying they should've held me back and made me repeat grades, well, that's sure no favor to me, ma'am."

"I'm saying they should have taught you to read. Why, I have half a mind to take it up with somebody at your school. But . . . okay. Maybe not. I saw the look on your face just now when I said that. Anyway, now that it's out in the open, I'm hoping you'll come back around and help keep my babysitting safe."

"I guess I could. But you have to stop bringing this up."

"I was thinking just the opposite."

"The opposite doesn't sound very good to me, ma'am."

"Let me finish. I was thinking I could read the book to you, the way you asked me to. And then maybe after a while we could go through and you could look at the words on the page and tell me which ones you know and which ones you don't. And maybe you'd get a little better that way. How does that sound?"

"Sounds like homework, ma'am."

"You said everybody likes having a book read to them."

"I did say that."

"Maybe we'll just start with that and push all that other stuff down the road."

"What road?"

"It's only a figure of speech."

"Oh. Well . . . yeah, I guess that would be okay."

He pulled to his feet and they walked out of the henhouse together. It was heavy dusk now, later than he realized. Stacey would want him in for dinner soon.

"I'm going to go home now," she said. "But I hope you'll come by tomorrow."

"How will you get home? Do you have to walk?"

"Yes, but I don't mind. Will you come tomorrow?"

"Okay. But wait. Don't go yet. I have to get you your eggs."

He sprinted away from her in the fading light.

He burst into the bright kitchen and past Stacey, who was stirring a steaming pot of some kind of pasta. He opened the fridge and pulled out a carton of eggs.

"Dinner in five minutes," she said.

"That's fine. I'll be right back. I just have to go give Marilyn her eggs."

"She's *here*? What's she doing *here*?"

But Stewie dashed out the door without answering.

She was waiting for him in the last light of the day, her shoulders looking stooped. It gave her a discouraged look. It made her look the way Stewie felt.

"You sure you'll be okay walking home?" he asked her, and handed her the eggs. "Maybe I should walk you."

"That won't be necessary," she said. "But thank you."

"But it's almost dark."

"And your sister will want you in for dinner. I have a little flashlight in my pocket."

"Oh," Stewie said. "Then I guess that's okay."

"I owe you four dollars."

"No, ma'am," he said. "This one is free."

"The last one was free. Can you afford that?"

"It's fine," he said. "Just take them. I have plenty of eggs."

"Well, then . . . thank you."

He stood for a long time, watching her walk back to the road in the gathering dark. She turned on the little flashlight when she got to the end of his driveway, and he watched the circle of its light bounce up and down along the road.

Then he went inside for dinner, grateful that Stacey and Theo had not heard anything they'd discussed.

Chapter Fourteen

Float

Marilyn

Marilyn stood at the edge of the playground, looking at the entrance to the school.

She felt as though she had simply found herself there. As though she had napped unexpectedly and then woke up in a new place. She knew she must have walked down to the school, but she had no memory of having done so.

What felt most troubling was the subject of why she had decided to come.

On its simplest level it was quite plain. It bothered her that they hadn't seen to it that the boy could read. And it was a kind of aggravating feeling that did not wish to be ignored. It reminded Marilyn of a scratchy tag on a new blouse. It was nearly impossible to hold your attention elsewhere, and there was no way to stay calm in the face of it.

But under that . . . underneath it there was something, and she had lost it, as she lost so many things these days. There was a reason she had initially wanted to come here but then decided against it. But the more she reached for the spot where it should have lived, the more empty that spot became. It had come to feel like a soft black hole, able to absorb and destroy more of her thoughts if she allowed it to do so.

Meanwhile, standing at the edge of a playground felt emotionally uncomfortable, because she had been tormented by her peer group on playgrounds as a child. And she couldn't help marveling—though not in a good way—at the fact that she could remember that ancient past, but not what might have stopped her from making this trip.

Tired of the mental tug-of-war, she sighed, made her way to the visitors entrance, and pulled open the door.

There was a yellow line on the floor inside, an arrow with a very long tail, that was clearly marked "office."

She followed it, and stepped inside.

A woman of about forty stood behind a desk, reading a book and drinking a mug of coffee. Her hair was stringy and limp, and she looked positively exhausted. Marilyn was curious as to whether she had lost sleep the previous night, or if this was simply the way you looked when you worked around all these children day in and day out. But of course there was no way to know. It was certainly not a question a polite person could ask.

"What can I help you with?" the woman said, without ever looking up from her book.

"I'd like to speak with the principal."

"Regarding . . . ?"

"One of your students."

"I figured that. I was hoping we could narrow it down to which one."

Marilyn felt a deep jolt of panic in her chest. Because she had forgotten his name again. But then she remembered that she had prepared for this. It was not that she remembered it in her head so much as she felt it in her fingers. She had brought the book, in case she forgot the boy's name.

She glanced down at its ancient, oddly comforting cover.

"Stewart Little," she said.

The woman looked up then, and her face brightened. But in a quirky way. As if the name amused and bemused her at exactly the same time.

"Ah, yes," she said. "Our Stewie." And her eyes drifted down to her book again.

"Why do you say it like that?"

"Oh, we love Stewie. Don't get me wrong. How could anybody not love Stewie? He's just so . . . loveable."

"Yes," Marilyn said, realizing the truth of the thing as the conversation moved along. "Yes, he is oddly loveable."

"Odd and loveable," the woman said. "That's our Stewie." Then she looked up again. Suddenly. Guiltily. As if only just realizing her mistake. "I didn't mean any offense by that. I didn't mean odd like . . ."

"No offense taken. I think it goes without saying that he's a bit odd, but in a way that's charming for some reason. Now . . . may I see the principal?"

"Let me see if she's busy."

The woman stepped away from the desk and rapped lightly on a closed office door. When a muffled word came from the other side, she opened the door a crack and stuck her head in. More muffled words were exchanged.

Then the woman motioned for Marilyn to come ahead in.

Marilyn stepped inside the principal's office, and the woman closed the door gently behind her.

Marilyn stood a moment, adjusting. Adjusting her eyes to the relative dimness, but also adjusting to the differences in the energy of the woman and the room.

The principal sat behind her desk, her hands clasped and folded on its top. She was not half involved in a book or a cup of coffee. She drilled her attention into Marilyn like a hawk watching a mouse scurry across a field. She looked to be in her late fifties or early sixties, but Marilyn had begun to have more and more trouble judging ages. Everyone just looked young to her.

The woman's hair was dark—likely dyed—and cut bluntly just below her ears, which Marilyn thought a silly and unbecoming style. She was wearing a dress that fit too snugly on her solid frame, and a waist-length jacket.

That's wrong, Marilyn thought. The more stuffed into one's clothes one appeared, the longer one's jacket should be.

Then she realized she was being judgy, and that it's best not to be if one can help it.

The principal motioned for her to sit, and she did.

Marilyn had worn a dress from her business days, making her look and feel quite professional. She folded her hands in her lap, on her linen skirt, feeling proud that it still fit her after all these years.

A little burst of lightning seemed to go off in her brain, reminding her that there had been some reason not to do this. But it remained beyond her reach.

"You're here to talk about Stewie Little," the principal said.

It knocked Marilyn away from trying to remember.

"I am."

"Good. I'm glad to see someone take an interest. We want very much to talk about his schoolwork with someone, but we can never get anyone in here. Not that I blame his sister, mind you. Poor young woman. Why, she was barely an adult herself when she found herself the guardian of two helpless young boys. I'm sure just supporting them all has been an adventure. But of course a child needs more than just financial support."

"Yes, of course," Marilyn said.

Meanwhile her thoughts ran elsewhere. She had come down here to be angry at the people in charge of the boy's school, because they were uncaring, and falling down on their jobs. But her anger had already begun to seep away, abandoning her. *And anger is such a safe tool,* she thought. She felt it like an inflated raft that one would cling to in the deep end of a pool. She had no idea how to handle this meeting once it was gone.

"And you are . . . ?" the principal asked. She had a pen poised over a small yellow tablet, prepared to write it down.

It set off another thread of lightning in Marilyn's brain. A little jolt. This was one of the reasons. One of the obvious aspects that had kept her from coming before today. And now it was too late.

There was something else as well, but it stayed out of her reach.

"Marilyn Higgenbotham," she said.

Because it was the name she gave to everybody these days. She hoped that the fact that it wasn't her real name would offer some protection.

The principal wrote it down, which made Marilyn uneasy.

"And what is your relationship to the child?"

Marilyn's head filled with a confusing jumble of thoughts. Her son was an attorney, and she remembered how he had talked about a case that involved "standing." The legal definition of the word. Whether or not the person bringing the case had legal standing to do so. Marilyn needed to have some relationship to the child to come to his school and take his educators to task. And she hadn't thought of it. And she knew that the fact that she hadn't thought of it was a problem—the same type of problem as having to carry the E. B. White book because she would inevitably forget the boy's name.

"I'm his grandmother," she said. And instantly regretted saying it.

The principal looked up quickly, and met her eyes.

"But Stewie's grandmother is . . ."

"Everybody has two grandmothers. At least as long as they both live."

"Yes, of course. I'm so sorry. You're his other grandmother. I'm surprised we haven't met you before. Do you live around here?"

"Not until recently."

"I see. Understood. All right, then. Was there something specific you wanted to discuss?"

"There is, yes," she said, grasping again for the safety of that pool float. "I want to know why you haven't taught him to read."

That hung in the air for a moment like something wounded. Like that split second between the moment you hurt yourself and the moment the blood begins to flow, and you really get a look at what you've done.

"Mrs. Higgenbotham," the principal began. Her voice had taken on a grave, overly professional tone. "I want you to know that we offer the same level and quality of instruction to all of our students. But it's not always received in the same way. How can it be? Every child is an individual."

"Are you saying Stewart is unintelligent? Because I don't think he is."

"No! Not at all. Nothing of the sort. When Stewie first came to us, we knew how bright he was immediately. And he loved school. He was so involved in his learning, and so proud of his schoolwork."

"And then what happened? Because it doesn't seem that way now."

"And then his grandmother—his other grandmother, who lived with the family—she began to deteriorate. She had Alzheimer's, but maybe you know all this. I'm not sure how close the two sides of the family are. Stewie adored her, so it was traumatic for him. We see this all the time, I'm sorry to say. I've been in education for decades, and I've seen it over and over. You have a very bright, involved student, doing very well in class, and then their family life falls apart in some way. There's trauma at home. And at that juncture we just . . . lose them. In a very real way we just lose that student. I'm sure you're familiar with the old saying 'You can lead a horse to water but you can't make him drink.' I don't mean it to sound callous. I know your grandson is not an animal. All I'm trying to say is that we've been delivering the same education all along. All through Stewie's school life. But then there came a time when he stopped accepting what we had to offer. Trauma does strange things to the human psyche. I don't know if it's that he can't concentrate well enough to do his work, or if he simply lost track of a reason why he should care. Depression does that to the mind. Makes it hard to care."

"You don't have to lecture me on depression," Marilyn said. "I know it as well as anyone."

"I'm sorry. Genuinely. I didn't mean to lecture you at all. I just wanted to describe what I see in your grandson's case. I'm sorry if I offended you."

"No," Marilyn said. And sighed. In her mind, the inflatable pool float drifted toward the horizon. Sucked out to sea, miles beyond her reach. There would be no safe, comfortable anger to protect her. That was over and done, and she knew it. "You didn't, really. Just . . . well, what do we do about the situation?"

"My first thought is that you're here now. You didn't use to live close by, you say. Now you do. That has to be a help to him."

"Perhaps so," she said.

But it was making her unhappy. She had come here to tell these people that Stewie was their job. And that they were falling down on that job. Failing him. Now she realized she would walk away having been assigned that job herself.

It was a decidedly sinking feeling.

She shifted uneasily in her chair, and the principal seemed to notice the book on her lap. Maybe she had inadvertently covered it with a hand or arm, and had just moved it away. Or maybe the woman simply looked at the book for the first time.

"Oh, you have his namesake book."

"Yes. I was hoping to get him to read it. But it seems to be beyond him, which is discouraging."

"Of course. But keep trying with him. It can only help."

"I agreed to read it to him. And then I said we could go over it word by word and see what words he knows and what ones he doesn't."

"Excellent!" The principal clapped her hands together, startling Marilyn. "That could make such a difference. I feel very optimistic now."

Clearly a great weight had been lifted off the principal's shoulders. Marilyn had lifted it away. And it had been dropped squarely onto her own.

They both stood, an agreement that the meeting was ending.

No good deed goes unpunished, she thought as she stepped into the outer office.

Somehow it had fallen to her not only to teach the boy to read, but to heal his traumatic life. And all she had wanted was to buy a few cartons of unusually fresh eggs.

Chapter Fifteen

Crashing

Stewie

When Marilyn opened her front door, she didn't say hello to Stewie, nor he to her. She just stepped out of his way and he walked in without comment.

He wasn't sure why she was being unusually quiet. He knew why *he* was. He was trying to avoid saying, "Why did you come to my school?"

Stewie lived his life on the basic tenet that, compared to an adult, he had no rights whatsoever. An eleven-year-old simply didn't say whatever he wanted to a grown-up. Especially a not particularly welcoming grown-up. Still, every time the thought came into his head, his question seemed so obvious, so . . . *justified*, that he felt anyone should have the right to ask it of anyone.

And yet to open his mouth and speak those words to her felt unthinkable.

He walked past Izzy, who was watching loud cartoons, but she didn't look up at him.

Nobody in this house seems all that happy to see me, he thought.

He walked into the kitchen and Marilyn followed.

"You brought your book," she said. Her voice sounded the way people sound in the morning when they've just wakened up and haven't used it for hours.

"Yes, ma'am." An awkward pause fell. "I said I would."

"And then you did."

"I always try to do what I said I would."

"That's a good quality in a person."

"I know that."

He sat at her kitchen table, his hands folded together over the book.

"I'm going to make myself a cup of tea," she said. "Do you want any?"

"No thank you, ma'am."

"Do you want anything?"

"No thank you. I'm fine."

Izzy stuck her head into the kitchen and frowned at him. "I wanted to play something," she said.

"I thought you would want to watch your cartoons."

"What made you think that?"

"Last time you just wanted to watch TV. Plus, when I came in just now, you were watching something."

"Not something *good*," Izzy said, her voice taking on that whiny quality on the final word.

"Well, it's going to have to be later," Stewie said. "Marilyn and I are going to work on reading this book."

"You *suck*," she said.

Then she stuck out her tongue at him and disappeared.

He shifted around in his chair, trying to let the insult move through him with the least possible amount of damage. He glanced up at Marilyn, who was lighting a paper match from a small matchbook.

"She's hard to get along with," Stewie said.

"Ha!" Marilyn said. "*Tell* me about it!"

Then she held the match to the stove burner to light it.

The stove was a modern enough variety, but Stewie had noticed how the burners wouldn't light on their own. Probably just the pilot flames had gone out, he figured. Stewie knew how to relight gas pilots, but he didn't figure he would in this case. He was more comfortable with the idea that those burners would only come on if the lady was entirely sure she wanted them to.

She was faced away from him at the stove. Not really doing anything. The kettle was on, and could heat by itself, but she was only staring at the wall behind the stove, as far as he could see.

The question barged into his head again. *Why did you come to my school?*

Almost as though his thoughts were on display for her to see, she spoke.

"I have a confession to make," she said.

"I'm not sure about that word."

"It means I need to admit something I did."

"Oh. Okay. Go ahead, then."

"I went down to your school."

And now, thankfully, the figurative door into that difficult question was open. And he could ask it.

"Why did you do *that?*"

"I was troubled by this reading thing. Or I guess I should say lack of reading."

Stewie felt an odd and uncomfortable stirring in his chest, like something that won't lie flat so as to stop getting in your way. He figured it was anger, which was unfortunate. Kids don't get to be angry at grown-ups.

All the same, his voice as even as possible, he did express his concerns.

"You told me you had a mind to do that. And before I could even say, 'No, please don't,' you took one look at my face and said you knew by my face that I didn't want you to. But then you went and did it anyway."

"And you want to know why," she said. A flat statement, not a question. She knew what he wanted from her.

She was still addressing the wall behind the stove, her back to him. That made things easier. Made it easier for him to talk. Maybe it was easier for her that way, too. Maybe that's why she was doing it.

"Yes, ma'am, I do."

"Then I'll tell you the truth, even though the truth doesn't make me look very good. I forgot that exchange."

"That what?"

"That moment when I realized I shouldn't do it. I saw on your face that I shouldn't, and then I went and forgot it. Just like I forgot to turn off the fire under my bacon. It just slipped out of my mind."

He waited for a few beats, thinking she was about to say more. Specifically, that she was about to say she was sorry. He could almost hear it hanging in the air, waiting to be said. *Wanting* to be said. But it never came along.

"Well, that's pretty honest," he said. "I'm glad you brought it up so I didn't have to."

She glanced over her shoulder at him. "Oh, you knew?"

"Yes, ma'am."

"You saw me there, or they told you?"

"The principal told me. She said something like 'I just had a talk with your grandmother.' And I said, 'My grandmother is dead. You know that. Everybody knows that.' And she said, 'Oh, no, not that grandmother. Your other grandmother.' And I said, 'My other grandmother is dead a lot longer than that. Like, before I was born.' And then she told me the name of the person who she just talked to, and I said, 'Yes, ma'am, I know her, but she's not my grandmother.'"

Stewie looked up suddenly as the big shadow of Marilyn appeared over him. Her face looked wild with alarm. It made him feel panic as well.

"You said that? Why did you say that?"

"Because it's true!"

"I know, but couldn't you have just said I'm your grandmother? What would it have hurt you to say so?"

"Okay, it's like this. If you need me to say something for some reason, I will. Even if it's not true, if it doesn't hurt anybody and you need me to do it, I will. But you have to tell me. How can I say what you want if I don't even know what it is?"

She sank down into the chair next to him, her alarm fading and morphing into what looked like some sort of depressed dread. She dropped her face into her hands, one palm covering each eye.

"You're right, of course," she said.

That made Stewie feel a little more relaxed, despite her evident darkness. He still didn't know what was so terribly wrong, but at least she wasn't blaming *him*.

"I don't see what the big deal is. I mean, you said you're something, but you're not. Kind of weird, but they can't arrest you for that."

"No," she said, her voice oddly quiet. "They can't arrest me for *that*."

Stewie had no idea what to make of her comment, so he moved things in a different direction.

"It's just so embarrassing," he said. "Thinking about you sitting there with her, talking about how stupid I am."

She did not remove her face from her hands as she spoke.

"No," she said. "It wasn't like that at all. Nobody said you were stupid. Quite the opposite. She said you were a bright boy with a lot of interest in learning. But then things turned for you when you started having trouble at home."

"They *know* that?"

"Of course they know it. Everybody knows your grandmother got sick and died."

"But they know I couldn't learn the same after that?"

"Of course."

"How do they know that?"

"Because you're not the only child it's happened to. When we have trauma in our life, it affects everything. It's a normal reaction to that stress."

Stewie sat quietly for a moment, feeling those words settle in. Almost wanting to memorize them for whatever hard times might come later. Seemed there were always more hard times out there somewhere, waiting to move in.

"I still don't really know why you went, though," he said. "I mean, I get that you wanted to go, but there was a reason not to, but then you forgot the reason. But why did you want to go in the first place?"

"I told you. I was troubled by the reading situation. Children should be taught how to read."

"All children? Or just me?"

"Well, of course all children. How could I possibly think that you're the only child in the world who ought to be taught how to read?"

"But you're not going to all *their* schools. That's what I'm trying to say."

"Obviously it makes a difference if the child is one I . . ."

But she trailed off. Just as she'd gotten to a sentence Stewie desperately wanted her to finish, she seemed disinclined to finish it.

"What? One you what?"

"You know what I'm trying to say."

"Not really."

"A child I take some interest in."

The teakettle began to whistle. Marilyn only sat there with her face in her hands. She did not get up to tend it.

"Sounded like you were about to say I was somebody you care about."

"Well, I'm not sure what exact words I was about to use."

They fell quiet again—though it was not the least bit quiet in the kitchen with that noisy teakettle whistling. Stewie got up to turn off the fire under it, since it didn't seem she had any intention of doing it.

"Okay," he said in the blessed silence left behind after its shriek faded.

"Okay what?"

"If it's really important to you that I learn to read better, then I will. But I really hope you'll help me. Because it would be totally embarrassing to have to go to my English teacher and tell her I need her to teach me again everything she already taught everybody in the first place."

"Yes, of course I'll help."

"Don't you want to get up and make this hot water into tea?"

She still had her palms pressed over her eyes. She still hadn't popped back from his news that the principal knew she had lied about being his grandmother.

Maybe grown-ups get embarrassed too, he thought.

But she had made some cryptic comment about arrest. It had been impossible to understand, though—he simply did not know enough about what was going on in her head to know how she'd meant it—so he pushed it out of his mind again and tried to focus on the lesson at hand.

—

There were four more reading lessons. Exactly four, over the same number of days, if you count the one that was interrupted. Stewie chose to count that one when he looked back on the lessons.

During the fourth lesson, it happened.

They were sitting together at the kitchen table, working on chapter four of the mouse book. The mouse with human parents and Stewie's name. Marilyn had asked him to point out all the words he didn't know. He had the book turned toward her, but angled so that he could just barely see it, and he was running his finger down the page, pointing to any word he couldn't understand.

Before he could reach the end of the page, Marilyn said something that hurt him.

She said, "My goodness, son." She had taken to calling him son. He suspected she might have forgotten his name, which also hurt. "It would be faster if you just pointed to the ones you *could* read."

He went silent then, and tried not to let on that he had been hurt.

To make matters worse, Izzy came stomping into the kitchen with her usual complaints.

"You never *play* with me anymore! I want to *play* something!"

Stewie didn't answer, because he was busy being wounded and keeping it to himself.

She turned her scathing attention to Marilyn.

"I'm hungry!" she shouted.

"Get some string cheese out of the fridge, and then when this lesson is done, I'll heat you up some soup."

The little girl sighed. "You guys are so *boring*," she said. She stomped to the fridge, opened the door, and stared inside for a moment. Then she closed it and turned away without taking anything to eat. On her way by Stewie's chair she punched him on the arm. Surprisingly hard for such a little thing. "You used to be fun," she said. "Now all you want to do is read."

She stomped out of the room. Stewie just sat there, rubbing his arm and watching her go.

Then it happened. The moment that sent Stewie's world crashing about his feet yet again. It came in the form of a very loud noise. A knock, but more than a knock. A huge, ominous pounding on the door. As though someone were striking it with the back of a fist, using all of their strength.

He jumped in his chair. Marilyn jumped, too. He looked at her face and watched all the blood drain out of it. Watched it go white.

"Police!" a big male voice shouted from just outside the front door.

Stewie only sat. Marilyn only sat. Her face grew even whiter, if such a thing were possible.

"Jean Clements?" the big voice shouted through the door. "Open up. We have a warrant for your arrest."

Stewie felt relief when he heard that, because clearly they had the wrong party. They were at the wrong house. He watched her face, waiting to see that same relief.

It never came.

Another huge pounding made them both jump.

"Get the door," she said. Quietly. "Talk to them. Keep them occupied. I'll go out the back."

She rose and tried to hurry out of the kitchen, but he grabbed her by her sleeve.

"Wait!" he hissed. "What do I say to them?"

"Anything. I don't care. I just need time to get away."

"But you're not Jean Clements."

But it was too late. She had pulled her sleeve out of his grasp and gotten away from him, and she was headed fast for the back of the house.

Stewie made his way to the door, hands shaking. Knees weak. He had to walk carefully, so they wouldn't buckle underneath him.

He reached toward the knob, then couldn't bring himself to do it.

He just stood, frozen in his fear, for what felt like minutes. His hand remained suspended in the air, almost but not quite to the knob.

Then he heard a noise behind him, and he turned.

Marilyn was being led to the front door by a man. He was a tall, broad-shouldered man with a grim expression. He wasn't wearing a policeman's uniform, just nondescript clothing—black pants and a dark blue short jacket. But he had a gun in a holster at his waist.

He led her to the front door and opened it, nodding to the plainclothes officer on the front stoop.

He was a shorter man, this second one, and pudgy, and he shook his head at Marilyn in disdain.

"You really think we're so stupid that we don't have someone wait at the back door?" he said to Marilyn. He said it flatly, and simply. Just stating a fact. As if he were surprised that she hadn't noticed the sun was out that day, or something equally obvious.

Marilyn made no reply.

The man who had her by the elbow moved her through the open door and out onto the stoop.

"Wait!" Stewie cried. "Her name is not Jean Clements! Marilyn! Tell them! Tell them your name is not Jean Clements!"

Oddly, she did not.

She was halfway down the stairs, one plainclothes policeman at each of her elbows, when she stopped suddenly and turned back.

"I can't go," she said. "I have to look after the little girl."

"I can stay here with Izzy," Stewie said.

"You're too young," the tall, broad-shouldered cop said. "I'll drive her in," he said, more quietly, to his partner. "You stay with the girl."

Then he led Marilyn to a long black American-made car and placed her in the back seat.

The other cop walked back up the stairs to Stewie.

"Her name is not Jean Clements," Stewie said.

"It is," he said flatly. "No matter what she told you. You don't live here, do you?"

"No, sir."

"Go home, then. I'll stay with the girl."

Completely out of options, his gut heavy and his mind spinning in a dizzying swirl, Stewie did as he had been told.

Chapter Sixteen

Hit the Ground Flapping

Marilyn

At first, she said nothing. She felt as though it might be more prudent to keep her mouth closed. She had been read her Miranda rights, after all. There was a reason they made sure you knew you had the right to remain silent.

They had driven along the lake for what seemed like a strangely long time. She hadn't realized how many miles it covered if you followed the length rather than the width of it.

Now the lake was long gone, and they had reached the outskirts of the dreaded city. And she was overcome with curiosity regarding how much this policeman knew about her situation.

She was in the back seat of his unmarked car, even though there was no one in the passenger seat. She was on the right side, not directly behind him, looking at the side of his head from behind.

The thrum of the tires on the surface of the highway created a vibration that would have put her to sleep under more normal circumstances. In that moment she was too shot through with pins and needles of fear to find it relaxing.

Curiosity got the best of her, and, after finding what felt like a safe door into a mild, uncontroversial topic of conversation, she spoke.

"I hate this city," she said.

For a beat or two, he didn't answer. He cocked his head like a dog trying to understand commands spoken in non-dog English.

"According to your file, you lived here all your life. It's not like you were just sent here because Eastbridge is here."

That's a bad sign, she thought. *He knows something about me. He wasn't just given an address and told to go pick somebody up.*

"And your point would be . . . ?"

"When people hate cities, they move away."

"I got married young. My husband wanted to stay."

He made no reply. Which didn't feel particularly strange. What was there, really, for him to say? It was her life, and it had nothing to do with him.

The highway had turned into the broad boulevard of Central Avenue, the long main drag with stoplights at every intersection. He missed the first light and had to stop, which meant he would miss all of them. They were timed that way.

They both stared at the red light together.

"Are you sure what I did is even against the law?" she asked.

He only snorted a short laugh.

She rushed to say more.

"I mean, yes. I ran away. And I was ordered to be there by a judge, but do you arrest someone for that? Or do you just find them and take them back?"

He said nothing for a strange length of time. As if his next words required much careful consideration. The light turned, and he drove.

He glanced over his shoulder, catching her eye. It froze her, all through her insides.

"Look. Mrs. Clements," he said. "We both know what you did to get arrested."

So he knew. That was too bad.

He pulled up to the next intersection, and the light, of course, turned red.

"Where are you taking me?" she asked, feeling a bit desperate now. "Are you actually taking me to a jail?"

"I'm going to take you back to Eastbridge and turn you over to them, and then they get to decide if they want to press charges. And, look. Just between you and me. If you still have the money . . . or even some part of the money . . . I know you've probably spent some by now, but if you still have some of it stashed somewhere, I'd have someone go and get it, and you can offer it back to them. If they get at least most of the money back, they're more likely to let a thing like that go without jail time."

The light turned, and he drove again.

"I have most of it," she said. "I figured it would have to last for a long time, so I was very thrifty with it."

"Good. That'll help your situation."

They missed three more stoplights before she spoke up again. And even then she surprised herself. A thought floated through her mind, but she hadn't seen it coming, and she definitely hadn't meant to say it out loud.

"Now I won't be able to teach that boy to read."

He caught her eye in the rearview mirror.

"What boy? That kid who was there at the house when we picked you up? He doesn't live there, right? We were told there was just a single mom and a girl."

"No. He doesn't live there."

"What's his story?"

She sighed, and let her mind go blank. She vaguely wondered if she even knew his story.

"He's had a lot of loss in his life. He just needs someone to need him around."

"Maybe he could come visit you."

"Where? In Eastbridge? Or in jail?"

He caught her eye again in the rearview mirror. His curiosity had been replaced by something that looked like a mild revulsion.

"Well, that remains to be seen," he said. "Doesn't it?"

———

She sat in the plush administration office, waiting to see who would come in to read her the riot act.

Please be Boris, she thought to herself. Over and over. It had become a loop in her brain. *Please be Boris. Please don't be Lynne.*

The door opened, and Lynne strode in.

She was a tall, bizarrely thin woman of maybe forty, with long arms and legs. She looked as though she had been stretched into her current height.

She sat down behind the desk, making a steeple of her fingers. Marilyn made a point of looking down at the green wall-to-wall carpet.

"Well, then," Lynne said. "What do you have to say for yourself, Mrs. Clements?"

Marilyn sat quietly for a long time. Or maybe it only seemed like a long time. She was hoping the question would go away on its own. It didn't seem to.

"Most people think chickens can't fly at all," she said at last. "But they do. They try. They're just not all that good at it. I looked it up online after someone told me that. They flap and they flap, but they never seem to gain much altitude. Sooner or later they hit the ground again. Generally sooner."

Silence. A strange, awkward one.

Then Lynne said, "Is this a metaphor?"

"Seems that way. Doesn't it? The longer you live, the more you come to believe that pretty much everything is. Yes, I hit the ground, but you have to give me credit for trying, though, right?" She waited. She glanced at Lynne, hoping the woman would at least smile. Even wryly. Lynne did not smile. She seemed utterly devoid of humor. Then again, Marilyn reminded herself, she always had been. "Well. Never mind. Of course you don't. What was I thinking? I have most of the money. I could give back what I still have. Maybe one of my children could make up the difference."

"You don't think we already approached your children about the money?"

"But that was all of it. This is only the difference. It's not really that much. You'd be surprised how little I got by on while I was gone. If I give it back . . . would you consider not pressing charges?"

"I'm not making any commitment about that," Lynne said. "Get it all together and bring it back here, and then we'll see what's what."

"How did you find me?"

"Oh, no you don't."

"Oh, no I don't what?"

"I'm not going to draw you a road map for how to do it more effectively next time."

"I would think it would only convince me that you're very smart and have a lot of tools at your disposal."

It was worth a try, anyway.

"I'll say this and this only: It didn't help your case that you tried to take on your deceased roommate's name. We all spent a lot of time wondering why you would do that. Boris had a theory. He thought it was your unusual way of showing that you actually cared about her. You go around trying to convince everybody that you care about nothing and no one. But since then I've found myself wondering if Boris was on to something."

"It's because I went to talk to the principal at that boy's school, isn't it?"

"I'm not saying any more."

"I know it is."

"Then why did you do it?"

"Now that's a very good question," Marilyn said.

But she didn't go on to answer it.

"Well," Lynne said, when she seemed to grow tired of waiting. "Go on back to your room. You have some phone calls to make."

Marilyn looked up at the younger woman, blankly. She wasn't sure if her face was blank, but her mind certainly was.

"What kind of phone calls?"

"The kind that will get that money back here. Call one of your children. Tell them how much hangs in the balance."

Marilyn moved to open her mouth to speak, then realized it was already open. Hanging open. Her jaw had dropped without her realizing.

"You won't even take me back there to get my things?"

"We have all of your things that you didn't pack to take with you. You couldn't have carried all that much. But . . . to answer your question . . . no. Absolutely not. We want you right here on the premises. We're not taking any chances with you after what happened. We want you where we can keep an eye on you. Make some calls and get whatever you need to come to you. And, more importantly, get what *I* need to come to *me*. And the sooner the better. And then, when you're done, get down to the cafeteria as fast as you can. It's steak night, and you know how long the line gets on steak night."

———

She sat in her old room, staring out the window. It was on the second floor. A bird had nested in the branches of the big maple tree outside her window. She could see the little birds moving about inside the bowl of the nest. They were not babies, from the look of them. They looked half-grown. Soon they would fly away. Really fly. With altitude. With real range. Marilyn envied that.

She took a deep breath and picked up the phone on her bedside table. Dialed her daughter's number by heart. It struck her as odd that her mind, which dropped so many details so regularly, still held on to that. It seemed as though the older memories had a firmer foothold. Many days she remembered with startling clarity the day when one of her children was born—but not why she had gotten up and walked into a new room.

The line rang. And rang. And rang.

Marilyn found herself relieved that Betty wasn't home. She could leave a message. It would hurt less to talk to her daughter's voice mail. It felt safer.

Then she was struck with an unpleasant thought: Maybe Betty *was* home. Maybe she was staring at her caller ID and choosing not to pick up.

The thought was just disturbing enough that, when the outgoing message in her daughter's familiar voice finished playing, Marilyn didn't speak. Couldn't speak.

The beep, and a long, panicky silence ticked by.

"Betty," she forced herself to say. It came out too sudden and loud, betraying her fear. "I need you to call me. I need you. I'm back at Eastbridge and I need your help. Please call me here." A pause. Then she added a humiliating second "please."

She held the phone to her ear in silence for several seconds, then realized her message was still recording. She hung up the phone.

Then, because she was not at all sure Betty would call her back, she made a similar begging, humiliating call to Gerald.

When she was done, she lay back on her bed and watched the little birds. Robins, from the look of them.

She did not go down to the cafeteria for steak night. She didn't feel the least bit hungry.

She realized she was physically and mentally exhausted from the experience of her terrible day, but she didn't notice herself falling asleep.

———

When she woke in the morning, she checked the message light on the phone beside her bed. When she saw that neither of her children had returned her calls, she felt depressed but not in the least surprised.

She decided to wait until close to the end of the day—just in case they came through—before falling back on her last-ditch option.

———

She skipped dinner again, eating a cup of cherry gelatin in her room instead.

What she really had a taste for was a meal of some very fresh eggs, but there was nothing of the sort to be had around Eastbridge.

She had no roommate, she had finally gathered. The bed next to hers was empty and perfectly made. Which meant either they had never filled that bed when the world lost Marilyn Higgenbotham, or they had filled the bed with someone who had then also died.

It felt discouraging either way, she decided.

She picked up the phone, called directory assistance, and asked for a listing for Stacey Little in Lake View.

She was prepared with a pencil to write down the number she was given.

She dialed it, and waited while it rang, nursing a surprising load of fear. It jangled in her belly like something sharp and electric.

Please let the boy answer, she thought. *Or his brother. Please don't let Stacey answer.*

Stacey had come to represent, to Marilyn, a sort of "guard at the gate" for her little brother's life. More to the point, Marilyn had the distinct impression that the young woman was not her biggest fan.

Stacey answered.

"Hello?" Stacey asked, as though it were an actual question.

"It's Marilyn," Marilyn said quietly.

A long, stony silence fell. Marilyn wanted to fill it, but she couldn't imagine with what.

"Where are you?" Stacey asked.

"That's kind of a long story. Can we maybe save it for another time? I was hoping I could speak to him."

"Are you in jail? Stewie told me you got arrested."

Stewie, she repeated in her head. Because she had forgotten it, and this was a bad time not to know it. *Stewie, Stewie, Stewie. Like the mouse.*

"I'm not in jail. I'm just in an assisted living facility."

"Since when do they arrest people and take them to an assisted living facility?"

"They arrested me for running away from one," she said, purposely leaving out the actual reason they had arrested her. Stacey wasn't saying anything, so she added, "Please may I speak to Stewie?"

"I don't know, Marilyn. I'm not sure if that's a good idea or not. He's been very upset since the . . . incident. You know. Yesterday. Watching you being taken away like that. He's been just completely . . . I don't know the word. But you know Stewie. He takes things very hard. He doesn't cope well."

"I understand. But don't you think he'd be better off talking to me and hearing that I'm okay?"

She waited for an answer. Waited for what felt like a long time. Those electric knives of fear seemed to be doing a little dance in her belly as she sat waiting, cutting her with every step.

Then she heard Stacey call his name, and she breathed for what felt like the first time in days.

A moment later she heard his welcome, breathy little voice on the line.

"Marilyn?"

He *sounded* like a mouse, too. That thought struck her when he spoke her name, but she quickly dismissed it again.

"Yes, it's me," she said.

"Where are you? Are you okay?"

"I'm more or less okay. I'm at a . . . home. For older people. I don't like it here, but I'm not in danger or anything of that sort. I'm not in jail. But I could be. In jail, I mean. I need a favor from you. It's hugely important, Stewie. It's to keep me from having to go to jail. That's how important it is."

She waited for him to ask why she could be about to go to jail, but heard only silence. She tried to watch the little birds in the nest outside her window, to calm herself, but she was losing her view of them to the evening twilight.

It occurred to her that maybe Stacey was listening to his end of the conversation. Maybe that was why he didn't ask.

"Okay," he said. "What?"

"I have some money at the house. The house where I've been living. I need you to go get it and bring it to me."

"How much is it?"

"A little over five thousand dollars."

Another long silence on the line.

Then, his voice smaller than she'd ever heard it, he said, "Marilyn, that's too much responsibility for me."

"Please. It's so important. I have no one else to help me."

"Ask your daughter."

Marilyn was vaguely surprised that he knew she had a daughter. Had she mentioned it to him and then forgotten that she ever had?

"I tried that, but she won't return my call."

"I'll go over and tell her to do it for you."

That's when she realized what he had meant by "your daughter."

"Oh, Sylvia's not my daughter," she said.

"She's not? So Izzy's not your granddaughter?"

"No."

"Well, who are they, then?"

"I was just living with them because I needed a place to stay. She needed a babysitter for the girl, and I offered to do it for room and board."

"Oh," the little voice said.

She opened her mouth to tell him where the money was hidden, but he cut her off.

"Why did they say your name is Jean?"

"Oh, that's such a long story, love. Please, can we talk about it when you bring me the money? We'll have a nice visit. We can even do another reading lesson if you want."

"But what do I call you?"

"Marilyn. You call me Marilyn."

"Okay."

Again she opened her mouth to tell him where to find the money. Again he cut her off.

"Are you a grandmother *at all*? To *anybody*?"

"Yes," she said. "I am. I have four grandchildren. Now, please, Stewie. This is important. The money is at the very back of my closet in the room where I was staying at Sylvia's. It's in a pair of shoes. It was my only spare pair, so they're the only shoes in there. They have orthopedic insoles. The money is underneath. They're much too lumpy to wear, because it's a lot of money. But I figured nobody would notice it there. There's some in each shoe. Maybe best if you just grab the shoes and put them in a bag and bring them to me."

She waited. He said nothing.

"Stewie? Are you there?"

"Yes. I'm here."

"You'll bring them to me, right? It's so important."

"I don't know. It's so much responsibility. Can't I just go ask Sylvia to bring them to you?"

"No!" she shouted. It came out far too loud.

"Jeez," he said. "You don't have to yell at me."

"I'm sorry. I really didn't mean to yell. But under no circumstances are you to tell Sylvia about the money. I don't trust her. I think there's a chance she might take it for herself. Please, Stewie. I hate to ask this of you, but it's just so important. I know you're uncomfortable with it, and I'd ask somebody else if I could. If I *had* somebody else. But you're my last hope. I need you to do this for me." She paused, wondering if she should break out the big guns. It seemed she had no other viable options. "I need you."

Another silence on the line, but it was brief this time. Just long enough for the boy to sort things into place in his brain, she figured.

"Okay," he said. "Okay. If you need me, then I'll be what you need me to be."

She heard herself blow out a very long, deep breath.

"Thank you," she said, her voice still breathy with the fear flowing out of her. "Really, thank you. I won't forget this. Let me give you my address and phone number here."

"Okay. Wait, please, while I go get a pen to write it down."

Chapter Seventeen

She Stole

Stewie

Through the whole conversation, Stacey had been hovering over Stewie as he sat at the kitchen table talking on the phone. She seemed to be trying to hear as much as she could, which made him uneasy.

Then again, most everything did.

The minute he hung up the phone, she lit into him.

"What did she want, Stewie? Why was that woman calling you?"

"Don't call her 'that woman,'" he said, getting up and walking the phone back to its base, so it could charge again.

"I have no idea what you're talking about," Stacey said. "She's a woman. What's wrong with calling her that?"

"It just doesn't sound very nice the way you say it."

He tried to slip off to his room, but Stacey was having none of it.

"You stop right where you are, young man. This conversation is not over."

Stewie stopped.

He hung there in the kitchen doorway, waiting. In his head, he was seeing a picture of a knight in a suit of armor. It was something he'd seen once in a museum on a school field trip. He tried to imagine himself safe like that. Inside the thing.

"What?" he said.

"What's this thing she wants you to do? I didn't like the sound of it."

"It's nothing. She just wants me to bring her something. There's nothing wrong with that."

"I don't know, Stewie. I don't like it. I'm losing patience with that woman. Her name isn't what she said it was, and she just got arrested. She said it was for running away from assisted living, but I honestly don't think they arrest people for that. And now I hear you saying that wasn't even her daughter and granddaughter she was living with. We don't really even know who she is. And I think she asks too much of you. You do so much for her, and I don't think you get much in return. I don't want you being used."

"She's not using me!" he shouted. It came out on a surprising burst of anger. "She cares about me. She just almost said so. And she does plenty for me in return."

"Like what?"

Stewie opened his mouth to say she was teaching him to read. Then he closed it again. Stacey would have been shocked to hear that he didn't already know how. She would be hurt. She would feel she had fallen down on the job of raising him.

He couldn't do that to her.

He opened his mouth again, and took the argument in a slightly different direction.

"She bought me that book for a present. The one about the mouse with my same name. Just to be nice, she did that. And she came to see me when Mabel died."

"Oh," Stacey said. "That's true."

Stewie thought she sounded almost disappointed to have to say so.

They both just hovered there for a moment, looking away from each other. Though he could not have put the thought into words, Stewie was noticing how hard it was for two people to really talk to each other. Even when they're supposed to be closer to each other than to anybody else in the world. Or maybe especially then.

"What does she want you to bring her?" Stacey asked. She was still looking away. Down at the kitchen linoleum, as if noticing a spot she had missed on the last mopping.

"Just a pair of shoes," he said.

He felt bad about leaving out as much information as he did. As it stood, what he had told her was sort of the truth but also sort of a lie. But there are some things everybody knows are better left unsaid.

"It's up to you," Stacey said. "I don't have time to drive you. You'll have to take the bus into the city. But if it's really what you want to do . . ."

"I already said I would," Stewie said quietly.

"Yeah, I heard that. That's what I was a little unhappy about."

"I can't go back on my word."

"I know you can't."

"I never go back on my word."

"I know you don't. I guess you can go after school tomorrow, and after your egg route. But it'll be dark by the time you get home. Are you sure you're up for that?"

"It's only a half day of school tomorrow. It's the last day before summer."

"I thought that was the next day."

"No. Tomorrow."

"Well, okay then," she said. "I guess that's what you'll do."

He slunk off to his room, wondering exactly how furious she would be if she ever found out that he had failed to mention the more than five thousand dollars hidden in the shoes. He hoped he would never have to find out.

———

He showed up on the lady's doorstep—that lady he had been so sure was Marilyn's daughter—at a little after seven the following morning, his stomach buzzing with nerves. The whole thing about the money and the shoes made him edgy, and he wanted to get them and stash them away properly before his half day of school.

He had to knock three times, and when she finally came to the door, it was clear he had wakened her. She did not look happy.

"Oh, you," she said. And she did not make it sound like a good thing. "What do *you* want?"

She was wearing a faded corduroy robe over a blue nightgown, and her hair looked a fright. She seemed nearly unable to look out her open door into the light of morning. It made her squint and blink.

"I came to get some of Marilyn's stuff."

"Whose stuff?"

"Marilyn's."

"You miss my point, kid. We *thought* her name was Marilyn. Now it turns out it was Jean Clements, and she was lying to us the whole time. And to think I left my daughter with that woman. I don't know what I was thinking. Total stranger. She just took my number off that bulletin board outside the market. I was looking for a babysitter, but I expected somebody from town to offer. She seemed okay enough. But why did I let her move in? We could've been murdered in our sleep! And now it turns out she didn't even give her real name."

It made his stomach buzz harder, but he ignored it as best he could and stood his ground in the conversation. He had to. He had as good as promised.

"Whatever," Stewie said. "Whatever her name is. I have to get some of her stuff."

She squinted hard at him, then pointed over his shoulder toward the street.

He spun around to look.

The trash cans had been hauled out to the street, and the area around them was strewn with items that apparently had not been able to fit in the cans. Clothing, and a cardboard carton of ladies' toiletry items. Two small suitcases, which definitely looked nice enough to keep. A purse. Another box of something, but Stewie couldn't make out its contents.

He briefly wondered why he hadn't registered their presence on his way up to her doorstep. Too much intense focus on confronting her, he figured.

"You threw her stuff away?" he asked, genuinely shocked.

"You bet I did. And it's trash day. If you're going to rescue her things, you'd better hurry up and do that."

And with that she slammed the door in his face. Well, not literally in his face. But close enough to his face to leave him with that uncomfortable sensation.

Stewie ran down to the street.

He rummaged around in the two cartons, but found no shoes. He looked under all the clothes, which were mostly just stacked on the sidewalk, getting dirty.

Finally, desperately, he began plowing through the two trash cans themselves.

In the second one, he found a pair of shoes. They were pushed halfway down to the bottom of the can, and covered with coffee grounds and eggshells, and what looked like the peelings from the outsides of carrots. He brushed them off as best he could. Set them on the curb with the rest of her belongings. There were no orthopedic insoles in them. There was no money.

He kept digging, growing more desperate, thinking there must be another pair of shoes. But there was only the one pair. And he remembered her saying she only had the one spare pair of shoes.

He straightened up, closed the lids of the cans again, and stood panting, trying to shake the coffee grounds and other wet garbage off his hands.

He wiped them off as best he could on the weedy, overgrown grass of the lady's lawn.

Marilyn must have forgotten where she'd hidden the money.

Of course. It made perfect sense to think so, and explained everything. She forgot all kinds of things, all the time.

He would have to go get his wagon and take all of her belongings home. Then he could go through it all and find where she had really hidden all that cash.

Unless she'd stashed it in the bed, or someplace that was still inside the house. That would present a thornier problem.

He pushed the thought away again, wanting to believe it wouldn't come to that.

He carefully moved all of her belongings, in two separate trips, to a spot in the side yard where they would be hidden from the street by a hedge.

Then he ran all the way home.

———

He was just heading out running again with his wagon when he ran into Stacey coming home from work. She was just pulling into the long dirt driveway.

He tried to get away before she could stop him, but she powered down her car window and called his name.

"Stewie!"

He stopped, because he couldn't think of a way to avoid it.

"What?" he called without looking over his shoulder.

"Where on earth are you going? You have school."

"Sylvia is throwing out all Marilyn's stuff. I have to hurry up and go get it before the garbagemen come."

"I thought she just wanted one pair of shoes."

"Well, she asked me to bring her the one pair of shoes. But I'm thinking she doesn't want the rest thrown away."

He waited, still not looking over his shoulder at her. He could hear the engine of her car humming softly.

A moment later he saw a shadow fall over him. He looked up to see that she had gotten out of her car and was standing right behind him.

"I know you think I do too much for her," Stewie said quietly. "But it's *all her stuff.* I can't just let it all get thrown away. How bad would you feel if somebody threw away *all your stuff?*"

"And what about school?"

"We never really do very much on that last half day. Ever. We mostly say goodbye, and the teachers have us get up and say if we're going to do anything special over the summer like if our family is going on a vacation or something. And I never have anything to say. It's kind of embarrassing."

Then he felt guilty, because he knew what he'd just said would hurt Stacey's feelings. And he'd more or less done it on purpose, because he desperately wanted her to say he didn't have to go.

For a time, no one spoke. Nothing moved. Even her shadow held perfectly still.

Then he saw and heard her sigh.

"Okay," she said. "You go do that. I'll call them and tell them I gave you permission to be absent today."

He thanked her, but they were breathy, barely audible words thrown over his shoulder. Because he was already running.

———

He left her belongings in neat piles on his bedroom floor and padded into the kitchen to use the phone.

The house was blissfully quiet. Stacey was asleep, and Theo had gone off to the last half day of school.

He would have to talk fast, because it was a toll call. Stacey would hate seeing that when the phone bill came in.

He unfolded the scrap of paper on which he'd written Marilyn's new address and phone number, and then carefully dialed, his heart hammering.

She picked up on the first ring.

"Stewie?" she said in place of hello.

She sounded desperate, and he caught her desperation like a contagious disease. It made him feel downright panicky.

"Yes, it's me," he said, sounding breathless to his own ears.

"Did you get the money?"

"No, it's not there. It's not in the shoes. It's not in any of your things. She threw away all your stuff. She took it all out to the curb, and it's garbage day. I got there just in time. I got the shoes back, but they didn't have those soles inside like you said they would, and there was no money. I brought all your stuff back here in my wagon. Partly because I figured you'd want it sometime, but mostly because I figured you were wrong about where you hid it. But I went through everything. I went through *everything*, Marilyn," he said again. It felt as though his desperation was trying to claw its way up and out through his throat. "It's just not here. Where else could you have hidden it? Maybe it's still in the house? Like under the mattress or something?"

He waited for her to answer, but heard only silence on the line. It stretched out into a truly painful length of time.

"Oh dear God," he heard her breathe quietly into the phone. "I'm going to jail."

"No!" Stewie shouted. Louder than he had meant to. "No, it doesn't have to be that way. Just tell me where else you could have hidden it."

"Stewie," she said. And she sounded more defeated than he had ever heard her sound—than he had ever heard anybody sound. "Wake up. It's over. It was in the shoes. Don't you get it? She stole it. By the time she dug everything out of my closet and carried it down to the street, she would have seen that there was something hidden in the shoes. It was only a good hiding place because they were all the way in the back of my closet, where I never figured she would go. It's over. The money's gone."

The line fell silent again. It struck Stewie, during that silence, that the call was costing Stacey too much. Maybe when the bill came in, he would volunteer to pay it out of his egg money.

When he spoke again, it was without forethought. He hadn't known he was about to speak. He especially hadn't predicted what he'd been about to say.

"I'll make her give it back," he said.

"I don't think you can," Marilyn said. "Seeing as you're just a little boy and all. And I can't ask you to. It wouldn't be right to ask it of you."

"I'll make her give it back," he said again.

"You can *ask* her for it back. It would certainly mean the world to me if you asked her and that was enough. But I don't want you doing more than that."

"I'll make her give it back," he said for a third time.

His voice sounded steadier the third time. As if he was somehow sure he actually could.

———

When he got back to Sylvia's house, she was just pulling into the long, steep driveway. She had Izzy with her, which made sense. She had no one to leave her home with anymore.

He wondered how she would go to work now, but he had neither the time nor the attention to wonder long, not to mention arrive at any conclusion. His heart was pounding, and he had to do something the likes of which he had never done before. He had to be brave, even as he knew in his hammering heart he was anything but. He had to do something he couldn't do, and be something he knew he was not.

He ran up the driveway and stepped in front of her car.

She slammed on the brakes and lurched to a halt just a foot or two in front of his belt buckle.

She powered down her window and leaned out, frowning at him.

"What the hell are you doing? You could've been killed!"

He opened his mouth to speak, and that's when it hit him. Beyond and behind everything he was consciously paying attention to, a realization dawned.

This was not her car.

This car was much nicer than the one he had always seen her driving. It was a deep midnight blue, and still had some numbers pasted onto the windshield, the way cars do when they sit in dealers' lots. A couple of numbers seemed to have been scraped off, and Stewie wasn't sure if the remaining numbers represented the model year, or the price, or both.

"You got a new car?" he asked her, ignoring her earlier complaints.

"It's not new. It's a used car. It's almost six years old."

"But you just went out and got a better car."

"So? What's it to you?"

"You really did steal the money."

She pulled her head back inside the car and powered up the window. Then she revved the engine to let Stewie know it was time to jump out of the way.

It startled him, so he did.

The minute she could get by him, she drove into her own garage, closing the automatic garage door behind her.

"I'm going to tell the police!" he shouted, pounding on the closed garage door. "I'm going to have them come arrest you. I'll tell them you stole!"

All he heard was the click of the door that separated the garage from the laundry room.

He ran around to the front door and pounded until his fist hurt. Then he took to leaning on the doorbell instead.

She never answered.

Chapter Eighteen

My Power

Marilyn

When she walked to the administrative office the next morning, it was of her own volition. She figured it would go over better that way—if she sought them out. If she didn't wait until they came after her.

She rapped on the door, and was inordinately relieved to hear Boris's deep, booming bass of a voice in reply.

"Come in."

She stood a beat or two, nursing a feeling of all her tension and panic running down through her gut and out through her feet. Well, maybe not all of it. She still had to speak to him. But enough to pass for all of it, strictly at the level of her feelings.

She opened the door.

He sat behind the desk, looking out the window, one huge, beefy hand running back and forth over his freshly shaved scalp. It took him a second or two to look at her.

"Ah," he said when he did. "Our very own prodigal daughter. I thought it might be you."

His face looked as though he was trying to frown at her, but without much success. He liked her, and she knew it. Maybe in spite of all he knew about her at this point, but he still did. That was one small point in her favor. It was the only point she had now.

"I came to talk to you about the money."

"Good. I was hoping so."

"It's in progress."

"Meaning?"

"I'm working on getting it back here."

"Since you came on your own to tell me this, I'm going to assume it's true."

Which affirmed why she had come on her own.

She stood in front of his desk. She did not sit. She felt that sitting would make her feel small. She already felt too small. She did not say more voluntarily.

"You broke our hearts with what you did," he said. His voice sounded even. As though he could strip all the judgment out of a statement like that.

"I'm not sure what you expected of me," she said, trying for the same tone. "I told you I don't belong here."

"Everybody says they don't belong here," Boris said. Without hesitation. "The point is that your children thought differently and the judge agreed with them. And to answer your question, Mrs. Clements, what I expected of you was not to slip away with all the money the residents raised at the Christmas choir performance and the auction. That money was for charity. But of course you know that."

It was the most harshly he had ever spoken to her, and she braced against her own emotional reaction. She assumed it would be shame. To her surprise, it was a flame-like burst of anger. It felt welcome, and clean.

She stopped bracing.

"You gave me no choice!" she shouted. She surprised herself by slapping her palm down on his desk, hard enough to make him jump. "You took all my money. You take my Social Security checks. I had a home. I loved my home. I had enough money to get by and live happily in my own home. That's a kind of power, to have what you need to get by. It means you can make your own decisions. Shape your own life. And you took that away from me. You made me helpless. You took all my power. What was I supposed to do? I took it back. I have a right to live my own life."

A silence fell. Her words seemed to bounce around the office like an echo. But not a real, audible one. Just the impact of them seemed to come back around again and again.

"I think you know," he said, "that a judge and your children made that decision. We just offer the care."

"Right," she said, her voice still hard. "You don't arrest and convict me. You're just the jailer."

She thought she saw him wince slightly. She felt bad then. She felt she had been too hard on him. Gone too far.

"Look. Mrs. Clements. In my business we're not without empathy, and we know this can be a difficult adjustment. For some of our residents more than others, of course. Some people have a terrible time losing their independence. It's something they can never really accept. Others of our residents appreciate the care we have to offer."

"I'm not like them."

"So I've noticed. Well. Thank you for coming in. I'm sure you'll keep us posted about the repayment. And I'm sure that once we have it, we can settle this whole unpleasant matter amicably. Reasonably so, anyway."

She heard a tight reserve in his voice that he had never used with her before. She had offended him, or wounded him emotionally, or both. She just stood a moment, wondering if there was any way out of this uncomfortable new situation.

Then she remembered that she probably could not get the money to repay what she had stolen. That, of course, sealed the deal. And not in her favor.

"Anything else?" Boris asked.

"No, I suppose not."

She walked out of his office, nursing that knot of regret in her lower belly.

She turned right and walked toward her room. And nearly ran smack into Betty, her daughter.

—

They sat on a bench, outdoors, overlooking the little artificial pond. There were a few ducks that had just begun to fly back for the summer, hunkered over their own webbed feet as if napping. There was a fountain shooting up from its center, tumbling this way and that. It made a fair amount of noise with its tumbling and splashing.

Meanwhile Betty was staring at her. Marilyn could see it in her peripheral vision, and it was making her uneasy.

They hadn't spoken for quite some time.

Marilyn felt that anything she said would invite a wrath she would prefer to avoid, or even delay. For an awkward and truly admirable length of time—at least, in her mind—she had kept her mouth shut. But the staring had become too much.

It just burst out of her.

"Oh, will you stop looking at me that way!"

It opened the exact can of worms she had expected.

"How am I supposed to look at you, Mom? What would be exactly the right way to look at you after five months of being worried sick about you? Five months without so much as a phone call or a postcard to let us know you were okay. Gerry and I figured there was just as good a chance you were dead as alive. How do you suppose that made us feel?"

"Relieved?" Marilyn asked.

She kept her eyes on the ducks as she spoke.

"See?" Betty said. "I can't deal with you when you're like this."

"You can't deal with me ever. No matter what's going on. That's why I thought you'd be relieved."

Another strangely protracted silence fell. This time Marilyn knew better than to break it.

"Well, you were wrong," Betty said after a time.

"I need six thousand dollars."

"I'm sure you do."

"That's all you have to say?"

"It's not like it's the first time it's ever come up. Gerry and I have been dealing with calls from the Eastbridge people for months. They even had one of their attorneys call a couple of times. I told them the same thing I'm telling you now. I have three teenagers. People with three teenagers don't have six thousand dollars lying around. Anything extra we get our hands on goes straight into their college fund. In less than three years we'll need tuition for all three of them. Imagine how that makes me feel."

"Maybe Gerald can help."

She heard her daughter let out an odd sound that she took, at first, to be a sneeze. A moment later she realized it had been meant as a sarcastic bark of a laugh.

"That's a good one," Betty said. "Gerry's going through a nasty divorce. You know how he is. He won't stand up for himself. Greta got a pit bull attorney and she's bleeding him dry."

"And why didn't I know about this?"

Even as the words flowed out of her mouth, Marilyn realized her mistake. It was too late, though. She could only wince and blink against the wrath she knew her words would incite.

"Oh, let's see, Mom. Maybe he didn't tell you, because . . . *we didn't know where the hell you were!*"

"Right," Marilyn said. "My mistake. Sorry."

"Why did you do it?"

"You know damn well why. I loved that house. I lived forty years with your father in that house. We raised two children there. I wanted to live out my life in that house. I wanted to go straight from that house when the time came, in a body bag, right out to a mortuary van parked under that nice oak tree out front."

"You almost burned that house to the ground," Betty said, her voice cool and even.

"But I didn't."

"But you didn't only because the neighbor happened to be walking by with that terrible dog. If that dog didn't ask to be taken out every other minute, that house would be gone anyway, probably with you in it. It's not to your credit that it didn't burn down. It was sheer luck."

Marilyn dug around for an answer, but found nothing.

"They're going to put me in jail," she said.

"Probably just for a couple of months."

"That's a couple of months too long for my tastes."

"Remember what you used to tell me when I was a kid?"

"I told you all kinds of things. Can you be more specific?"

"You used to say, 'You got yourself into this trouble, so it's nobody's job but your own to get yourself out of it.'"

"Oh," Marilyn said. She could hear the lack of strength and spirit in her own voice. It felt alarming, yet somehow it was an alarm she could barely feel. Or only very distantly feel. "Yes, I guess I did use to say that, didn't I?"

Chapter Nineteen

Sylvia Stole

Stewie

He sat in the psychologist's office, staring at his own knees. He was wearing shorts, and it was hot, and the skin on the backs of his legs felt sweaty, and stuck to the leather chair in an uncomfortable way.

The doctor had told him once that the office was equipped with air-conditioning, but he didn't like to use it. He'd said he didn't care for the feeling of artificial cold, and would rather be too warm. It seemed rude and a bit cruel to Stewie—like saying, "I could solve your problem, but I've decided not to." It also seemed like he was saying he was more important than Stewie. Stewie figured he probably did think so. Most adults seemed to think that.

Neither of them had spoken for a weirdly long time.

"Anything you want to tell me about your grandmother?" Dr. Briggs asked suddenly.

At least, it seemed sudden. It made Stewie jump a little.

He shook his head. "No, sir."

"You don't have to call me sir."

"What am I supposed to call you?"

"Dr. Briggs is fine."

"Okay."

Then they sat in silence for a minute more.

"Anything you want to tell me about anything?"

"Yes, sir. I mean . . . Yes, Dr. Briggs. Two things. Well, one thing is more of a question. And then the other thing is more of a thing. You know. Like a thing to tell. Here's the question: What about people who steal?"

"What about them?"

"Is that just, like, the worst thing ever?"

The doctor shifted around in his chair. It struck Stewie that he seemed genuinely surprised to be having a conversation that required his attention and thought. He seemed to be manually screwing himself back into the necessary mode.

"That's a complex issue," he said. "Yes, it's wrong. Of course it is. It breaks our social contract, and anything that does that is a problem. But certainly not everyone who steals is a bad person."

"Tell me more about *that*," Stewie said.

He could feel himself leaning forward more in his chair. Leaning toward the doctor and his words.

"Sometimes a person will steal to survive. If they don't have food, let's say. Or medicine. Or if someone in their family needs something to survive, and they can't afford it. This is not a bad sign about the person's character. They're simply being put in a bad situation, and they're trying to choose the least destructive option. Sometimes a person will steal because they're poor, and they feel the corporation they're stealing from, like a chain of stores, for example, is unfairly rich. They're objecting to the way society is structured."

"I was pretty much keeping up with you until that last sentence," Stewie said, feeling the area around his eyebrows scrunching down.

"I'm sorry. I should just say they resent having to live in poverty."

"Okay. But if they're not a poverty person?"

"Well, it's relative. They may think they are. They might look around and see so many people who have so much more. But there are also people who steal for a different reason. They steal things they don't even need. It makes them feel alive to break the rules. But you have to understand, Stewie, that I'm a psychologist. It's not my job to label people good and bad. If I see a person with kleptomania, for example—which is a stealing problem—I see that person as a sick person, not a bad one. It's my job to help them understand why they do what they do, and to get better. Very few people actually set out to be bad. Most people just have psychological wounds, or a sense of lack, and they're trying to fix themselves the best way they know how. Do you understand what I mean by all that, Stewie?"

"I think so."

"Now I have a question for you. Have you been stealing?"

"No! No, I would never! No, I was talking about this lady named Sylvia. She lives in the house where my friend Marilyn lives. I mean . . . used to live. Marilyn had some money, and Sylvia stole it. And now I have to try to get it back."

"That's a big job for a little boy. What if you can't do it?"

"I have to."

"But what if you can't?"

"But I have to. I told her I would. Well. I told her I'd try. But I have to, because if I can't get the money back, then she said she'll have to go to jail."

He shifted uncomfortably in his chair, trying to unstick his sweaty legs from the slick leather. He expected the psychologist to say something, and he assumed it would be something that would make him unhappy.

But Dr. Briggs only waited for him to go on.

"Here's the thing," Stewie said. "I was sort of asking about Marilyn. Not so much about Sylvia. Because I don't really care about Sylvia, so I don't really care if she steals. I mean, except that now I have to get the money back from her, and so that's a problem, especially since I'm pretty sure she spent it on a car. But I don't care so much what it means about her as a person. But I care about Marilyn, and I've been thinking about it, and if Marilyn needs the money back so she won't get put in jail, then that probably means she stole it, too. I mean, I figure it probably means that."

"I think you're correct," Dr. Briggs said. "And I think you were smart to figure that out on your own. And also . . . I guess . . . *wise*, for lack of a better word. But don't give up on Marilyn just yet, because we don't know for a fact that she did it, and even if she did, we don't know why."

"That's true."

Stewie noticed himself sitting back in his chair more. He heard himself sigh. Not so much a contented sigh, exactly. Maybe more of a relieved one.

He decided this Dr. Briggs was probably more okay than he'd been giving him credit for being.

"You said there were two things," Dr. Briggs said.

"I did?"

But he knew he had. He simply felt uncomfortable about the thought now, and not at all sure he cared to express it.

"Yes. You said you had a question, which we just now covered, and then also something you wanted to say."

"I don't know if I want to say it anymore."

"I wish you would."

"I'm afraid it would sound weird."

"But I want you to think of this as a place where you can say anything, and where you never have to feel concerned about how it will sound. I've been in this line of practice for forty years. There's very little I haven't heard. I hope you'll trust me on that."

Stewie wiggled in the chair slightly, a series of subtle movements with no real purpose.

"I don't know," he said.

"I can only help you if you'll begin to trust me."

Stewie sighed again. But this time there was no relief in it.

"I guess I could."

But then, for a minute, he didn't.

He sighed again, and forced himself to speak.

"A couple of nights ago I was lying in bed. I couldn't sleep. And I started feeling like . . ."

He paused, feeling the impossibility of going further.

"Go ahead and tell me what you felt. There are no wrong feelings."

"Really?"

"Yes, really."

"I thought there were."

"I don't think there are."

Stewie took a big, deep breath and raced through to the end. It seemed like the only way to get there.

"I felt like I missed my mom."

"Well, that's certainly normal," Dr. Briggs said, scribbling on a pad of paper with his nice silver pen.

"But I told you I don't remember her. I tell everybody I don't remember her. And I'm not lying."

"But you were inside her body, Stewie. You survived on the blood she pumped through your own body as it formed. You felt her heart beat every minute of every day for nine months. Some part of you knew her intimately, whether you consciously remember her or not."

"That's how it feels!" Stewie shouted. He was growing excited now, but it was a scratchy, uncomfortable sort of excitement. "I feel like there's part of me that remembers her, but it's not the brain part of me."

"I'm very pleased that you told me that, Stewie. I'm afraid our time is up for today, but I think we made good progress this session."

"You do?"

"Absolutely I do. You shared a lot with me."

"I don't see what it changes, though."

"I'm sure you don't, but it will become clearer over time. It takes time, Stewie. Most things worth having take time."

———

He was in the car with Stacey, on the way home, when he decided to tell her. Though actually "decided" was not quite the right word—not quite what happened. They were just driving along, Stewie staring at his bare knees, when he noticed that some truth was about to arrive.

"I have a confession to make," he said.

He looked over in time to see her furrow her brow and twist her mouth around.

"That's a weirdly adult way to say a thing," she said.

"It means I need to admit to something."

"I know what it means. It just seemed odd."

"You want to hear it or not?"

"Of course I do."

"I'm not a very good reader."

"Well, I know you're having trouble with your schoolwork these past couple of years. Since things got bad with Gam. I sign your report cards, so it's not like I don't know. I feel bad that I'm not doing more to help, but . . . you know. I'm trying to support us and all."

"See, this is why I didn't want to tell you. I figured you'd feel bad. Like it was your fault or something."

"Well, it kind of is my fault, Stewie. I'm more or less asking you kids to raise yourselves."

"You're doing good, Stacey. Really."

"Well, thank you for telling me, anyway."

He watched the fence posts flashing by outside the window. Maybe for a minute. Maybe for two. His neighbor's black-and-white cows came into view. That always made him feel better. It struck him that he could just let the whole thing drop, leaving it right where it had fallen. Then another part of him said no, he couldn't.

"I don't just mean I'm falling a little behind in class," he said. "I mean I can hardly do it at all. I can read *some things*. I'm not saying I can't read *anything*. I just can't really read the kinds of things kids my age usually can."

She didn't answer, so he braved a glance at the side of her face. She looked as though she had a headache.

The car lurched to a stop, and Stewie looked through the windshield to see that she had pulled into their dirt driveway and into her usual parking spot in front of the garage. They just sat a moment, saying nothing. Stewie wasn't sure if that was a good sign or not. Well, that's not entirely accurate—he knew it was a bad sign. He just wasn't sure *how* bad.

"Did you already know that?" he asked.

"I did and I didn't," she said.

"Marilyn was helping me catch up. We were taking lessons for reading."

"That was nice of her. I'm sorry I didn't give her more credit."

"But now she's gone."

"True."

Stacey turned off the car's engine and pulled on the parking brake. Then she unbuckled her seat belt and threw her car door wide. Stewie did the same.

He followed her into the house, hoping she would say she'd find the time to teach him. He had no idea *where* she would find the time. But he still wanted to hear her say she would try.

She said nothing until they had reached the kitchen door. Until she had her hand on the knob.

Then she said, "Maybe we can get you a tutor."

They stepped inside, Stewie nursing a sharp sense of disappointment in his chest. It felt like swallowing something a person was never meant to swallow.

He heard Theo say, "Oh, here he is."

He looked up. Theo was holding the phone out to him.

"Who is it?" he asked in a too-loud whisper.

"It's that lady."

"Marilyn?"

"Yeah."

He took the phone. "Hello," he said.

Then he instinctively spun around to see if Stacey was hovering over his shoulder, listening to the call. But instead he only saw her back, retreating into her bedroom.

"Hello," Marilyn's voice said on the line. "Maybe I shouldn't have called."

"Why not?"

"I don't want to seem like I'm pressuring you."

"It's okay."

"Is it?"

"I think so," he said. "I mean, I don't mind if you call. I don't have the best news, though." He instinctively scanned the room again, this time to see if Theo was listening. But Stewie was in the kitchen blessedly alone. "I don't think I can probably get it back. She bought a new car. Well, not new exactly. But nicer than what she had."

A long silence fell on the line. He listened to it as though it had something to tell him. But the only thing that came through was how much he hated to be the bearer of bad news. Especially twice, with two people and two pieces of bad news in just a few minutes.

"Do you know where she got it?" Marilyn asked, startling him a little. He had just gotten used to the silence.

"What, the car?"

"Yes. The car."

"No, how would I know that?"

"But do you know if she bought it from a car dealer or from a private party?"

"What kind of party sells cars?"

"A private party just means a person selling their own car. Like a neighbor or someone like that."

"Oh. I think she bought it from a car place, because it had those numbers on the windshield."

"Then she has three days to take it back. By law they have to give her three days to change her mind."

"But what if she doesn't change her mind?"

"Well," Marilyn said, and then paused. Her voice sounded dense and heavy, like something that weighs more than you'd expect it to. "Then I guess I'd go to jail. I suppose I was hoping you could talk her into changing her mind. Though I realize that's an awful lot to ask a young boy to do. I shouldn't ask. I didn't want to. But I'm just so desperate. I'm only suggesting talking to her. If it doesn't go well, you can always leave."

"Will you be mad if I can't?"

"Of course not," she said. "Sad, and a little disappointed. But not angry. It's a big job, and it's really not your job to do."

But it felt like Stewie's job. Because there was nothing worse than telling somebody something that made them sad and disappointed. Anger would have been a step up.

"Where does she work?" Stewie asked.

———

Theo came into his room and looked over his shoulder, silently at first, watching him make the cardboard sign. It was unlike Theo to wander into his room for no special reason, so Stewie figured Theo must have noticed his sign-making activities from the hallway.

"That's not how you spell *stole*," Theo said.

Stewie looked down at his sign.

He was making it from one panel of an extra-large cardboard box. He had written the words SYLVIA STOLL in big block letters with a bright-red marker.

"Are you sure?"

"Positive."

"Well, how do you spell it, then?"

"S-T-O-L-E."

"Hmm," Stewie said, feeling his forehead scrunch up. "I guess I'll have to start all over then."

"Or just add two lines to the second *L*. What are you doing, anyway? And who's Sylvia?"

"She's a lady who stole money from Marilyn. I need to try to get her to give it back."

"Marilyn asked you to do that?" Theo sounded almost alarmed.

"No. I said I would. She said she shouldn't ask it. But I said I could just talk to her and try. I can ask, anyway."

"And what if she gets upset?"

"I don't know. Then I guess she just does, then."

"You should let me go with you."

"Oh, no. Please, Theo. Don't. If she got upset with me, that's not so bad. But I would really hate it if she got upset with you and it was all my fault. Please let me do this on my own. Please?"

"I don't know, Stewie. I don't like the feel of it."

"I promise I'll be careful."

"Well. I guess. I guess if you really promise."

He turned to walk out of Stewie's room, a slightly involved process.

"Wait," Stewie said. "Tell me again, please."

"S-T-O-L-E."

—

Stewie pushed the door of the pharmacy halfway open and leaned inside. He stood for a time, watching employees bustle back and forth. Back and forth. From behind the counter to the back room where the drugs were kept. They were serving a line of people standing between velvety ropes. Two older women leaning on canes, and three or four men, one of whom kept nervously glancing at his watch.

Stewie did not see Sylvia. He regretted not having asked Marilyn *when* she worked, in addition to where.

He stepped back and let the door swing closed.

In that exact moment, he heard her voice.

"What're *you* doing here?"

Stewie opened his mouth to say, but she never gave him the chance. Her surprisingly strong hand locked onto his shoulder, spinning him around. It reminded him of the big talons of the raptor birds who fished in the lake.

"Wait, what does your sign say? I *stole*? You can't go around telling people that!"

With her hand locked even more tightly around his shoulder, her fingers digging into his flesh, she dragged him around the corner and into the alley.

"Why can't I?" he said. Bravely, he thought. "It's true."

She threw him up against the brick wall of the pharmacy's south side. He hit his head slightly.

It struck Stewie that he probably would never get that money back, but that this slight roughing up would be a badge of honor for him. It would prove how hard he had tried, and how courageous he had been in his attempt to help Marilyn. He could visit her in jail and tell her what he had gone through for her.

"Because you'll lose me my job!"

It was an odd kind of shrieky thing, her sentence, shrill and desperate, yet almost in a whisper voice. She clearly did not want anyone inside the pharmacy to hear.

He wondered briefly who was taking care of Izzy, but of course it was not the time, nor his place, to ask.

He heard a little "oof" sound come out of her. A sudden, unexpected release of breath. He looked beyond her face to see that Theo was standing behind her, poking her in the back with one of his crutches.

"Leave my brother alone," Theo said. "Pick on somebody your own size. It's one thing to talk to him, or even to let him know you're mad at him. But you can't start pushing him around. I won't have that."

She turned mostly away from Stewie to face this new threat. Stewie felt a huge breath come out of him. He felt a swelling in his chest, knowing his big brother had come to stand up for him, even though he had told him not to. For a moment it overpowered his embarrassment at having pulled Theo into this mess.

"Your little brother," she began, sounding hopelessly sputtery, "needs to learn to mind his own business. He's going to lose me my job."

"I think if you lose your job for stealing," Stewie said, "it's because you stole. Not because somebody told on you."

His voice sounded brave to his own ears. Much braver than he felt.

She turned back to face him, her face red and livid.

"What do you want?" she said, her voice a deep, threatening hiss.

"I want the money back so I can give it back to Marilyn."

"I already spent it on a car."

"You have three days to change your mind about the car. By law they have to give you that."

"I don't want to change my mind about it."

"Well, I don't want to go away. I want to stand here for the rest of the day with my sign."

She pulled the sign out of his hands. Roughly. He watched helplessly as she tore it in half down the middle. It wasn't easy to tear, being corrugated cardboard. But she was angry, and she managed.

She dropped the two halves onto the concrete sidewalk of the alley and stomped on them several times. Stewie watched, wondering what she thought that would do. Nothing really happens to cardboard when you stomp on it. It left a few dirty footprints on part of her name, but not much more.

Theo also merely watched, a puzzled look on his face. After all, she was only assaulting cardboard. Not anyone he cared deeply about.

"I can just stand out front and hold the two pieces together," Stewie said.

Her eyes alive with rage, she picked up one of the two pieces and tore it again. He watched, realizing that her anger was scary. Not so much that he was scared, but that it was scary. He probably *was* scared, somewhere inside, but he wasn't able to feel much of anything in that moment. He was disconnected from the scene, and from himself.

"It didn't really take me very long to make it," he said. "And we have lots more boxes at home."

She moved in closer, her face much redder. Weirdly red. Her eyes looked shiny and wet. There was something jerky about her movements, as if she couldn't decide whether to move toward him or back up. It took Stewie a minute to notice that Theo was tugging at the back of her shirt to force her to keep her distance.

"Have you ever heard of slander and libel?"

"I'm not really sure," Stewie said, a bit more aware of his own fear.

"You can sue somebody for saying harmful things about you and getting you fired from your job."

"Oh. Right. Yeah. Stacey was watching a lawyer show about that a couple months ago. Kind of boring. And I didn't understand some of it. But I'm pretty sure you have to prove that what the person said wasn't true."

He watched the redness drain out of her face. She was still standing close, making him feel pinned to the brick wall. Threateningly close. But she didn't look or feel threatening anymore. She mostly looked discouraged and tired.

Stewie heard a man's voice. It startled them both.

"Sylvia?"

He looked in the direction of the voice. They both did.

A tall older man stood at the end of the alley, watching them. He was wearing a white coat, like a doctor, and a name tag. It was too far away for Stewie to see what it said.

"What are you doing out here in the alley?" he asked. "Is there some kind of problem? You were ten minutes late when you first walked up to the door, and I've been waiting for you to come in and start your shift."

His eyes scanned down to the torn cardboard sign. Stewie and Sylvia looked down, too. But she was still standing on the pieces, and there wasn't much of it that could be read.

"No problem, sir. I'll be right in."

"I certainly hope so," he said.

He stood a minute, frowning at her. Then he spun sharply on his heel and disappeared from their view.

Stewie looked back up at Sylvia's face. He felt as though he could see her deflate. As if he were watching all the air flow out of a punctured tire.

"I can't lose this job," she said. "I have a daughter to support."

"I know it," Stewie said.

"What do I have to do to make you go away?"

"I already told you."

"Yeah," she said. And sighed deeply. Noisily. "Yeah, I guess you did."

———

They walked home together, Stewie purposely matching his brother's pace.

"Think she'll really do it?" Stewie asked.

"Not sure," Theo said. "She might. She seemed really worried about losing her job."

"Why did you come, Theo? And how did you know where I was going?"

"I followed you. And to keep you safe, dope. That's the easy part to figure out."

"But I told you not to."

"Sorry," Theo said. "Some things just won't let you not do them."

Chapter Twenty

The Cavalry

Marilyn

Marilyn sat in the cafeteria, frowning at the bacon. The scrambled eggs were a little dry, but they did not seem inedible—though she knew they were not the fresh eggs she'd grown accustomed to eating. But the bacon was worse. It was pale and limp, as though someone had run out of time halfway through cooking it.

She lifted a piece, which sagged over her fingers before she could take a bite.

A movement caught her eye, and she looked up to see Lynne standing over her table.

"Is it too much to ask that the bacon be cooked?" Marilyn asked, her voice dripping with judgment. "I swear that's reason enough to go on the lam from this place all by itself."

She had been trying for humor, in the hope of defusing the tension she felt between them, but a quick glance at Lynne's face revealed that the woman was not the slightest bit amused.

"That was meant as a joke," she added.

"Too soon," Lynne said.

"Sorry."

"We're having a meeting. Your presence is required."

Her voice was enough to rob Marilyn of what little appetite she had managed to muster in the first place.

"Before I even have breakfast?"

"Yes. Now, please."

Marilyn rose, and followed Lynne out of the cafeteria. She found herself nursing a distinct sense that she was marching to her own execution. To an old-fashioned gallows, perhaps, or a sharp and menacing guillotine. In her peripheral vision she could see table after table of other residents, mostly with their mouths full, staring at her as she passed. Based on the expressions on their faces, they seemed to think she was on the way to her demise as well.

She followed Lynne down the carpeted hall, her heart pounding.

They stepped into the office together.

Marilyn's eyes focused first through the window. It was a lovely early-summer morning, and there was a flowering tree of some sort just outside the window, with a carefully tended grassy green slope beyond. It would have been a much nicer place to be, which was probably why her eyes had gone there.

She pulled her gaze back into the room. Boris sat on the leather couch. Behind the desk sat an official-looking older woman Marilyn had never seen before.

"Sit down, Mrs. Clements," the woman said.

It made Marilyn's heart race faster, which made her a little dizzy.

She lowered herself into a chair in front of the woman's desk. Lynne stood with her back up against the office door, as if Marilyn might make a run for it at any moment.

"Let me get right to the point," the woman said. Her voice was full of authority and devoid of any lightness or humor. "We were hoping to get this cleared up a bit more quickly. You've been back at our facility long enough. That is, it seems like time enough has passed to have someone bring the money back here . . . if it's true you still have it. If the problem is only transportation, let us know. I can send someone out to pick it up. But if you don't still have it, you'd best come clean about that right now."

Marilyn opened her mouth to speak, but no words came out. Another slight wave of dizziness passed through her and moved on.

"I'll take your silence to mean you don't have it."

Marilyn had a quick flood of thoughts and impressions, mostly involving the very real possibility of incarceration, and how much she didn't want it. It helped her muster words in her own defense.

"I might still be able to get it. Most of it. I spent some, just living on it. But I was very frugal. I lived with a single mother and babysat instead of paying rent. I only spent what I absolutely had to for my own personal needs. I had most of the money when I was arrested. I could have gotten it and brought it back then, but the police handcuffed me and dragged me out of there. The money was hidden in my room. I had somebody go over to get it, but the woman I was staying with had dumped all my belongings at the curb, and found where the money was hidden. And she took it."

"Then you can't get it back. And this is now a matter for the police."

Marilyn's eyes darted outside again, and she tried to breathe normally. She was not entirely successful.

"I was working on having somebody get it back from her. I'm not sure how that's going."

"We've reached the end of our patience."

"Yes," Marilyn said. "I sensed that."

A knock sounded on the office door. It was loud, and made the door rattle. Lynne had been leaning her back against it, and it startled her forward.

She turned and opened the door just a crack.

"We're in a meeting," she said.

The voice of a woman on the other side of the door said quite a bit, but not at a volume that allowed Marilyn to make out most of the words. But she thought she heard the words "He won't take no for an answer."

The door opened wide, and Janet from the reception desk walked in. She had that little boy with her.

Marilyn struggled for his name. At first it evaded her. But then she thought of the book. She remembered that if she knew the title of the E. B. White book, she knew the name of the little boy.

"Stewart," she said. "What are you doing here? How did you get here?"

"I took the bus," he said.

He walked past her chair and stood leaning his belly against the woman's desk.

"I have money," he said, and pulled a huge wad of cash from his shorts pocket. "I have five thousand four hundred thirty dollars. Here, I'll count it out for you."

"That won't be necessary, young man," the woman said. Marilyn still had no idea who she was, but she was clearly higher in rank than anyone who worked every day at Eastbridge. "Boris, come here and count this cash, please."

Boris stepped in. Stewie stepped backward, until he was standing near the arm of Marilyn's chair. They all watched in silence as the money was counted.

"Five thousand, four hundred and thirty dollars," Boris said. "Confirmed."

"Wait," Marilyn said. "How is that possible? Don't get me wrong. I think it's wonderful. But how is it possible? I only had a little over five thousand two hundred left."

"I put some to it from my egg money," Stewie said. Then he turned his attention to the woman behind the desk. "I can bring more, if I know how much more you need, but I just don't have it right now. I make pretty good money from my egg route, but it'll take me a few months to get the rest. But I'll bring the rest, if it's not too much, and if you're willing to be patient that long. I could get it faster, except I give half my egg money to my sister, Stacey, because she supports the family and she needs it. And I don't want to break my promise to her. But please, please trust me and don't put Marilyn in jail. Please?"

The woman's face changed as he spoke. Marilyn watched the changes. The softening. The sudden presence of empathy. Her heart still hammered, unable to catch up with the rapidly changing developments, but her mind knew she was not going to jail.

"You don't have to give me any more of your egg money," Marilyn said. Her voice sounded a little shaky to her own ears. "I'll talk my children into making up the rest."

"You really love your grandmother," Boris said. "Don't you?"

The boy opened his mouth to speak. Marilyn knew him well enough to know he would be utterly honest, and admit that they were no blood relation.

She cut him off.

"I'm only his adopted grandmother," she said. "But, yes. We're very close."

———

"That was nice, what you said in there," Stewie said.

There were sitting on the same bench where she and Betty had sat the day before, looking down over the man-made pond and fountain. This time the ducks were wildly active, chasing each other about and flapping their wings. Fighting, maybe, she thought. Or maybe mating. The line between those two had always struck her as a bit unclear, and not only in the animal kingdom.

"It's all true," she said. "You're very much my hero right now. You came in here like the cavalry. I couldn't be much happier about it."

"Like the what?"

"The cavalry. It's a kind of army that rushes in and saves you."

"I'm glad I saved you," he said.

"I'm glad you saved me, too. I don't know how you did it. But thank you."

He didn't answer.

He was sitting with his hands between his bare knees, twisting and fidgeting with his fingers. He seemed to enjoy her gratitude at the same time as it made him squirm. He looked unable to hold it all up.

"How *did* you do it?" she asked when it was clear he did not plan to speak.

"I made a sign telling everybody she stole. And I took it down to her work at the pharmacy. And she got scared she'd get fired over it, so she took the car back to where she bought it and gave me back the money. She wasn't very happy about it. She doesn't like me anymore. Or maybe she never really did. I don't know. It kind of seemed like she never really did. Anyway, she got mad, but I don't really care. It was the truth. And it was her own fault for stealing in the first place."

"It was brilliant," Marilyn said.

It made him twist his fingers around and fidget again.

"It was?"

"Absolutely. A very smart way to handle the thing. Now I know why you asked me where she worked. You're a very intelligent boy."

She expected more squirming. Instead his body went still on the bench.

"One thing, though," he said.

"What's that?"

"You stole, too. Right?"

Marilyn felt herself pull in a big, deep breath. She let it out in a noisy sigh.

"Yes. I'm afraid I did."

"Why?"

"I suppose . . . because I felt they'd taken away my freedom. My children, and a judge, and the people here at Eastbridge. And it meant something to me. It was all I had. I had no more money because my Social Security went directly to them. I guess I felt that without my own home and my own money I had no power. No say over my own life. I felt helpless. And I don't like feeling helpless. I never have. It was the only way I could see to get back what I'd lost."

"But you don't have your freedom now," he said.

"No."

"You lost it again."

"Yes."

"So that's bad."

"It's not very good, no. But it's better than prison. I have you to thank for that. I just feel like . . ."

But then she wasn't sure how to go on.

"You feel like what?"

"It's hard to say it. I'm not sure how appropriate a feeling it is."

"You should say it, though. Know why? Because it turns out there are no wrong feelings. I thought there were. But then it turns out I was wrong. There aren't."

"I guess I feel as though I should've been nicer to you all along."

"You were nice enough."

"I could have done better."

"Everybody can always do better."

"Yes. I can. And I will. Why aren't you in school?"

"It's out for the summer."

"Oh. Well. If you're willing to ride the bus, you should come out and see me here. We could go on with the reading lessons."

"That would be good. Stacey wants me to have a tutor. I'd be a lot happier if it was you."

"It'll be me."

"I'm sorry you lost your free . . . whatever. Again."

"Not your fault."

"I know. But I can be sorry anyway. Right?"

"I suppose so. Thank you."

She reached across the bench and rested a hand on his shoulder. And left it there. He didn't seem uncomfortable with the arrangement.

"We could go have breakfast in the cafeteria," she said. "I haven't really eaten. Have you eaten?"

"No. I was in a hurry to get here."

"They don't cook the bacon very well. And you won't like their eggs at all, because they're not fresh like yours. But you should get something in your stomach."

"Do they have oatmeal?"

"Oatmeal *and* Cream of Wheat. Both."

"That'll work."

Without further discussion they rose, and moved off toward the main building, side by side. He reached over and took her hand. She allowed it.

Chapter Twenty-One

How Lucky You Are

Stewie

He had escorted her back to her room after breakfast, just to be gentlemanly. He figured that's what a young gentleman should do with his grandmother, adopted or not. He should escort her places.

As he stepped out of her room again and into the hall, a hand gripped his shoulder. Hard.

"Ow," he said.

For the second time in just a couple of days, he was reminded of the talons of a big bird. Reminded of the time he saw a ground squirrel being lifted, shrieking, from their corn patch by a red-tailed hawk. But it wasn't a big hand. Just strong, and insistent. Not afraid to dig in.

"Who are you?" the voice asked.

It was a woman doing the asking.

"Could you let go of my shoulder, please?"

She did, and he turned around.

The woman was about fifty, as best he could figure, with a thick waist and reddish hair. She held her eyebrows knitted down, and she stared at him as though she were about to shoot lasers out of her eyes.

"I'm Stewie Little," he said.

"That doesn't help even a little bit."

"Well, I don't know what more I can tell you about who I am," he said.

"What were you doing in my mother's room?"

"Just walking her back after breakfast."

"But why? How do you even know her? What's your relationship to her?"

"She's my grandmother," he said.

The look on the woman's face changed. She no longer seemed to want to vaporize him with eye lasers. Now it seemed as though proving him wrong would be good enough.

"She's not your grandmother."

"She is. She said so herself. You can ask her if you don't believe me."

"Look. Sonny boy. I'm her daughter. I'm the mother of three of her grandchildren, and my brother is the father of her fourth. If she had another grandson, don't you think I would know it?"

"Well," Stewie said. "*Adopted.* She said I was her *adopted* grandson. But that still counts."

Stewie watched the woman's face grow alarmingly red as he spoke.

"She can't adopt a grandson!" she shouted, her voice sounding sputtery.

"Why can't I?" Stewie heard a different voice say.

He looked up to see Marilyn standing behind him—hovering over him, as if to protect him from harm, such as the wrath of a relative. He felt one of her hands rest on his shoulder. It was a comforting feeling.

"Because you have grandchildren of your own!"

"And if I want to adopt another, I just will. I don't even know why it upsets you. I owe him more than I owe you. He helped me when you wouldn't lift a finger to try. Why, I'd be on my way to jail right now if not for this young man."

"I don't even know what all that means, but I know you have four grandchildren you never pay attention to as it is! How do you think my sons would feel if they knew you just picked a new grandson after all this time of not seeing you? Not even knowing where you were?"

She was raising her voice as she went along, Marilyn's daughter. By the end, she had crossed the line into yelling. It made Stewie uncomfortable. Yelling always did.

"Oh, like they would even notice!" Marilyn said, raising her voice in return. "Like they even care. They're so busy with their noses in their expensive little electronic devices. They don't care one way or another about me."

"How dare you say that, Mother!"

It was full-on shouting now. It made Stewie rise up onto his tiptoes and open his eyes wider. He could feel it.

"We had no idea if you were alive or dead!" the daughter added. "You don't get to tell us what we felt about that!"

"Stop!" Stewie shouted.

Everything fell silent. It was such a relief.

A young woman in an Eastbridge work uniform swung around the corner and raced down the hallway in their direction, one raised finger to her lips.

"No yelling!" the woman said in a terse whisper. "If you want to have a conversation at that volume, you'll have to take it outside."

She pointed to a glass door at the end of the corridor that looked out onto the tops of trees, and a set of railed stairs leading down to the yard. Through it Stewie could see the green boughs swaying in the wind.

The three of them walked together down the corridor, toward the outside world, where Stewie sincerely hoped they would not feel free to begin shouting again.

He held the door open for both of the ladies, to be polite.

"Thank you," Marilyn said.

Her daughter said nothing at all.

They made their way downstairs, where they stood together in the gathering heat of late morning, looking down over the fountain and the pond. Or, at least, that's where Stewie was looking. Because he wasn't looking at either of the ladies, he couldn't say for a fact where their eyes were resting.

For a moment, blessedly, nothing was said.

"Don't you know how lucky you are?" he asked quietly.

For a moment his comment was met with only silence.

"Which one of us?" the daughter asked, finally.

"Well, both of you, but I meant you."

"Why am I so lucky?"

"Because you have your mother."

"I'm not sure that's as lucky as you think it is." There was a harshness in her voice. As if nothing satisfied her. As if everything existed for her judgment, and she wasn't afraid to deliver it. "She's just about the most infuriating woman on the planet."

"Probably not," Stewie said, his eyes still glued to the pond and the ducks. One of them had spread its wings and just held them that way, as if asking the sun to warm them. He could hear the tumbling water of the fountain from where he stood. It comforted him. "I mean, I can't say for a fact, but there are an awful lot of people on the planet, so probably not. But even if she was. She's your *mother*, and you *have* her."

"So what? Everybody has a mother."

"*I* don't."

That shut her up. It was a relief to hear her say nothing.

"Stewie lost his parents when he was just a baby," Marilyn said quietly.

"Oh," her daughter said, quieter now herself, and seeming chastened. "Well, that's too bad. I'm very sorry for your loss. But as far as I knew these past few months, I might have lost my mother, too. We didn't know if she was alive or dead."

"Well," Stewie said, "maybe instead of yelling at her, maybe just tell her you were scared because you thought you'd lost her."

A long silence.

Then the daughter said, "Okay, I see your point. I suppose you're right."

"No, I mean really. You should say it to her."

For several minutes, nobody said anything. Stewie had begun to figure nobody ever would.

Then Marilyn's daughter spoke, startling him slightly.

"Mom . . . I'm sorry I've been yelling. But we were worried sick about you."

He heard Marilyn sigh softly.

"Thank you, Betty. I'm sorry I gave you such a fright."

"Are you?" Betty asked, her voice beginning to harden again. "Are you really?"

"Stop!" Stewie barked. "You can't keep talking to each other like this. You're a family. You're so lucky to have a family. You can't just waste it."

In the silence that followed, Stewie heard two soft sighs.

"Yes," Marilyn said. "I really am sorry. I guess I didn't realize people cared about me as much as they did."

Stewie heard the daughter suck in a breath of air, and he knew she was about to shout again. He shot her a warning look, and she seemed to rethink the moment.

"Well, we do," Betty said at last.

"Then I'm genuinely sorry I worried you."

"Thank you."

"There," Stewie said, "was that really so hard?"

———

They sat in Marilyn's room together, after the daughter had gone, not talking. It was quiet, and they both seemed to like it that way.

Marilyn sat perched on the edge of her neatly made bed, her hands folded in her lap. Stewie sat on a hard wooden chair. They both faced the window, seeming content to watch the hot wind swirl the trees around.

Then something caught Stewie's eye, and he got up and moved closer to the window.

"Ooh," he breathed, his voice a reverent whisper. "You have baby birds right outside your window!"

"Yes, I saw that."

"And didn't it just make you so happy you could barely stand it?"

"I don't know that I'd go that far. I thought it was a pleasant thing to see."

He watched their tiny beaked heads wobble on their bodies as they tried to look around. At least, he perceived their flurry of movement as looking around themselves.

"Oh, but for me it's much more than that," Stewie said. "It makes it hard to hold still. It makes me want to jump up and down. But I won't, because they might see me through the glass, and I don't want to scare them."

He walked to Marilyn's bed, turned around to face the window again, and leaned back against the edge of the bed, a respectful distance from her. He folded his hands in front of himself the way her hands were folded.

"I just remembered," she said. "You were about to leave."

Stewie jumped upright, his face burning suddenly with shame.

"Oh. You want me to go?"

"No, I'm not saying I *want* you to go. I'm just remembering that when you ran into Betty in the hall, you were on your way home. Did you need to get back for something?"

"Not really," he said, daring to lean back against the bed again. "But I can go if you want me to."

"Stay and talk to me," she said. "It's all right."

A long silence fell. But Stewie thought it felt comfortable.

"Talk about what?" he asked after a time.

"I don't know. Anything you like."

"We could do another reading lesson."

"I don't have my copy of the book," she said. "Did you bring yours?"

"No, I didn't think to bring mine. Where's yours?"

"It's in with my belongings that I was forced to leave at Sylvia's house."

"Oh. Right. I have all of that. I could bring it back to you now."

"That would be very nice. Thank you."

"I'd have to bring it a little at a time, because it's too much stuff to bring all at once on the bus."

"However you bring it, I'll be grateful," she said. "You're a very helpful boy. But bring the book first, so we can go back to our reading lessons."

"Yeah. That would be good. Stacey wants me to have a tutor for reading. And I wanted it to be you."

"There's a library here. I could go get a different book."

She shifted as if to rise, but Stewie stopped her by speaking quickly.

"No," he said. "I mean . . . no, thank you. I don't think it should be just *any* book. I think it should be *that* book, the one you gave me. Because you gave it to me. And because no other book has a mouse in it with my same name."

She settled again, and for a time they did not speak.

"I liked what you told Betty," Marilyn said.

"About not wasting family?"

"Yes, and about having your mother."

"Did you have your mother for a long time?"

It struck him, as he asked it, that they were talking in a way they had not talked before. As far as he could remember, he had never dared to ask her anything about her life before she'd met him.

"Oh yes," she said. "She only died a handful of years ago. She was a hundred and three."

Stewie felt his eyes go wide.

"*A hundred and three?* Nobody lives that long. Do they?"

"Oh yes. People do. It's not especially common, but it happens."

"Did you know how lucky you were all that time?"

"No, I'm afraid I didn't. I'm afraid I wasted it. She was a difficult woman. There were some good things to be said for her, but I'm afraid I didn't clearly focus on them until after she passed. When she was alive, all I could see were her maddening qualities."

"That's sad," he said.

"Yes, it is. I wish I'd known you when she was alive, so you could have given me that wise advice."

"When did she die?"

He watched her look up and off at an angle, as if the answer were up above her head and to one side.

"Eight years ago," she said.

"Eight years ago I was only three. I might not have said that same thing. You know. That advice you liked."

She didn't answer him. Only smiled a little smile at one corner of her mouth, but Stewie didn't quite know how to interpret it. She seemed to think he was funny, but he wasn't sure why.

"This feels like really talking," he said. "We didn't used to talk like this."

"We know each other better now."

He sat with that for a moment, contented. Then a difficult question came up in him. And he thought he might know her just well enough now that he could ask it.

"Can I ask you a question?"

"I suppose."

"If you were in that same situation again . . . like if you could go back to the moment you stole money and ran away . . . would you still do it? Or would you not do it this time?"

"That's a complicated question," she said. "First of all, I'm not sure if you mean if I had a second opportunity, or if I had the first one to do over. If a second chance arose, I wouldn't take it. It got me exactly nowhere, and I got in trouble, and I hurt people more than I realized I would. But if I had that first time to do over, and I didn't do it the same, then I would never have met *you*."

"Oh," Stewie said, genuinely surprised by the answer. "I hadn't thought of that."

Then they didn't talk much for the rest of the visit, because it *was* complicated, and Stewie was busy thinking about it.

———

"She's not happy," Stewie said.

They were at the kitchen table, eating dinner. Spaghetti with plain marinara sauce, because it was getting near the end of the month, and Stacey couldn't buy anything very fancy at the grocery store until her next paycheck.

His words seemed to wake her from some kind of daydream.

"Who isn't happy?"

"Marilyn."

He thought he saw a faint cloud blow by behind her eyes, but then he told himself it might only have been his imagination. Theo seemed to be listening, but he clearly did not plan to step into the conversation.

"Well, I'm sorry to hear that, honey. But I'm not sure what we can do about it."

"She hates where she's living."

"But didn't a judge say she needed to live there?"

"Yeah. But maybe if she had people to look after her . . ."

"Stop right there," Stacey said. She had one hand up like a crossing guard—like a stop sign—and her voice was firming up fast.

"I just—"

"Don't even go there, Stewie. We can't. We just can't. It's out of the question. We have enough on our plate as it is."

"But we have Gam's old room and it's just sitting there empty."

"But she needs someone to look after her."

"I could look after her. I sort of did anyway when she was living at Sylvia's, but I could just do it more. And it would be easier, because she'd be here."

"No. You couldn't, Stewie. You're not thinking clearly. Because you'll have to go back to school in the fall."

"Oh," Stewie said. "Right. But maybe she'd be okay on her own. You know. Just part of the time. Just a little bit."

"Stewie . . ."

"What?"

"You remember when Gam started forgetting things, don't you?"

"Yeah."

"Did it get better? Or did it stay the same? Or did it just keep getting worse?"

Stewie never answered.

He twirled spaghetti onto his fork until it turned into much too big a nest to ever shove into his mouth. He had lost his appetite now, and his stomach felt twisty and tight.

"I wish you would eat that instead of playing with it," Stacey said.

"I'm not hungry anymore."

"Try. Please."

He picked at the food for another couple of minutes, watching her at the corner of his eye. Then he saw and heard her set her fork down with a slight clang.

"Look. Stewie. I know you feel like when somebody has a problem you need to fix it for them. But sooner or later there's going to come a time when you need to accept that people will have problems you can't solve."

"I already did that," Stewie said. "I couldn't help Gam remember things and not get older and sicker and have to die."

He braved a look up at her face, but it was a mistake. She had that look again. The one he hated so much. The pity look.

"I guess that's true," she said. "I'm sorry. Maybe it's something you can talk to Dr. Briggs about."

"Maybe. I don't know how much that helps, though. I mean . . . he doesn't really know how to fix any of this stuff, either. He just listens."

"What I'm trying to say, Stewie, and I think you're not quite getting it yet . . . is that sometimes we need to accept things the way they are and not let it tear us apart."

"I don't know how to do that."

"I know you don't. That's why I got Dr. Briggs to help you with it."

"Oh," Stewie said.

"Now please eat your dinner."

He ate most of it, because her concern over his refusal to eat was the only problem in his life he knew how to solve. It didn't taste like much of anything, though, and it sat in his stomach in a lump, as though he'd forgotten to chew.

Chapter Twenty-Two

Don't You Get Tired?

Marilyn

That little boy came bouncing into her room at a few minutes after nine in the morning. He had a plastic trash bag full of something heavy-looking over his shoulder—her belongings from Sylvia's, she assumed—and he held the *Stuart Little* book up proudly with his free hand.

She couldn't help noting that there was something almost elating about his presence now. As though he figuratively turned on the lights in this dim and drab place every time he walked into a room. Then she put the thought away again because it embarrassed her to feel emotional about anything or anyone. Especially anyone.

"I brought the book," he said.

"I see that," she replied.

"We can do a reading lesson."

"Good."

"And I brought about half the stuff you left at Sylvia's."

"Thank you. That was very thoughtful."

He dropped the heavy trash bag on the floor of her room and crossed to the window, seeming relieved to be out from under all that weight.

"Oh, look! The mom bird is feeding the babies!"

"Or the dad bird," she said.

"Does the mom or the dad feed them?"

"I think either. Or both. But I confess I'm not entirely sure I know."

"I thought confessing was when you had to say something bad you'd done."

"It can be. Or it can be anything you'd be happier not having to admit."

She stepped over and stood beside him and watched the display. Just for a moment she had a flash of why he found it so exciting. Why he was so completely drawn in by the smaller moments in life, the ones she'd spent her years ignoring.

There were five babies, all tweeting up a storm, trying to get the attention and a piece of the worm. With their tiny beaks stretched open absurdly wide, they reached out for feeding. The adult bird seemed to do more than simply present food for them to take, or drop it into the waiting beaks. Instead she, or he, seemed to stuff it down their throats with several sharp plunging movements.

"You're so lucky," the boy said. "To have this happening right outside your window."

"Yes, I suppose I am."

"Even though I know you don't like it here."

"Thank you for pointing out that there are small things to like about it, though."

He stood looking around the room for a moment, as though it had never occurred to him to notice it.

"How come you have two beds but no roommate?" he asked.

"I had a roommate. But she died."

"What was her name?"

"Marilyn. Her name was Marilyn."

"That's a coincidence," he said, sounding a bit confused.

"Not really. My name is really Jean, don't forget."

"Oh. I did forget that." He stepped closer to the window, seeming to rivet his attention to the nest of birds again. She got the impression that he saw them as a path onto more solid emotional ground. "I never really understood that," he said.

"What's not to understand? I was on the run, and I used somebody else's name."

"Did you purposely use *her* name? Your roommate who died?"

"I suppose I did."

"So you liked her."

"Not at first, I didn't. At first it was just awful, having to share my space like that. But after a time I grew to care about her."

"And they never gave you another roommate?"

"Not yet."

He glanced quickly across his own shoulder at her, then took the conversation in an entirely different direction. She could tell it would be a more serious direction, even before he opened his mouth.

"I tried to talk Stacey into letting you come live at our house, but I don't think she thought it was a very good idea."

"Oh, honey," she said.

"What?"

"Come sit down a minute."

They walked to the edge of her bed and sat. He seemed apprehensive, as though he already didn't like the words she hadn't yet said. He trained his gaze to the patterned linoleum floor, seeming careful to avoid her eyes.

"Don't take this the wrong way," she said, "because it's really not any reflection on you or your family. But I wouldn't be happy living at your house, either. That wouldn't be any better to me than living here. Both my son and my daughter offered to take me in."

"They did?" He sounded surprised. And he must have been, because he almost looked up at her. "And you didn't want that?"

"Oh my goodness, no! All that commotion and chaos. It's not for me. I wanted to live in *my* house."

"We have to figure out a way to get you back to your house, then."

She sighed deeply, and allowed herself not to answer for a few beats. He was so sweet, and yet his sweetness felt like a kind of pressure on her. It seemed as though every time she spoke, she had to break his delicate heart.

"It's gone, honey. My children sold it to pay for this place."

"Oh," he said.

For what seemed like quite a long time they sat without speaking. She found herself wishing she could offer him a penny for his thoughts, but it seemed a little silly. Old-fashioned, maybe, and even a bit trite. Still, she wished she could know how he was doing inside himself with that news.

"Then I guess I really *can't* solve your problem, then."

"No, you really can't. I'm sorry. Sometimes the people around you will have problems, and you'll wish they didn't, but there won't be anything you can do. You just have to trust them to get by as best they can."

"That's pretty much what Stacey said."

"It's unfortunately true. And the sooner you accept that simple truth, the happier your life will be."

His eyes came up to hers. Just for a flicker of a second. As if they were a shield that could hold back anything he didn't want near him. Then his gaze careened back to the floor again.

"But I don't like that," he said.

"No, of course you don't. But it's *what is*. And if something is a certain way, and you can't accept that, and you need it to be another way, well . . . if you can change it, that's great. You go ahead and change it. But if you can't change it, and you can't accept it, it just gets so exhausting. Don't you get tired?"

"Very tired," he said.

She could tell by his tone that he had dropped all his defenses. That seemed like a decent start.

"Now let's just forget about me and my situation for a while and help you learn how to read."

"Yeah, okay," he said. "That would be good. It just seems too bad that you can fix my problem, but I can't fix yours."

"Be that as it may," she said, "let's just focus on what we can change."

Part Two

Winter

Chapter Twenty-Three

A Scholarship

Stewie

He sat at the kitchen table, staring at Stacey's closed bedroom door and buzzing with excitement. Literally buzzing. He could feel it all down the bones in his arms and legs, and in his belly. As if he were battery powered and his electricity was arcing slightly.

The report card was upside down on the table in front of him. He had one hand over it, to make sure it stayed a surprise. Even though there was no one else in the room.

In time Stacey's door opened, and she came slouching out, still in her nightie. Her hair fell in a wild tangle halfway over her face, and she scratched her shoulder as she walked down the hall. He watched her nose twitch as it worked the air.

"You made coffee for me," she said. She slid by behind his chair and kissed him on the top of his neatly combed hair. "That's very sweet."

"Stacey, I—"

But she held one hand up like a stop sign. She had taken to doing that more and more lately, as if to stop life from piling up on her, deeper and higher.

"Let me just have my coffee first, Stewie. Please. It was such a long night at work last night."

"It's a *good* thing, though."

"I'm glad to hear that. But please. Just a few sips."

She filled the largest mug they owned with plain black coffee and sat down at the table with a thump.

"Ooh. Nice and strong," she said, staring down into the cup as if in a trance.

"I know you like it that way."

She looked out the window, over his head at the snowy yard. She seemed to be turning something over in her head. She blew on the coffee, took a long sip, then sighed contentedly.

"So good," she said. "Now why aren't you at school?"

"It's Saturday."

"It is?"

"Yup."

"Are you sure?"

"I'm positive."

Apparently Stacey was not. Because she pushed to her feet and walked to her purse. It was on the little table by the front door—the one that held mail and keys and such. She reached in and pulled out her phone. Touched it a few times with her thumb.

"Well, I'll be damned," she said.

She sat back down and took a couple more sips. Stewie began to buzz again with the waiting.

"Now?" he asked, when he couldn't stand another moment.

"I suppose," she said. "Go ahead and lay it on me."

He slid the report card until it rested in front of her coffee cup. She looked down at it with widening eyes.

"Your report card."

"I wanted to show it to you when I got home from school yesterday, but you'd already left for work."

"Okay . . . let me see . . . it's your report card. And you're very anxious for me to see it. Which can only mean . . . it's a good report card."

He leapt to his feet and pointed wildly at a note the teacher had written.

"Read this part first," he said.

"Okay. Let's see. Oh, this is very good. This is very nice, Stewie."

"Read it out loud. Please."

"'Stewie's reading comprehension has improved by close to two grade levels between the end of last school year and the end of this semester. The tutor you arranged for him is clearly doing a world of good. Though he tells me they work only on reading, his grades in almost every subject have gone up a letter or more, and overall he seems more relaxed and enthusiastic about learning, and less hesitant and frustrated by the work. We are so happy to see this change!' Oh, Stewie. This is *very good*. B-plus in English. B in math. B-plus in history. There's nothing under a B on this whole report card."

"I know! I told you it was good news!"

"Well, I'm very proud of you."

"Thank you."

"Are you going out to see her again today? Since it's unexpectedly Saturday and all?"

"It's not unexpected. Yesterday was Friday."

"Unexpected for me."

"Yes. I'm going. Please don't make it seem like a bad thing. I know I go out there a lot."

"I'm not. After a report card like that, I wouldn't dare."

———

When he arrived at Eastbridge, he went first to the big industrial kitchen, as he always did. The ladies there all knew him by name.

."Why, Stewie Little," Marjorie said. She was a big, solid woman, easily six feet tall, with her hair up in a food service net. "Did you bring eggs for your grandma?"

"I did," he said.

He very carefully withdrew the carton from his backpack and handed it to her. She had a coffee mug of pens and markers sitting on her counter, and he watched as she wrote the name "J. Clements" on the carton in big block letters.

"It's nice of you to make hers separate," he said.

Marjorie snorted a laugh that seemed critical. Not of him, he didn't figure.

"What would really be nice is if Eastbridge would buy their eggs from you, because they're better. Then everybody could have fresh ones that taste better and are better for 'em. But it's all about the bottom line to them."

"I don't know what that is," Stewie said, ducking out of the way as a rack of fresh bread came rolling through, pushed by another member of the kitchen staff who liked him.

Everybody here liked him.

"Money. The bottom line is money. If they can save a dollar, they will."

"Oh. Well, I couldn't bring enough eggs for everybody here anyway. I don't have enough hens. We don't have any roosters, so no new hens ever get born. And a lot of the older girls have stopped laying. More all the time. All my gam's hens are starting to get old. Even the young ones are starting to get old."

"Couldn't you just go out and buy more?"

Oddly, he realized, the idea had never occurred to him. Now that it had been presented, he immediately disliked it.

"I'm not sure I'd want to go out and get hens that weren't Gam's hens. The whole idea was just to take care of them after she died. My sister wanted to sell them. But I didn't want them sold, because most people eat them the minute they stop laying."

"I know Mrs. Clements will miss these if they're ever not around. But I'll make sure she gets this dozen on her breakfast plate this week."

"Thanks, Marjorie," he said.

Then he ran up to the second floor, taking the stairs two at a time.

———

When Stewie walked down the hall to Marilyn's room, there was a man there. Sitting on the wooden bench outside her door. A man Stewie had never seen before. He was fiftyish, and balding, wearing a short-sleeved shirt even though it was cold outside. His forearms and the backs of his hands were strangely hairy. He was sitting with both palms over his eyes.

Stewie tried to walk right by, but the man stopped him with a word.

"Wait."

He had a deep voice, and Stewie thought it sounded sorrowful. Even though it was hard to judge by only one word. Or maybe it wasn't the voice. Maybe sorrow just surrounded the man, hung in the hall all around him like a misty cloud, and Stewie could feel it. It was hard, sometimes, to find your way around in the difference between what you saw and heard, and what was there to be felt. For Stewie it was, anyway.

"What?" Stewie said.

He stopped, even though he very much wanted to walk in and see Marilyn. The man moved his hands and looked Stewie over.

"Who are you?"

"I'm Stewie," he said. "Who are you?"

"Oh, you're that boy. The one she decided is her grandson now."

"Yeah," Stewie said. He was thinking it was just like a grown-up to insist you answer their question, and then ignore yours. But of course he didn't say so out loud. "You didn't say who you are."

"Gerald," he said. "Her son."

"Oh. I never see you here. I've never once seen you here in all these months."

"I come out. I come see her."

"I didn't say you never did. Just that I never saw you."

"Well," he said, and then stopped talking for several seconds. Even though that clearly hadn't been a complete thought. "I guess not as often as I should."

"Why don't you go in?"

"I was in."

"Why didn't you stay in?"

"She's having a bad day. Brace yourself. She won't know you. If she didn't even know her own son, she won't know you. I told her I was her son, and do you know what she said? She said, 'Don't be absurd. You can't be Gerald. You're a grown man.'"

"Oh," Stewie said. "That *is* a bad day."

"Plus they just gave her a new roommate. It's not pretty in there, son. She's totally up in arms about it. She thinks that room is her old house. She thinks she owns it, and nobody else gets to live there unless she says they can. And she's not about to say they can."

"Uh-oh."

"You don't have to go in," Gerald said. "You can go home. You can save yourself."

"No, thanks," Stewie said. "I'd rather go in."

When he stepped inside, Marilyn was pacing. She was fully dressed in a blouse and yellow slacks, with nylons showing at her ankles, but she wore loose white slippers on her feet. They shifted around and made a shuffling noise as she walked. Especially when she turned to pace in an opposite direction. Then she almost left the floppy things behind.

When she saw him, she looked up suddenly, and stopped moving. It was a relief to Stewie, who tended to catch nervous energy the way other people caught a cold.

"Oh. Stewart," she said. "I'm so glad you're here."

Stewie heard a little noise behind him. Something breathy, like a sigh. He glanced over his shoulder to see Gerald standing in the doorway. Then the older man ducked away again.

Stewie wanted to say something to Gerald. Maybe some kind of apology, because his mother had recognized the wrong one of them, and that was hurtful. But the man was gone, and anyway it had all happened too fast.

"Tell this maddening woman that she can't live in my house, Stewart."

The woman in question sat on the edge of the bed, rolling her eyes and gesturing broadly with her hands, as if to make a counterargument. She was younger than Marilyn, but not young. She had a wild shock of gray hair, and big, loose upper arms that Stewie could see flapping as she moved them around, even though she wore a thick brown sweater.

"*Maddening woman,*" she said in a gravelly, deep voice. Actually damaged-sounding, rather than naturally deep. "If that's not the pot calling the kettle black. This is just about the most disagreeable woman it's ever been my misfortune to meet. Tell this difficult woman, young man, that this is a nursing home. This is not her privately owned house."

Stewie just stood a moment, overwhelmed, his thoughts swirling. He remembered Gerald giving him the option to save himself by not stepping into this fray. But he couldn't have done that, regardless. Marilyn needed him.

"Maybe . . . ," he said, ". . . they could put you in a different room. Since you two don't seem to get along."

"I tried that," the woman said. "Twice. They are . . . all. Full. Up. Now *tell her.*"

"Okay," Stewie said. "Okay. I'll try. But everybody needs to stop yelling at everybody else. And especially everybody needs to stop yelling at *me*. It gets me all muddled up and confused. Marilyn and I can go down and look over the pond like we do. And I'll see if there's anything I can say to help."

"Too cold out there, honey," the woman said.

"Oh. Well. There's that nice sunporch. With the big windows and the fireplace. That room looks over the pond, too. Come on, Marilyn. Let's go."

He took her by the hand and tugged lightly, but she didn't budge.

"I'm not sure about leaving this . . . *person* alone with all my things. Why, I don't even know her."

"And now she just called me a thief," the woman said.

"Please, Marilyn. Everything will be fine here. I promise you. Let's just go someplace quiet where we can talk."

—

"Remember when there were ducks?" Marilyn asked.

She was sitting in a rocking chair on the glassed-in sunporch, an afghan draped around her shoulders. One of the ladies on the staff had brought her a cup of herbal tea, and she was sipping on it.

"Sure I remember them," Stewie said.

"They all flew south for the winter."

"I guess."

"But they'll be back next season. And I'll still be right here. Because I'm always right here. Where would I go? I'm not a good flier the way they are."

"People can't fly," Stewie said.

"I was speaking metaphorically."

"I have no idea what that means."

She never told him. She took the conversation in an entirely different direction instead.

"I know that room is not the house where I raised my children."

"You do?"

"Most of the time I do. I just pretend. Maybe sometimes it doesn't feel like I'm pretending. But most of the time I know it's not real. But it's been the only tiny little space that's been *mine* this whole time. Since I had to come back. A blessed little piece of privacy. It's made the whole situation livable for me. And now I'm just so unhappy about this turn of events. I'm not at all sure what I'm going to do, Stewart. It's really such a problem."

"You wait here and look at the pond," Stewie said. "I'll go talk to the people and see if there's anything at all I can do."

———

He stuck his head over the counter that opened into the administration office. Seeing no one, he set his hands on the counter and jumped up, supporting himself on his arms and leaning his belly against the counter, hoping to see farther into the room.

"What can I do for you, Stewie?" a woman's voice said.

It was Joni, the woman with the beautiful, lilting accent. Stewie had never known exactly what kind of accent it was, but it always sounded like music to him.

"Where are you, Joni? I hear you but I don't see you."

She stuck her head out of a private office in the back and frowned at him, furrowing her forehead. She tended to, when she spoke to him. It was a gesture that suggested that she had better things to do than Stewie. He never took it as an insult, though, because he never got the sense that she intended it that way. It seemed to be the way she approached anything that demanded her attention.

"How 'bout if I come to the counter," she said, still furrowing, "and then you can stand with your feet on the rug like everybody else."

"That would be okay."

He slid down to the carpet. She arrived on the other side of the counter, rested her forearms on it, and leaned toward him until their faces were only a foot or so apart.

"What can I do for you *now*, Stewie?"

"I want to know how we can get Marilyn into a private room."

"You want to know how to get *who* into a private room?"

Stewie rolled his eyes dramatically.

They went through this every time. If someone else was taking care of the counter, Stewie and that other person still went through it. There must have been a memo passed around that read something like "Always challenge Stewie on this particular point."

"You know who I'm talking about. My adopted grandmother. The only person I *ever* come to visit. I know you know exactly who I mean, Joni."

"And her name is . . ."

Stewie sighed deeply.

"Jean Clements."

"All right. Now we're getting somewhere. You want to know how you can get a private room for Jean Clements."

"Right."

"You can't. We are all full up."

Stewie felt his heart sink. He knew it couldn't be the literal organ of his heart, literally sinking, because he paid attention in science class, especially since it first happened to him, and he knew hearts were attached pretty firmly inside their chests. It sure felt like his heart sinking, though.

"You couldn't have just told me that in the first place?"

"I'm sorry, Stewie. But we've told you before, there is no one named Marilyn Higgenbotham living at this facility. There was, but she is unfortunately deceased. You can call your adopted grandmother by any name you like, but when you come and talk to us, we are talking about Mrs. Jean Clements."

"Yes, ma'am. If you say so."

"I say so because it's the truth. Would you like to be on a waiting list for a private room for Mrs. Clements?"

"Yes, ma'am! That would be great."

"But you do know that a private room costs quite a bit more, don't you? The monthly rate would go up a lot. We'd need to know who would be paying for that extra charge. Medicare won't pay for a private room, and we've had precious little success trying to get extra money for her care from her son and daughter."

"Oh," Stewie said. And he felt his heart slip a little lower. "How much more a month?"

"I can't tell you for a fact until a room comes up vacant. Some cost more than others. Some are a little bigger and some have nicer views."

"Can't you even give me an idea?"

"The least expensive private room we've got would be six hundred dollars a month more than the double room she's in now."

Stewie felt his eyes go wide.

He had *begun* to understand that there were problems other people might have that he couldn't solve. At least, in his head he'd made a little progress. Dr. Briggs talked to him often about that. But he definitely needed to solve this one. Because the upset he'd absorbed in her room earlier, as the mean words flew back and forth, well . . . he knew he couldn't live like that for very long. Besides, no matter how many times Dr. Briggs explained that it was not a good way to be, it was still the way Stewie was put together.

"Six hundred dollars?" he repeated, his voice full of awe.

"I know. I'm sorry. Eldercare does not come cheaply. I know this is probably out of the question for you, since you're . . . you know . . ."

"No. What am I?"

"Like . . . ten."

"I'm *twelve*," Stewie said, pulling himself up as tall as possible.

"I was close."

"You weren't close at all! Twelve is much older than ten."

"I'm sorry. I didn't mean to offend you. I'm only saying that I don't suppose you make that much money by selling your fresh eggs."

"No, ma'am," he said. "I don't suppose I do, either."

———

He looked for her in the sunporch, but she had left her half-full mug of tea on the carpet and the afghan on the back of her chair and wandered away. Which probably meant she had forgotten all about him.

Part of him was relieved that she wasn't waiting right there to ask him what he'd managed to accomplish on her behalf. Since the news was not good. Still, he couldn't avoid telling her indefinitely. He climbed the stairs to her room. He did not vault up them two at a time as he normally did.

Gerald was still sitting on the bench outside her door, still holding his face in his hairy hands.

Stewie walked up to him, stood a few feet away, and spoke.

"I need to ask you something."

Gerald, who apparently hadn't known anyone was there, jumped the proverbial mile.

"You scared me," he said, after dropping his hands and visually considering Stewie for a beat or two.

"Sorry."

"What do you need to ask me?"

"If you could help pay for a private room for her."

He watched the man's face as he asked. Gerald was clearly skeptical.

"Help?"

"Yes."

"Meaning someone else would do part of it?"

"Right."

"And who would that someone else be?"

"Well. Kind of . . . me. I could put all my egg money into it. But the egg money isn't as much as it used to be. Now that the hens are getting older and all. I could get a job."

"How can you get a job? Aren't you, like, eleven?"

"I'm twelve!" Stewie said, nearly shouting now. "Why doesn't anybody get that I'm twelve? Kids my age get jobs. I could mow lawns or something."

"In the middle of winter."

"We have a snowblower. I could do people's driveways. And then later it won't be winter anymore, and I can mow lawns. I know it's a lot to ask, because I know you already put out extra to pay back the rest of what she stole."

"I didn't pay for any of that."

"You didn't? Who did? Betty?"

"Nobody did. They accepted less than the full amount. They'll probably take the rest as a tax deduction."

"I have no idea what that means," Stewie said. "But if you didn't help then, maybe you could help now."

"I doubt it. But go ahead and tell me how much extra we would need."

Stewie could have quoted the minimum figure Joni had given him, but he didn't want to. It was so much.

"We don't really know, because we don't know which room. Because right now they're all full, and we don't know which one will be empty first."

"Wait," Gerald said. "Let me get this straight. You're asking me to pay for a private room for my mom, but there are no private rooms."

"But there will be eventually."

"So we're waiting for someone to die."

That made Stewie uneasy, because it was such a terrible thought. He shifted his weight from foot to foot, trying to vent off that discomfort.

"Not necessarily *that*."

"We're waiting for someone to reverse the aging process and get young again?"

"Maybe someone will take their mother home to live with them."

Gerald's voice seemed to harden. But Stewie purposely didn't look at the man's face to confirm whether there was any anger there.

"Look. Kid. If people were willing to have their mothers living with them, and the mothers were willing to be there, they would have done that from the start. This place is a last resort. A last stop. People leave here one way, and one way only. In a body bag."

"I wish you wouldn't talk that way," Stewie said. "It's upsetting."

"Sorry, kid. It's the damn truth. And let me lay another truth on you. I don't have money. My wife took it all in the divorce."

"All of it? How do you buy food to eat?"

"All right, not all of it. But enough that there's nothing extra left over. And if I did have a little more, I have lots of stuff I need for myself. My mother is just going to have to adjust to life in a double room. I'm sorry, kid, but that's just the way things are."

Stewie sighed, and decided to say nothing more on the subject. Talking to Gerald wasn't very much fun. It was a lot like talking to Betty. He wondered what it had been like in that household, when they'd all lived together as a family. Then he decided he didn't want to wonder that anymore.

"I'm sorry you and your wife had to get a divorce," he said.

It seemed to take Gerald by surprise. He had placed himself in opposition to Stewie, ready and willing to defend himself. Now he had to shift gears to allow Stewie's caring in. Stewie could see him doing it. It was all right there in front of his eyes. It seemed to make the older man uncomfortable. Stewie was left with the uneasy feeling that Gerald had been more comfortable on the defense.

"Thank you," Gerald said quietly.

Stewie decided it was best to leave him alone after that exchange.

He stuck his head into his grandmother's room, but she didn't notice. She was sitting on her bed, looking out the window. Maybe looking at the bird nest, which was empty now, and dusted with snow. Her roommate was reading a book on her own bed. It struck Stewie as quite a peaceful scene.

He decided to leave well enough alone for the time being.

—

"Thank you for talking to me," Stewie said.

He sat in front of the desk, in the main office of Eastbridge, across from that lady. The same lady he'd given the money to on the day he'd brought it back. He couldn't seem to overcome slouching in his chair. It made him feel small. In that moment, everything did.

He didn't know the lady's name, because she hadn't bothered to tell him. But it was someone he did not see at Eastbridge every day. He got the sense that she was too important to be here often.

"Well," she said. She cleared her throat in a way Stewie decided had nothing to do with phlegm in her throat. It sounded like something a person would do to make themselves sound weightier and more in control. And that made him feel even smaller. "I had to drive over from the corporate office. But you said it was important."

"Yes, ma'am."

"Go ahead and tell me what's on your mind, then."

"I want to ask for a scholarship for . . . Mrs. Clements."

"A scholarship?"

"Yes, ma'am."

"This is not a school."

"Yes, ma'am. I know it's not."

"I think maybe you don't know what a scholarship is."

"Maybe I don't, ma'am. But I'll bet you know what I mean. When my sister, Stacey, wanted to go to nursing school . . . our parents had died, and she was trying to raise my brother and me on a regular job. The kind that doesn't pay very much money. So she told the university about how she couldn't pay what they usually get, and they let her go there anyway."

He waited, hoping she would speak quickly in return, and then he would know. Instead she made her fingers into those imitation church steeples. Stewie had no idea why grown-ups did that when they were talking to you.

"This is about her wanting a private room."

"Yes, ma'am."

"You realize there are none available."

"Yes, ma'am. I do know that. But sooner or later one will be."

"And you're hoping we'll give it to her at the double-occupancy rate."

"Yes, ma'am."

"That would be quite impossible, Stewart, and if you think about it, I expect you'll know why."

Stewie felt a deep achiness in his belly. He tried to ignore it so he could still talk.

"Because of your bottom line?"

His words seemed to stun her. She actually shook her head a little, as if to help his comment hurry away.

"That seems like a strange thing for a boy your age to say."

"I'm twelve," Stewie said quickly.

She hadn't accused him of being younger. But he'd been getting that a lot lately, and this time he was determined to "head it off at the pass," as they said in the old black-and-white cowboy films he watched on TV on weekend mornings.

"I'm not sure why you would say that. And if you fully understood what you just said, then you accused me of caring more about money than I do about my residents."

Stewie opened his mouth to issue some kind of disclaimer. Then he closed it again without speaking. He had no idea what this woman cared about most, so he was not prepared to issue a statement.

"The reason it's out of the question," she said, "is because it would be unfair to our other residents. Everyone else with a private room would be paying more. How am I to explain that to them?"

"Maybe they wouldn't know?" Stewie asked, his voice desperately hopeful.

"*I* would know," she said.

Her voice sounded like thunder. Booming and deep, the way someone might sound if they were trying to imitate God bellowing down from above.

Stewie sighed deeply, and as quietly as possible, and knew it was over. And knew that he had lost.

"But she's not *happy*," he said, his voice just above a whisper.

"I'm not convinced that that woman is capable of being happy. I might be wrong to say that to a young person your age."

"I'm twelve," Stewie said. Just in case the matter of his age was headed in a bad direction again. Then he realized he had told her that already. "I guess I should go now."

"I'm sorry I can't help you."

"Yes, ma'am. I'm sorry you can't help me, too."

———

"It just makes me . . . really . . . *mad*!" Stewie said, raising his voice to a shouting level on the final word.

He was pacing frantically in Dr. Briggs's office, even though it was hot. Oddly, the same man who wouldn't use air-conditioning in the summer was happy to overheat the office with a furnace in the winter chill. Or maybe that wasn't odd. Maybe he just always wanted to be warm.

For several minutes Stewie had been pacing, waiting for the doctor to order him to settle down and return to his seat.

No such order seemed forthcoming.

"That's interesting," Dr. Briggs said.

Those two words made Stewie even angrier.

"It's not *interesting*!" he shouted. "It's . . . angry . . . ing. It's . . . I don't know the word. It's mad-making."

"Infuriating?"

"I don't even know what that one means."

"From the word *fury*. Something that makes you furious."

Stewie stopped pacing for a split second.

"Is 'furious' 'mad'?"

"Yes, but even more intensely."

"Then yeah, I guess so."

He paced a minute longer before he was hit with a worry. He stopped. Turned to face the doctor. Looked into his eyes. The older man seemed oddly unperturbed.

"Not at you, though," Stewie said. Just to make sure Dr. Briggs knew.

"I didn't think you meant me. But thank you for clarifying."

"I don't know what 'clarifying' means."

"From the word *clear*. To make something clear."

"Then why don't they call it *clear*ifying?"

"Off the top of my head, I can't say. But I think we're getting off track, Stewie. With whom are you angry?"

Stewie stopped again. He was close to the window, so he looked out. There was a pigeon on the windowsill, pecking at some seeds. Stewie wondered if that meant Dr. Briggs put seeds out for the birds, which would make Stewie like him a lot more. He wondered why he'd never noticed birds on the windowsill before. It wasn't like him to fail to notice birds.

"'*With whom?*'"

"I mean who are you angry with?"

"Nobody. I'm angry all by myself."

"Let me try this again, Stewie. Who are you angry at?"

"Oh, *at*. Why didn't you say so? Well . . . maybe some of the people at Eastbridge, because they won't help me. And I feel like they could if they really wanted to. But mostly I think I'm just mad at life, because everybody's unhappy and that doesn't seem fair."

"Not everybody's unhappy," Dr. Briggs said.

"Everybody I know is unhappy. Why can't people just be happy?"

"All the time?"

"Yes, all the time. Why not?"

"First of all, because if we were happy all the time, it wouldn't even be happiness. It would just be the way we were all the time, and we would fail to even notice it after a while. I know this is a tricky concept, Stewie, but bear with me. Say, for instance, there's a sound. If I whistled, for example." He stopped speaking for a moment and created the whistling noise, a thin, quiet thing between his pursed lips. "First there's no whistling. Then there's whistling. Then there's no whistling again. The reason you notice the whistling is because of the contrast with the moments when there's no whistling. If that sound were present all the time, every minute of your life, if it had been going on since the moment you were born, you wouldn't even hear it anymore. It would just be what you considered normal. Does that make sense, Stewie? Or am I not explaining it well?"

To his own surprise, Stewie returned to his seat. He perched on the edge of the big chair, his hands resting on the knees of his khaki pants.

"I actually think I might get what you mean. I think you're saying the reason happiness is happy is because we're not always happy."

"Exactly. I'm glad you understand. Let me present you with another concept. The reason people are unhappy is because they're so sure they know what they want. And then it makes them unhappy when they don't get it. I personally think people would be happier if they weren't so sure they knew the difference between a good thing and a bad thing."

"That makes no sense," Stewie said.

"It's a very adult concept."

"Everybody knows a good thing or a bad thing."

"But do they, though?"

"Yes. They do. Like when my hen died. That was bad."

"Good example," Dr. Briggs said. "We think it's bad when someone dies. But their body is getting older and giving out on them. They're in more pain. Knowing that, is it really bad?"

"Well, then, it's bad that their body gets old and gives out."

"You would have nobody die, ever."

"Right, exactly."

"How would there be space for all of us in the world, if everybody who had ever lived was still here? How would there be resources? How could we grow enough food, or have enough fuel or water, for everything and everybody who had ever been born?"

Stewie realized he was holding his head, one palm on each temple, as if worried it might explode.

"This is making my head hurt," he said.

"I'm sorry. I just want you to try on some different kinds of thinking. You think Marilyn is unhappy because she has a roommate. And Marilyn thinks Marilyn is unhappy because she has a roommate. But I think Marilyn is unhappy because she thinks having a roommate is a bad thing. Not everyone would. Some people would be lonely in a room all by themselves, and would welcome the company."

"I think I see what you mean," Stewie said. "But I'm not sure how it helps solve the problem."

"I don't know if it does. I can't solve everybody's problems."

Stewie looked up quickly. Looked at the man's face. Because he hadn't sounded upset when he said that, which Stewie found nearly unimaginable.

"And you're *okay* with that?"

"Yes," Dr. Briggs said. Without hesitation. "Yes, it would be nice if I could solve everyone's problems for them. But I accept that I can't. But let's apply this directly to your situation. You tried to solve Marilyn's problem by getting her a private room, but you weren't able to do it. Maybe now there's some way you can help her see the company as not such a bad thing."

"Hmm," Stewie said. "She did tell me that she was upset when she got her last roommate, but then she ended up liking her."

"Maybe it would help her to remember that."

"What if it doesn't work?"

"In that case you'll have to fall back on accepting that you can't solve everybody's problems."

"Oh," Stewie said. "Too bad. We keep coming back to that one. And that's the one I hate the most."

"I know. I'm sorry. But maybe the fact that you hate it doesn't make it a bad thing."

"Wow. That's so much to think about."

A long silence fell. As though Stewie had begun thinking about it. But in reality, his brain had hit a point of exhaustion and he was thinking nothing at all.

"Just one thing, though," Stewie said suddenly. It surprised him when the question came up in his head. He had not consciously seen it coming. "Why did you say it was interesting that I was mad?"

"Because you've never shown any anger in my office before. I thought that was good progress."

"You think anger is good?"

"I think anger is a normal human emotion. And I think people getting in touch with their emotions is good. I think people tend to bury their emotions because they don't want to feel them. And I think we can't heal those emotions until we let them come out into the light."

"So you think we let things come up so they can heal?"

"Exactly. That's exactly what I think."

"Hmm," Stewie said. "That's interesting."

———

Stewie stood in the doorway of Marilyn's room. He had one hand extended to steady himself against the jamb. The other lady, whose name he didn't know, looked up at him and smiled.

Marilyn wasn't looking up. She was lying on her bed, and she had a book in her hands, but she didn't seem to be reading it. She seemed to be staring down at her own lap as if lost in thought. Her hair was messy.

It bothered Stewie that nobody at Eastbridge seemed to want to be sure her hair was kept neat. At least, not so far that morning. Maybe he just wasn't giving them enough time. Still, it bothered him. It just did.

It was a Saturday morning, and it was early. Stewie had set an alarm and caught the very first bus into the city.

"I wanted to talk to you," he said.

Her head came up, and she looked at him as though he had just wakened her from a sound sleep.

"Oh, Stewart," she said. "I didn't see you there."

"Maybe we could talk privately," he said, casting an apologetic glance at her roommate.

Marilyn looked in the direction of the window and frowned.

"It's awfully cold to sit outside."

"We could go down to the dining room and eat breakfast. Unless you already ate."

He shrugged out of his coat as he spoke, because it was hot in the hall.

"Did I eat?" Marilyn asked. "Did I? I'm trying to remember."

"You didn't," her roommate said. "You been right there on that bed since you got dressed this morning."

"Okay, then," Marilyn said. "We'll go down and have something to eat."

———

"Just take pancakes," Stewie said as they walked down the buffet table. "They'll bring you the eggs special."

"But there are eggs right there," she said, pointing in the direction of a male resident who was spooning an absurdly large helping of scrambled eggs onto his plate.

"But they bring you better eggs."

"Why do I get better eggs?"

"Because I bring them special for you. Come on. Let's sit down now."

He gently took hold of her sleeve, carefully balancing his plate with the other hand, and steered them toward a table, where they settled.

"How do you get eggs that are better than everyone else's eggs?" she asked. As she spoke, she shook out a folded napkin and draped it on her lap.

"Don't you remember? I have my own hens. They used to belong to my gam. It's how I met you."

For a moment, she simply looked confused.

Then she said, "I thought I had always known you."

"No," he said. "Just since last summer. Well. Late spring, really. But if you want to think you always knew me, that's okay with me. Because it feels like we always knew each other."

"It does," she said. "Doesn't it?"

"You should eat your pancakes," he said, because she was ignoring them.

She cut into them with the side of her fork, but then seemed to drift away again.

"I wanted to talk to you about something," he said again.

"All right."

"It's about your roommate. I was thinking that . . . maybe it only seems like you don't like her because you don't really know her yet. Because you told me once that you didn't like Marilyn Higgenbotham when you first met her."

She set her fork down on her plate, carefully.

"Are you sure I said that?"

"Positive."

"I don't think I would have said any such thing as that. Marilyn Higgenbotham was a lovely woman."

"You said you didn't like her at first. I remember it really well, like you just said it to me today. You said at first it was just awful, having to share your space like that. But then you said after some time you started to really care about her."

"That doesn't sound right. Are you sure?"

"Positive. I'd bet my whole life on it."

"I guess I'll have to take your word for it, then."

Just then the big tall woman, Marjorie, came through the swinging kitchen door and headed toward their table. She was carrying a small white plate with what looked like two scrambled eggs on it. Stewie knew they were his eggs, because they were a nice bright yellowy-orange. Not pale like the ones you got at the supermarket.

She set them down in front of Marilyn.

"Special for you, Mrs. Clements," she said.

"Why, thank you . . . ," Marilyn said, looking up at the woman with a soft look on her face. She seemed to be searching for the woman's name to finish her sentence. Not finding it, she simply stopped speaking.

Marjorie patted her on the shoulder and moved off toward the kitchen again.

Marilyn took a forkful of eggs and tasted them.

"Mmm," she said. "They have the best eggs here at Eastbridge. That's one thing I do like about being here."

"I bring those eggs specially for you," Stewie said.

"Now how do you happen to have eggs, Stewart?"

"Never mind. It's not important. I just wonder if you remember what we were just talking about. Because *that* was important."

"Oh. Let me see. That *did* feel important. And it's right on the tip of my tongue, too. Oh, I know. We were talking about Marilyn Higgenbotham. She was such a lovely woman."

"But at first you didn't think so. At first you hated having a roommate."

"Really? Are you sure?"

"I'm positive."

"Then I suppose I'll have to take your word for it."

"My point was that you think you don't like having a roommate now. But maybe you just don't know her yet."

Marilyn set down her fork again. Her gaze seemed to veer off into the distance, as though trying to chase an answer that was trying to run away.

"I don't think it's about the woman in particular," she said, her eyes still far away. "I think I just don't like having to share such a small space."

"But maybe that's because you're not used to it yet, and you don't know her."

"Well, I don't know, Stewart. I suppose I'd have to think about that."

"Right," Stewie said. "Thank you. Just think about it. Thank you. That's all I want."

Then he finished his pancakes. And, because she was only leaving them to get cold, he finished hers, too.

Chapter Twenty-Four

Magical Boy

Stewie

The following Saturday, when he stood in her doorway, she was talking to her roommate in a normal tone. She was sitting on her bed and wearing something yellow and knitted draped over herself. Not a sweater. It was something less fitted, like a small blanket wrapped around her shoulders.

She looked up and saw him almost immediately.

"Oh, Stewart," she said. "You remember Louise."

And she pointed to her new roommate, the woman with the huge gray hair. Took her in with an expansive sweep of her arm.

"Sure I do," he said. "I just didn't know her name."

"Louise made this for me. She asked me my favorite color, and I told her it was yellow. And then she crocheted it especially for me. Wasn't that just the most thoughtful thing for her to do?"

"That was very nice of her," Stewie said, taking a moment to offer Louise a relieved smile. "What is it?" Then, realizing that had sounded rude, he scrambled to correct his mistake. "It's very nice. I don't mean it's not nice. And I sort of know what it is. It's a thing to keep you warm. I just haven't really seen a thing quite like it. It doesn't exactly have sleeves or anything, and I just wasn't quite sure what you call one of those."

"You've never seen a shawl?" Marilyn asked, sounding genuinely surprised.

"No, ma'am. I don't think so. I mean, not that I can remember. It's nice, though. I like the fringe."

Stewie heard a slight noise behind him and turned to see one of the Eastbridge employees, a young woman, waiting to get by him to enter the room.

"Oh," he said. "Sorry."

And he moved out of her way.

"I need to take Mrs. Clements to physical therapy," she said.

"Oh. Really? That's too bad. I just got here to visit her."

"You can wait thirty minutes, can't you? Her physical therapy is important."

"Yes, ma'am. I can wait."

A new voice entered the conversation. It was the gravelly, deep, damaged-sounding voice of Louise, the new roommate.

"We'll wait together, honey," she said to Stewie. She crossed the room to where he stood in the doorway. Slid her arm through his. "I've been wanting to talk to you anyway. Get to know you better. We'll take a walk. Take a walk down the hall with me, honey. We got a lot of catching up to do."

———

Louise kept her arm threaded through his as they marched down the hall at a surprisingly brisk pace. She was a small woman. Not much taller than Stewie. But she seemed to have the constitution of a much younger woman. Stewie couldn't help wondering why she even lived at Eastbridge if she had that kind of health and energy.

"It was nice of you to make something for her," Stewie said as they passed the nurses' station—again.

The second floor was a continuous loop in the shape of a rectangle. A person could walk around it forever if they had the time and energy to do so.

"She's been nice to me," Louise said in that bullfrog voice. At least, it reminded Stewie of the bullfrogs that lived in the marshes in the shallows of the lake. "I'm trying to encourage that."

"I'm sorry I didn't know what it was."

"You don't have to be sorry. A shawl is an old-fashioned thing. An older woman would know what a shawl was. I wouldn't expect a young boy your age to know."

Stewie opened his mouth quickly to say he was twelve. Just in case he was about to lose a year or two in somebody else's eyes. Again.

She spoke before he could manage.

"Other women I know who crochet make sweaters. Or hats. But that's so complicated. You have to make things turn out in just this perfect shape. I learned how to do it, but then I decided I didn't want to. I guess I'm lazy. Well . . . I'm not sure 'lazy' is the right word. I do it to have something to do with my hands, and it helps my arthritis to keep my fingers moving. But I just do it for the fun of it. If anything stops it from being fun, I guess I just start wondering why I'm doing it at all."

"That makes perfect sense," Stewie said.

"Good. I had a feeling we'd see eye to eye, you and me."

They walked in silence for nearly a full loop around the second floor.

Then Louise said, "You know her mind is getting very bad, right?"

"Yes, ma'am. I do know that."

"It's a good thing she's in a place like this, where people with professional training can look after her."

"I get why she's here," Stewie said. "I'm not sure why you're here. Your mind seems good and you walk really fast."

"I sold my house," she said, "because I just flat-out got tired of taking care of it. Taking care of everybody and everything. Raised five kids. Took care of two husbands when they got sick and old. All my life I took care of everybody else. Now it's my turn. Now it's time for other people to take care of me."

"Wow," Stewie said. "You're really different from her. I wish she could look at the thing that way."

"Yes indeed," Louise said. "We are two very different people. Not really made for getting along, but we *are* getting along. Well enough, anyway. And it started last week when you came in wanting to talk to her over breakfast. I have a sneaking suspicion I have you to thank."

"I just reminded her of something she forgot. How she didn't like having a roommate last time she had one, but then she got to know the lady and really liked her a lot."

"Well, it's funny," Louise said, "because I just know she forgot all that again a minute after you told her. But some little bit of something you said stuck. Maybe underneath the part of her brain that doesn't hold on to things, the feeling of the thing stuck. Somehow you said just the right thing. You're a magical boy. You know that?"

Stewie stopped dead in the hall. Louise kept going a few steps, and tugged on his arm without meaning to as their linked limbs pulled her to a halt.

"Why would you say that?" he asked.

"Because I believe it."

"I'm not magic. I'm just a regular boy."

"I'm not saying you're not real like everybody else. I give you credit for being a real boy. But you wake something up in people. You remind them we can do better at getting along. You can be just a regular, real person and still be the magic somebody else needs in her life. We do it for each other all the time. It's that everyday sort of magic. We're all capable of it, I do believe, but still you don't always see people living up to that potential."

"I understood some of that," Stewie said.

He expected her to break it down. Dissect it. Dumb it down for a kid listener.

Instead she just said, "Good."

They walked again, more slowly this time.

"You remind me of my own grandson," she said.

"How old is *he*?"

"Thirty-three."

"Your *grandson* is *thirty-three*?"

"Yes, child, I have been on this earth for a few trips around the sun."

"How can I remind you of a thirty-three-year-old?"

She chuckled, a hoarse sound in her throat. "You don't. You remind me of him when he was your age. Like . . . thirteen?"

"Twelve," Stewie said. "But thank you."

"Just so you know, son, if you ever needed another adopted grandma, I'm adoptable myself."

"That's a nice thing to say."

"It's true."

They walked more slowly for another trip around before she spoke again.

"Ever notice how she forgets everything and everyone . . . but not you? Her own children come here, and half the time she doesn't know them. But she always calls you by your name."

"I did notice that. But I don't know why."

"Don't you? Seems clear to me."

"Because I'm magical?"

"Maybe. Maybe that, too. I was thinking because she cares about you. Maybe more than you know."

"I like your reason better," he said.

They walked for a while longer, but did not talk again. To Stewie, it felt as though they didn't need to talk more. As though everything that needed saying had already been comfortably said.

—

When they got back to the room, Betty was sitting on the bench in the hall out front. Louise walked right by her, but Stewie stopped.

Betty looked up at him, and offered a half smile, but it was strained and sad looking. So Stewie sat down beside her. He always tried to stay with people who looked sad, in case there was anything he should be doing to help.

"She's at physical therapy," he said.

"So I hear."

"You okay?"

"Not really."

"What's wrong?"

"I'm just sitting here wondering if I should even stay and visit. I drove over an hour to get here, and now I'm wondering if I should just give up and go home."

"Why would you go home without visiting her?"

"You don't know how it feels," she said. "You don't know what it's like to have your own mother not even know you."

"I don't even know what it's like to have a mother," Stewie said.

Then they sat without talking for an uncomfortable space of time.

"Is that why Gerald hasn't been coming out?" he asked. He shifted around on the hard wooden bench as he spoke, because it was uncomfortable. It made his sitting bones ache. "Because I haven't seen Gerald for a while. But maybe I'm wrong. Maybe he comes out, but I just keep missing him."

"No, you're right. He doesn't come out anymore. He told me there's no point visiting a person who's not there. He says it's just a waste of time."

"That's wrong," Stewie said, shaking his head hard.

He saw her consider him in his peripheral vision, turning her head to stare at him, her eyes narrowed.

"With all due respect," she said, "I'm not sure you get to judge. Since you haven't had the experience."

"But she's *there*," Stewie said, "and that's just a fact. It's not something I'm judging. It's just true."

"You're an opinionated little guy, aren't you?"

"It's not an *opinion*," Stewie said, growing quite a bit more agitated. "It's just the truth. You just look with your eyes and you'll see. She's *there*. You talk to her and she talks back. That's being there. That's all a person has to do to be there. You're just upset because she doesn't say the same things she would have said before. Instead of being so sure about exactly how you want her to be, why can't you just be glad because she's there? You know how happy I would be if my mother was there? Sometimes I think you and Gerald don't get how lucky you are."

Stewie was pretty sure she was about to tell him a thing or two. He thought he heard her open her mouth and begin a word. But he didn't let her go there.

"I know a man," he said. "A man who taught me that the reason people aren't happy is because they have these ideas about what the world should be. And the world is never just what they think it ought to be. If the world has to be a certain way for you to be happy, then you'll never be happy. Heck, I'm only twelve and even I know that. She's not the same as she used to be, but she's not gone. She's your mother. If you could just be happy she's here, then you could be happy."

Stewie paused, wincing slightly, to hear her reaction. It had been blunt advice. He didn't normally speak to grown-ups that way, and he knew there was a chance she would be offended.

For what felt like several minutes—but probably wasn't—he didn't get to find out much about her reaction.

Then she said, simply, "I'm not used to taking advice from a kid."

"Advice is just either right or wrong," he said. "It's not so much about who told it to you."

She opened her mouth to answer, but never got the chance.

They both looked up to see Marilyn shuffling down the hall in her loose, oversize bedroom slippers, the young Eastbridge employee clutching her elbow as if she might be about to fall off a cliff. She was still wearing the yellow crocheted shawl wrapped around her shoulders in the very warm hall.

"Stewart," she said when she saw him. "How lovely to see you. I hope you'll introduce me to your friend."

"This is your daughter," he said, his face burning red. "Betty."

"You're confused, dear. My daughter Betty is your age. This is a grown woman."

For a moment, nobody said anything.

Then he heard Betty sigh deeply.

"I came to visit you, Mom," Betty said. "Let's go ahead and have a nice visit. Or at least . . . let's go ahead and have as nice a visit as we can have. Under the circumstances."

She rose from the bench, brushed off her slacks, and followed her mother into the room.

Stewie continued to sit on the bench in the hall, even though he had been hoping for a nice visit, too. Because he decided that some things are more important than others, and that a woman just discovering her mother was still there was more important than anything he had come to do.

Part Three

Late Spring Again

Chapter Twenty-Five

Please Lay

Stewie

Stewie moved along the row of nesting boxes, gently sliding a hand under each of the newer hens. He kept his eyes closed most of the time, and on each reach he muttered under his breath, barely above a whisper, "Lay."

Just as he thought not a single one of the young hens had laid an egg in the night, his hand touched one smooth treasure.

He slid it out from under the new bird.

"Helen!" he said, probably too loud for a henhouse voice. "You laid an egg! You're the first of the new girls to lay an egg! You're a star!"

It was an expression he had picked up from his English teacher, who was increasingly enthusiastic about his reading-level progress.

The young hen seemed concerned by his excitement.

He slipped her egg carefully into the basket with those of the older, more veteran birds. That is, the ones who hadn't already stopped laying for good.

He scanned the basket. His eyes told him there were just a few more than two dozen eggs. Barely more than he had hoped to have for his own family.

He sighed and carried them into the house.

Stacey was in the kitchen, scrambling the last of yesterday's eggs.

"Any luck?" she asked. She looked into his basket and frowned. "Hmm. Not exactly a windfall. How many of those are from the new girls?"

"One," Stewie said. He could hear the absolute devastation in his own voice.

"How old are they supposed to be again, when they start to lay?"

"Guy at the feed store said eighteen weeks."

"And that's what they are, right?"

"No. They're nineteen weeks. Couple days past, actually."

"Well, it's not the same for every bird," she said. "And there are other factors, like the season or the stress of the new place."

"Yeah, yeah," Stewie said. "I know all that." Then, realizing he might have sounded rude, he added, "No offense."

"None taken. Go and get your brother and tell him breakfast's ready, okay?"

"Okay."

He set the basket of eggs on the counter and started down the hall toward Theo's room, but she was still talking to him.

"You going out to Eastbridge after school?"

"I was going to, yeah."

"If you're not home in time to eat, I'll hold your dinner in a warm oven."

"I should be home. I don't have to do my egg route first, because there's nothing to sell."

"Oh. True. I'm sorry, Stewie. They'll lay. I'm sure they will. They just need a little more time."

"I guess," he said.

He stuck his head into Theo's room. The door was standing open, and Theo was sitting on the bed, struggling his way into a purple T-shirt.

"Breakfast," Stewie said.

It took another minute for Theo's shaggy head to pop out through the neck hole.

"Did they lay?" he asked immediately.

"Not really. One did."

"Oh. Sorry, Stewie. That's too bad. They will, though. They just need a little more time."

Stewie found himself wishing he felt as sure as they both sounded. Then again, maybe they weren't sure, either. People did that all the time, he noticed. Somebody was always trying to convince you of something when they were barely sure about the thing themselves.

—

He looked for Marilyn first in the activities room, because it was sing-along time.

Sing-along was a daily event at Eastbridge, with that nice lady, Janet, playing the piano, and the words of the song projected onto a screen in big letters that most of the residents could read. Usually more than half the residents packed into the activities room for sing-along.

He leaned in the open doorway and scanned the faces carefully, but Marilyn was not there.

He tried to duck out again, but it didn't work. He was spotted immediately.

The piano music stopped, and the remaining voices trailed away.

"Stewie!" Janet called, her voice a delighted shriek. "Look, everybody. Stewie's here!"

That set up a chorus of "Hi, Stewie!" from the crowd. One person said, "Good morning, Stewie," even though it was afternoon, and one older man said, "Who's Stewie?" even though it was a resident who had met Stewie many times.

"Hi, everybody," he said, waving awkwardly. "Well. I don't want to interrupt sing-along. I need to go find my grandmother."

"You can visit us, too, Stewie," a woman in the front row said. It was Mrs. Baker, a nice old lady in a wheelchair who didn't have much vision left. "We always like to see you."

"Thank you, Mrs. Baker," he said, still mortified to have interrupted the singing. "But I need to put my grandmother first. I hope you understand. Maybe I'll come see you later."

"But we won't all be together later," she said.

The light in the activities room was blazing fluorescent, and it made Stewie wince and blink. It was warm in there—it was warm everywhere inside Eastbridge—and he could feel sweat trickling down the back of his neck under his collar.

"I'll come to your room and say hi, Mrs. Baker."

But of course the minute that was out of his mouth, he realized his mistake. Because Mr. Watkins loudly asked for a visit, too. And Miss Jenna. And Mrs. Balkerian.

"Whew," Stewie said, trying to get it in before anyone else could pipe up. "I hope I can remember all that."

He would be late getting home. But that was pretty okay, he figured, because Stacey would keep his dinner warm before going off to work her night shift. Or he could eat dinner here, in the cafeteria with the residents. Everybody was always inviting him to. It even flitted through his mind that he could eat dinner both places. He was, after all, a growing boy, and the prospect of too much food did not have a place on his worry list.

"Did you bring us any eggs, Stewie?" a voice asked from the crowd.

It was a voice he didn't recognize. Or at least he wasn't sure it sounded familiar. It rang out just as he was hoping to get away so he could stop feeling guilty about interrupting sing-along.

"No, I don't have enough right now," he said. "I'm sorry. The new girls haven't started laying yet. I'm worried about them," he added. It made his face flame red because he hadn't meant to share worries out loud. Worries were something you kept to yourself, he figured. You were supposed to hold them tightly to your chest, like a poker hand in those old western movies. "They might start laying any minute, though. They're supposed to. But even if they do, they'd have to lay an awful lot for me to bring all the eggs Eastbridge uses. And even if I could, I already asked and they don't want to pay that much for them. They want to buy the eggs that aren't very expensive."

"We had a plan," Joni's lyrical accent said. "We've been waiting to tell you our plan."

He spun around to see her standing in the hall behind him.

"A plan? What kind of plan?"

"We put together ten residents who want the better eggs enough to pay for them. And they were going to chip in to make up the difference in cost."

"Oh," Stewie said.

He looked back at the crowd seated in the activities room. No one was singing. Janet hadn't gone back to playing the piano. They were all just waiting. Staring at him. Waiting for him to say something about hens and eggs.

"Well," he said, his voice a little shaky. "I guess all that's holding us back now is getting the new hens laying. Whew. That's a lot of pressure."

"What did the boy just say?" a woman's voice called out loudly.

Then Mr. Peterson shouted out, "It's no pressure on *you*, Stewie. We're not asking you to lay them yourself."

And of course everybody laughed.

But it *was* pressure on him, whether they knew it or not. Almost as much as if he really did have to lay them himself. Impossible as that would be to do, it almost sounded like a relief to him, compared to being responsible for what his new girls did or did not accomplish.

"I have to go," he said. "But I'll come visit all the people that asked me to."

"Me too," a woman's voice said.

But Stewie had already scrambled out of the room and was able to pretend he hadn't heard in time.

No offense to the woman, who was undoubtedly a nice person, but he was already overcommitted and he knew it.

———

"She is *not* having a good day," Louise said when she saw Stewie leaning in the doorway.

He looked at Marilyn for a long time.

She was sitting on the edge of her bed, her back oddly straight, staring out the window. But there was nothing out the window. They were on the second floor, after all. The trees barely moved. The nest had long since been brought down by the storms of the previous winter, and no new family had decided to build outside Marilyn and Louise's window.

"Marilyn?" he said.

She did not look around. She did not offer any indication that she had heard.

He walked around until he was more or less between her and the window. Not blocking her view or forcing her to look at him, but in her field of vision.

"Marilyn?" he said again.

Still no response.

He looked over at Louise, who was giving him the pity look. Stewie still hated the pity look. It seemed there were just some things he would never get used to.

"Do you think she hears me?" he asked Louise.

"I don't know, child," Louise said. "They say it's nice to talk to people in a coma, though. Even if you think they can't hear you. I guess the doctors have some kind of idea that, deep down, on some level or another, maybe they do hear. I don't know what she's got going on right now, but I don't suppose it's as bad as a coma. Do you?"

"I have no idea," Stewie said. "But I guess it can't hurt to try."

He sat on the edge of her bed, next to her but a respectful distance away. He still always stayed a respectful distance away. If she wanted to reach out to him—put a hand on his shoulder or pat his head—that was always welcome. But, except for that one time he had been bold enough to take her hand, she had never let him into her life to such a degree that he felt physical closeness was his decision to make.

"Okay," he said. "Then I'll think of something to talk to you about." He had only one thing on his mind, so it wasn't hard to know where to start. "The new hens still won't lay. Well. One did. One egg. I think about it all the time now. It's all I can think about. It makes me really nervous, I guess because I can't control it. And all my regular customers in Lake View want me to bring eggs, but I don't really have them, and now all my friends here at Eastbridge want me bringing the Eastbridge eggs, and I don't have those, either. But here's the thing . . . those new hens could lay their heads off like no hens ever laid before, but I still wouldn't have enough to do both. I guess I could buy *even more* new chicks, but I can't even get eggs out of the ones I already bought. And I got pretty much no egg money now, so I don't know how I'm supposed to buy them anyway. I mean, don't get me wrong. It's nice that everybody here knows me and likes me and wants better eggs. I mean, that's great and all. I just don't have them, so that makes it hard."

He stopped talking suddenly and shot a glance over at Louise, who was the only person he was certain was listening. She still had a little bit of the pity look on her face, but also a look like she thought it was good what he was doing. She offered him a little smile that he figured was meant to be supportive.

"But I don't know if you want to hear about hens and eggs," he said to Marilyn, who still gave no indication that she was aware of his presence.

His eyes drifted around the room, landing on the *Stuart Little* book on her bedside table. It was her copy, the old one with the mouse wearing what looked like a dress.

"I know!" he said. It came out too loud, and he was afraid it would startle her. But she still gave no indication that she heard. "I'll read to you! Everybody likes to be read to."

He jumped up and grabbed the book off the bedside table.

Settling on the bed again, he opened to the first chapter, and read every word. Read all of chapter one from beginning to end.

At the end of the chapter he closed the cover of the book, almost reverently.

Marilyn still gave no indication that she had heard, or even that she knew Stewie was there with her.

"You're a very good reader now," Louise said.

"Better," he said, feeling sheepish. "I don't know about very good. I have a confession to make. I've read that first chapter so many times I sort of know it by heart. I mean, I really was reading. Honest. But there's not a single word in that book I don't know, except maybe that stuff about who published it and all, before the story even starts. I could probably leave the book closed and close my eyes, too, and still have it come out just the same. But it was real reading, though. I wouldn't lie about a thing like that."

"I never doubted you," she said.

"Well . . ."

He stalled on that word. Looked over at Marilyn again. She was still gazing out the window as though her thoughts were a million miles away.

For a split second Stewie wondered if she was asleep with her eyes open. Stewie used to sleep with his eyes open when he was little, according to Gam. But not sitting straight up and holding good posture, he didn't. So it didn't make sense to him to think that's what was happening.

It made him feel bad to think maybe he should give up on their visit and go. He could feel it like a slight queasiness in his belly.

"I guess I should visit a few more people before I go home. Since they asked me to."

"Who asked you to go visit them?" Louise asked.

Stewie rolled his eyes grandly.

"*Everybody!* I might *never* get home for dinner."

"If you're hungry, you can eat dinner here. You know no one'll mind."

"I just might do that," he said. He stood and straightened out his khaki slacks, even though they didn't need much straightening. "And if my sister has dinner warm in the oven for me when I get home, I might just eat dinner there, too."

"Why not? You're a growing boy."

"That's exactly what I thought! In just those words and everything."

"Great minds think alike," she said.

Stewie thought it was a wonderful thing for her to say, because his gam had used to say the same thing. Often. And, because of that, he even had a pretty good idea that he knew what it meant.

———

He tucked himself into bed at a little after nine.

He was physically tired, and he figured that would make it easy for him to sleep. But the slight soreness in his muscles seemed to keep him tossing and turning, and being tired wasn't quite the same as being sleepy in this case.

He lay awake for a long time, stressing about his hens. Feeling bad about his old regular customers, who were now reduced to buying their eggs at the supermarket. Feeling worse about his new prospective customers at Eastbridge, who seemed to think he was magical, and who could so easily be disappointed.

And what if he didn't even have eggs for his own family to eat, or egg money to help Stacey feed and keep the family? What a miserable turn of events that would be.

And then, underneath that, if he wasn't the boy with the best, freshest eggs around, then who was he? What did he have if he didn't have that?

While he pondered these dark avenues of thought, he chanted the word "lay" under his breath. As though the hens could hear his command.

It hit him suddenly when it hit, and made his eyes fly open wide. Then, having had the revelation, he wondered how he could ever have made such a mistake.

He rose and slipped quickly into his shoes, then trotted out the kitchen door and through the night to the henhouse, still in his pajamas.

When he opened the door in the dark, the hens set up a frightened ruckus. They weren't used to Stewie coming in at such an hour, and were clearly alarmed by the prospect of anything or anyone else coming along in the dead of night.

"It's okay," Stewie whispered. "You're okay. You're fine. It's only me, Stewie."

They recognized his voice, and believed him, and they settled slowly.

A thin crescent of moon shone through the dirty henhouse window, and it lit his way as he moved along the rows of nesting boxes.

"*Please* lay," he whispered over and over, at least once to each bird. "*Please*. I'm sorry if I was impolite before. I should've said 'please.'"

He said nothing to the older hens, because that might have been too much pressure. Even being asked nicely to do something was hard, if it was a thing you probably couldn't do. Stewie knew that as well as anybody and better than most.

Then he said good night to them at the henhouse door and put himself back to bed.

This time he slept.

Part Four

Autumn

Chapter Twenty-Six

The Woods

Stewie

Stewie burst through the front door and into the reception area of Eastbridge. Probably too loudly and too suddenly, and as stridently as a person can burst when he is carrying a cardboard box heavy with fully loaded egg cartons.

Everybody looked up.

There were two people behind the reception desk, both of whom he knew well. Janet and Ted. There were three women residents sitting near the walls in wheelchairs, their spotted and arthritic hands resting on blankets on their laps.

"They're laying!" Stewie cried, not meaning to be too loud. "All the hens are laying! The new-new ones and the sort-of-new ones. They're all laying, and now I have enough eggs to bring for all the Eastbridge people!"

He set the heavy cardboard box of eggs on the reception desk. It felt good to get out from under all that weight.

Ted caught his eye and put a finger to his lips to remind Stewie about speaking quietly.

"Sorry," he said.

One of the residents, Mrs. Wilson, waved him over to her wheelchair.

"What's this now?" she asked when he arrived. "It sounds like a happy thing, and we all like to see you happy, Stewart, so tell me all the details."

"Well," he said, feeling breathy and excited again. "My hens are getting old, and not laying so much or so regular, and some of the original ones aren't laying at all. I bought some new chicks with my egg money, but they didn't lay as fast as I thought they would, so then I didn't know what I would do, because I didn't have any egg money to buy more chicks. I barely had enough eggs for Stacey and Theo and me, and maybe a carton to bring for Marilyn, my grandmother, and meanwhile the people here at Eastbridge put together enough extra money to get all their eggs from me, because mine are so much fresher and better, but I didn't even have them to sell." He paused just long enough for a quick breath. "But then the new hens started to lay, so I sold those eggs to my old regular customers in Lake View, where I live, and then I got enough money to buy a whole batch of even newer chicks, and now they're laying, too. Now everybody's laying. Well, not so much the old hens, but still, it's enough. So I just brought as many eggs as Marjorie in the kitchen said she would take from me if I had them. Now I have them! That's why I'm so happy."

"You live in Lake View?" Mrs. Wilson asked.

It struck Stewie as an odd thing to take away from everything he had just said.

"Yeah, you didn't know that?"

"Why, no. I figured you lived here in the city. Lake View is so far. How do you get out here so often?"

"I take the bus."

"Why, that must take you an hour!"

"A little more, but I don't mind. No offense, Mrs. Wilson, but I've got to go now. I have to go tell Marilyn the good news. I don't know if she hears me or not. I never know anymore if she hears me when I talk to her, but I also don't know for a fact that she doesn't, so I talk to her a lot, and I still have to tell her everything that's important."

"All right," she said. "You run and do that, Stewart. But come see me again on the way out, won't you? I always enjoy your visits."

"Yes, ma'am. I promise."

He darted away from her wheelchair and headed fast for the stairs.

As he trotted along, he heard Janet talking on the telephone—heard her say, "He's here right now. He just got here a minute ago. Oh dear. Oh no. Yes, I'll try to stop him." Then she called his name. "Stewie! Stewie, wait!"

Stewie did not wait. He was too anxious to see Marilyn and tell her his good news, so he pretended not to hear Janet in time. Whatever she had to say to him, he figured he could hear it on the way back down. He had to come back down to the reception area anyway to pick up the eggs and take them to Marjorie in the kitchen. And he had promised Mrs. Wilson another visit.

He vaulted up the stairs two at a time and ran down the hall toward Marilyn and Louise's room.

Before he could reach their doorway, two of the Eastbridge nurses came out of the room, rolling a gurney. On it was something the size and shape of a person, but Stewie figured it probably wasn't a person, because it was completely covered with a bleached white sheet. He didn't figure you would cover a person all the way over like that, because if you did, how could they even breathe? Surely a nurse would know that.

The two nurses looked up to see Stewie standing there, and they stopped. And the gurney stopped.

"Oh, Stewie," one of them said. "Janet said she was going to keep you downstairs until we could talk to you."

"I was too fast for her," he said. "Talk to me about what?"

But the situation had already begun to stir up a funny feeling in his belly, and he found himself wishing he had never asked, and hoping they would never answer.

Louise appeared in the doorway before they could say more.

"I'll talk to him," she said. "Let me do this. Stewie and I are good friends. This will be better coming from a friend."

———

"I know you're old enough to understand that everybody and everything dies," Louise said.

Something about her voice felt troubling to Stewie. She was using that extra-gentle tone, the kind people used when they seemed to think Stewie was as fragile as fine china, and maybe already slightly cracked. It reminded him of the pity looks, and it was making the funny feeling in his belly even more troubling. It was not a pleasant sensation, to put it mildly.

They were sitting on the edge of Marilyn's bed, the way he and Marilyn so often had, looking out the window. The leaves had gone red and gold for autumn, and a warm wind rustled them around. Here and there it would shake loose three or four leaves at once, and they would swirl in the breeze before falling out of Stewie's view.

Looking back, Stewie would be clearer on the fact that, at the beginning of this talk with Louise, he already knew everything there was to know. Some part of him, at least. At some level. In the moment his mind was something like a fortress. It was a place to hunker down inside high walls and guard against anything that might attempt to breach them.

Meanwhile he wasn't answering.

"You do know that, right, Stewie? I think you do. Because I remember you told me you lost two of your gam's original hens, and how sad it made you feel."

"I know everybody and everything dies. But I don't understand *why* it has to be that way. I mean . . . I talk to Dr. Briggs about it. All the time. And he sort of told me why, so it's not really that I don't know why, it's that I wish it didn't have to be that way and I think it totally sucks."

"Nobody really likes it," she said. "But it's the way it is."

"Dr. Briggs says things like that all the time."

"Great minds think alike," she said again.

She smiled slightly, and sadly. Stewie did not smile.

He turned around and looked at the bed behind him, and wondered where Marilyn was. He had come all this way to visit her, and she wasn't here.

Then it all came together in Stewie's head, and he knew. Except, in a way, he had already known. But in that instant every part of him knew. The walls had been breached, and there was no saving the fortress.

"She *died?*" He could hear the effort not to cry in his voice. He could hear the way the inner sobs, the ones he would not allow, bent the words around all the same.

"Yes, child. I'm so sorry for your loss. I know you loved her. We all know that."

"Why did she die? That doesn't make sense."

"She was old, honey."

"But sometimes old people live longer than that. And you don't die from not remembering things. Do you?"

"I don't know, darling. I don't think they know the cause yet. Might have been her heart, but it's too soon to say. But she went peacefully in her sleep, and that's all any of us really wants. She's in a better place."

Stewie found himself on his feet, facing her. Which felt odd, because he had no memory of standing up. He felt now as though he were walking through a dark, heavy dream, with pieces missing.

"You shouldn't say that! That's a terrible thing to say!"

He could hear himself raising his voice. He could feel his hands balling up into tight fists, and his fingernails digging into his palms.

"What? That she's in a better place?"

"Yes. That. Don't say that. I'm not there with her. Are you saying it's better for her to be somewhere away from me? Like she's better off without me?"

"No, darling, I didn't mean it that way at all. I'm sorry."

She reached out to touch him on the shoulder, but he darted out from under her hand.

"Well, how did you mean it, then? Why did you say it?"

"I just mean that when we get old, we're in pain, and everything gets harder. And maybe at a certain point this is better."

"But how do you *know* it's better?" Stewie's voice had risen to a tight screech now, and he pumped his white-knuckled fists up and down just to have some way to move. Some way to release the energy balled up in his gut. Otherwise it felt as though it would electrocute him. "You've never been dead. So you don't know if it's better. So why do you say it's better?"

He was shouting now, and he half expected someone from the Eastbridge staff to come in and shush him. He felt himself braced against that, because he hated to break the rules. But no one came in.

"I guess," Louise said, "we just all want to believe it's better."

"That's not a very good answer," he said. Shouted, actually. He felt bad yelling at her, but he couldn't seem to control himself.

"I'm sorry," she said. "I guess you're right. I don't have all the answers, and I'm sorry you had to lose someone again, after everyone you've lost already. But the offer still stands. If you ever want to adopt another grandmother, I'm available for adoption."

"I have to go," Stewie said.

He purposely didn't look at her face as he ran out of the room, because he might have been hurting her feelings, and, if so, he didn't want to have to see that with his own eyes.

———

Stewie sprinted past the bus stop because of the possibility that someone from Eastbridge would have followed him, and would want to talk to him some more. Stewie was plain done with talking, and even more tired of listening to other people talk at him.

His chest began to ache and burn with the exertion. His lungs felt as though they might be about to catch fire, or maybe even as though they already had. Still, he kept running.

He ran all the way to the next bus stop. The second closest to Eastbridge. He leaned forward at the waist, braced his hands on his bare knees, and panted, and panted, and panted. And tried desperately to catch his breath.

When he looked up, the bus was there.

"You okay?" the bus driver asked when he got on.

It was Hank. One of his two favorites.

He dropped his change into the fare box. He didn't answer the question. Just took the seat directly behind Hank, where it would be harder for the driver to see him, in case he couldn't stop himself from crying. Then he remembered that Hank had a big, wide mirror to see all the passengers, but there was nothing Stewie could do about that.

It was a Sunday morning, still fairly early. Nobody had to work, so nobody was riding the bus except him. If he had stayed for a nice long visit with Marilyn, there would have been lots of people, mostly in their good Sunday clothes, taking the bus to church. But it was too early for that.

He rode most of the way back to Lake View in silence.

Two people got on and then got off again. But Stewie didn't know them, so they paid no attention to him and didn't ask him any questions. And that was good.

He got off one stop early. By the lake. Marilyn's old neighborhood, near the house where he had first met her.

Before Hank pulled the lever to open the rear door for him, he met Stewie's eyes in the big, wide rearview mirror. Stewie looked away again as fast as he could.

"You sure you're okay, Stewie?" the driver asked.

"I'm fine," he said, shifting from foot to foot. Wishing Hank would just open the door.

"This's not your stop, though."

"I want to walk the rest of the way."

Hank opened the door. It made that sighing sound that bus doors make when they open.

Stewie ran again.

And ran. And ran. And ran.

———

In time he found a spot at the very edge of the lake, as close as he could get to the water and still be on the part of the bank that was reasonably dry, not soupy with mud. There was a big hollow log—a tree that had fallen on its side and was now only a shell of its former grandeur. But Stewie did not go inside it to hide, because he was afraid of spiders. Especially if one of them was a black widow or a brown recluse, both of which were possible around those parts.

Instead he hid on the ground on the other side of the fallen tree, in a dense understory, its floor composed mostly of ivy.

From there he could see the house. Not his house, but the house where Marilyn had lived when he first met her. The one whose door she used to open when he came around on her egg-buying day. He should think of it as Sylvia's house, he supposed, but he had no idea if she still lived there after all this time.

He saw no movement. No indication that anyone was home.

He stared at the house for a few minutes, and then the tears caught up, and he couldn't have stopped them if he tried. But anyway, he had no reason to try. There was no one around to see.

He cried for hours. Literally hours. His eyes felt as though they were full of sand, and his head ached from stuffiness. He wiped his nose on his short sleeves because he had nothing else to use for that unpleasant purpose. He had to keep slapping at his bare arms and legs because the mosquitos were eating him alive.

But Stewie did not get up and go home.

———

At the end of the day it grew dark, as days always will. The only difference between that day and every other one was that Stewie still had not gone home and gone inside. And he had no plans to do so, even though it was too dark to see Marilyn's old house.

Just as dusk was turning to pitch-blackness, he heard several people wandering up and down Lake Road calling his name. One was clearly Stacey, but the others didn't seem to be anyone Stewie had ever known.

He did not let on that he was there.

The darker it got, the colder it got. And he had no jacket or sweater.

His bare, mosquito-bitten arms and legs developed gooseflesh from the cold, and his teeth chattered uncontrollably. Still he had no urge, no will at all, to end this strange moment of acting out.

But then it began to rain.

He had been looking up at the brilliant field of stars because they were beautiful, and because nothing else could be seen. There were no streetlights at the lake. Then, more suddenly than seemed realistic, the sky turned into a thick gray blanket of clouds, and what seemed like seconds later he was drenched.

And that was it. That was just too much.

It was one thing to be freezing. It was quite another to freeze while soaking wet.

He rose as quickly as he could manage, though his hips and shoulders and muscles ached from lying on the hard ground for so long.

He jogged home in the rain because the effort helped him warm up some.

He trotted up his own driveway, thinking Stacey would be at work. But he could clearly see her through the kitchen window. She was talking on the phone. He was too far away to see the expression on her face, but her mood seemed to surround her like a fog, or maybe Stewie could just imagine it all too easily.

All the lights were blazing in the living room as well, and as he walked by the window they illuminated him, and he caught a glimpse of himself in the big, long living room mirror. He stopped dead and stared at himself for several seconds, processing his shock.

His exposed skin was covered in angry red welts. His hair was a soggy mess, trailing onto his forehead, and matted with mud and twigs. His clothes dripped muddy water that trailed down his cold bare legs. His nose was still visibly runny and his eyes looked puffy and red.

Stacey was going to kill him.

He looked up then and saw her. She had spotted him, and opened the kitchen door. She stepped out to stare at him, even though it was still raining. Even though standing outside with him quickly soaked her to the skin. They considered each other in the glow of light from inside the house.

It was bright enough that he could watch her register his condition, which was a shame, as her reaction was something he would have preferred not to see. She looked him over from head to toe, her face hard.

She opened her mouth to say something, and Stewie winced, expecting a bellow of rage to come out of her. Instead she simply closed her mouth and said nothing at all.

Then, almost before he could see it coming, she was on him, crouching slightly to his level, and throwing her arms around him. She held him so tightly it hurt, and made it hard to pull full, deep breaths. But he didn't say so. He didn't say anything. Just stood shivering in her arms in the rain.

He waited for her to lecture him about how scared she had been, or what she had gone through to find him, but she never spoke a word.

When she finally pulled away, he saw that she had been crying.

"I need to see Dr. Briggs," he said.

"I'll call him again in the morning."

"Again? You called him today?"

"I called everybody today. Anybody who might've seen you."

"Can you call him tonight? I think I need to see him now."

"It's Sunday night, Stewie."

"Can you at least ask?"

A long pause, during which they continued to be soaked by that cold rain.

"Come inside and take a bath. I'll probably just get his answering machine, but I'll try."

"I'm sorry I scared you."

"Just come inside, Stewie. Just come in out of the rain."

While he ran himself a hot bath, Stewie heard her on the phone in the kitchen. Heard her call the sheriff's office and tell someone there, in a breathy voice, that the sheriff and his men could stop looking now, and never mind, and thank you all the same.

—

He was soaking in a hot tub with bubbles when she rapped softly on the door. Normally he didn't like bubbles, but on that night it was a luxury that made him sigh with relief. The hot water was allowing his teeth to stop chattering, but it was also making his bug bites itch fiercely.

"Stewie?" Stacey said through the door.

"Yeah?"

"He says he'll come into the office an hour early tomorrow and see you before his first client. Eight o'clock."

"Thank you. But what about school?"

"I'll write you a note."

"Thank you."

"I'm sorry for your loss, Stewie. I know you loved her."

"You knew about that?"

"Yes, I told you. I called everybody."

"Oh. Okay."

"You've had an awful lot of loss in your life for such a young guy. It doesn't seem fair."

"No," Stewie said. "That's exactly what I think about the situation. It really doesn't seem fair."

———

Theo stuck his head into Stewie's room just as Stewie was dropping off to sleep. Or maybe he already was sleeping, and maybe the Theo in his dream turned into Theo in reality when his brother spoke.

"You asleep?" Theo asked from the doorway.

"No," Stewie said. It was a lie, but somehow it didn't feel like the bad or wrong kind.

Theo came over and sat on the edge of Stewie's bed in the dark. Stewie assumed his brother was going to scold him for worrying everybody. But when Theo spoke, his voice sounded deep and soft.

"Remember when you used to go around and check all the hoses? Three times a day at least, you would check them all. Just to make sure Gam didn't forget to turn one off again."

"Yeah, I guess I remember. Why?"

"I don't know. No reason."

"Something must've made you think of it."

Silence for a beat or two. Stewie wished he could see his brother's face in the dark.

"I suppose I just wanted you to know that I miss her, too."

"I figured you did," Stewie said. Then, when Theo didn't answer, Stewie added, "You never said so, though."

"Neither did you."

"Oh. That's true." They sat in silence for a time. Then Stewie added, "You mean Gam, though. Right? Not Marilyn."

"I meant Gam."

"I didn't figure you miss Marilyn, because you didn't like her all that much."

"I didn't hate her or anything. I had nothing against her, and I don't want to say anything mean about her now that she's gone. Maybe you saw another side of her. I just sort of thought she wasn't the nicest person."

"Neither was Gam."

"True. But she was our gam."

"Marilyn was *sort of* my gam," Stewie said.

"Then I'm sorry you lost her."

He patted Stewie on the shoulder a couple of times and left his room without saying more.

———

Stewie sat in his regular chair across from Dr. Briggs, drumming his fingers on his knees. It wasn't like him to be so fidgety, but he secretly hoped it would draw attention away from his shivering. He was wearing his heavy wool slacks and a jacket, even though it was a warm day. And of course inside Dr. Briggs's office it was always warm.

He hadn't spoken much yet, which made him feel guilty, because the doctor had come to work an hour early just so Stewie could talk.

"Are you cold?" Dr. Briggs asked.

It made Stewie jump a little.

"I'm not sure," Stewie said. "Maybe. I caught a bad chill last night and somehow it seems like it never quite went away. But I can't exactly tell if it's that or if it's something else."

"Tell me about the something else."

"But I'm not even sure if there *is* a something else. I was just trying to explain that."

"What if there is, though? Imagine there's something else there, and just tell me your best guess as to what it might be."

Oddly, Stewie spoke without so much as a hint of hesitation. It just burst out.

"I didn't get to say goodbye to her."

"I can understand why that would trouble you. But I don't think anyone knew she was about to pass away. Did they?"

"No, not Marilyn," he said. "Well, that too. Her too. But, like you say, nobody knew, so how could they tell me? I was talking about my gam."

Stewie sat very still for a moment, waiting to hear how the doctor would respond. But no words came back to him. Doctor Briggs just scribbled a quick note on his pad and left space open for Stewie to say more.

As he opened his mouth to speak it struck him that he was no longer shivering.

"They took her to the hospital and I wanted to go visit her but they said I couldn't. The hospital people. They said I was too young to come in and that you have to be fourteen to visit. And then she died and that would have been the last time I ever got to see her and they didn't let me have it. And that makes me really mad."

He waited, in case it was wrong to be mad and he was about to be taken to task for it, but then he remembered that Dr. Briggs seemed to have a different opinion than most people about such things.

"You don't sound mad," the doctor said, leveling Stewie with an almost alarmingly direct gaze. Under normal circumstances it would have made him squirm, but these were not normal circumstances. "You just sound down and sad."

"If I tell you I'm mad, I think you ought to believe me."

"I'm not saying you're not. I'm just noting that the last time you told me you were mad, you looked and acted mad. I just think it's interesting that you're expressing it in such a different way today."

"I wish," Stewie said, "that when I'm having a hard time with something, you wouldn't keep saying it's interesting."

"Maybe I haven't been clear about what I mean when I say that. I don't mean that you're a curiosity to me, like a butterfly pinned to a card."

"That's a terrible picture to have in my head," Stewie said, shaking his head as if to dislodge it. "What a horrible way to treat a butterfly. Why would anybody pin a butterfly to a card?"

"That's the way they used to study them. Or maybe they still do, I don't know."

"Alive?"

"No, I think they probably kill them first."

"And that's supposed to make me feel better? Can we please talk about something else?"

"Sorry. What I was trying to say is that I don't find you interesting like a curiosity. When I say I find something interesting about you, I mean it's something that helps me know you a little better. And the reason it's of interest to me is because the more I know you, the more I feel I can help you."

"Oh," Stewie said. "Well . . . I guess that's maybe okay, then."

He shrugged out of his jacket. It was harder and more awkward than he would have wanted it to be, especially with the doctor staring at him.

"Here's the thing about being mad," Stewie said. "Stacey always says it doesn't do any good to get mad."

"It may or may not do anything to help your situation, depending on the case. But I do want to note that anger is not without its purpose."

"It's not?"

"Not at all."

"What does it do?"

"It protects you. When somebody treats you in a way you don't wish to be treated, you get angry with them, and that's a clear sign that you don't want them to do it again."

"But you can't use that with a person dying."

"No."

"So in this case Stacey was right. What good does it do?"

"But the problem with a statement like that—'It doesn't do any good to get angry'—is that by the time a person says it, you already *are* angry. Good or bad, helpful or unhelpful, when you're angry, you just are. You really only have two choices at that point: keep it in or let it out."

"Safer to keep it in."

"I'm not so sure I agree. A lot of trouble in this world comes from people who hold their anger in too long, and then it comes out on its own and there's no controlling it, and it's destructive. I honestly think the world would be a much safer place if people knew how to express their anger appropriately."

Stewie scratched his mosquito-bitten legs through his irritating wool trousers, which he now realized had been a mistake to wear.

"How do I do that?"

"Maybe start by telling me what makes you angry."

"I just did. They wouldn't let me in the hospital to say goodbye to Gam."

"Anything else?"

"Sure. Lots of things. Everything. Why does everybody have so many people but me? Just about every kid I know has two parents and four grandparents, and most of them have aunts and uncles and cousins, and some even have great-grandparents, and even those that don't have all of that have most of it. All I had was my gam and then she died and then I had Marilyn and then *she* died and I don't think it's fair. Every time I have somebody, they die. I mean, I have Stacey and Theo, and I'm not saying that's not a good thing to have, but I'm talking about the older people. Older relatives. You know? There's Louise at Eastbridge. She always says I can adopt her, but I don't know. Now I'm just sort of thinking . . . if I adopt her, I'll probably get to liking her real well and then she'll die. Why even start liking people if they're just going to die?"

"This is another situation," the doctor said, setting down his pad, "where you really only have two choices. Have no one at all in your life or have people in your life at the risk of losing them. You never had parents, in a very real sense, as most people do. You did, of course, but you were so young that you couldn't even experience what it meant to lose them. It's almost as though they were never there. Do you really think that's better than loving someone and then losing them?"

"No, it's worse. Because I didn't even get to have them. I didn't even get to know them. Everybody knows their parents but me. I got totally robbed."

"So we agree. 'Tis better to have loved and lost / Than never to have loved at all.'"

"Isn't that that Tennyson guy? The one with 'Lord' in his name?"

The doctor seemed shocked.

"I'm a little surprised that you recognized that."

"Our teacher taught it to us in English class last year."

"I see."

"So you think I should adopt Louise."

"I absolutely do."

Stewie sat for a long time, feeling around in something. Some vague feeling of dissatisfaction. Or maybe it was a sense of incompleteness.

He heard a tapping sound, and looked to the window to see a little brown bird, probably a sparrow of some sort, beating its wings against the glass. The doctor didn't seem to notice, but Stewie couldn't take his eyes off it. He couldn't figure out why a bird would try to beat its way into a room. It just seemed to need to be someplace other than where it was, which Stewie found almost painfully familiar.

A few seconds later it was gone in a flash of wings—it had given up and soared in a new direction.

"Here's the thing," Stewie said. "You tell me these things, and I believe you. And I sort of get it. But another part of me . . . I just don't see what it changes. I come in here and I'm all upset because Marilyn died. And we talk about it. We talk about all these things, and then we're done talking, but I'm still upset because Marilyn died. I'm just not sure I see the point of the whole thing."

He waited for Dr. Briggs's reaction with a slight inward wince. After all, he had just maligned his life's work.

The doctor shifted in his seat. Sat back. Cleared his throat. He didn't seem upset, the way Stewie had feared he might.

"All right. I'm going to try a different way of explaining it to you. Imagine you're in the woods and you're completely lost. You've been wandering around and around for ages. And you really have no idea which way is out, so you could wander almost indefinitely and still not be found again. Now let's say I come along and give you a compass and a map of the woods. Would you look at me and say, 'Dr. Briggs, this is useless to me because I'm still in the woods?' Or would you see that you'd been given the tools to begin to solve your problem and that you're better off for that? Yes, you're still in the woods, but you're no longer hopelessly lost. Does that make sense to you, Stewie?"

Stewie sat for a long time, thinking. Or possibly not thinking. Maybe he was only letting the doctor's words settle in, and feeling his way around in them as they settled. He had every intention of giving Dr. Briggs an answer that was both honest and well thought through.

"You know," he said after a time, "I think it does make sense. When you explain it like that, I really do think I get it."

"Good," Dr. Briggs said. "Then our work together has begun in earnest."

Chapter Twenty-Seven

The Better Side of Fair

Stewie

Stewie waited a full week to go back to Eastbridge, because he no longer had a grandmother there, and maybe he wasn't welcome for a visit until his Sunday egg delivery.

Or, at least, that was the story he told himself.

But during the week, people from Eastbridge called.

He never actually spoke to them. He would be at school, or out with the hens, or taking a bath. Later he would see a note on Stacey's little yellow pad by the phone. It was filling up fast with names and short messages.

"Joni called, and hopes you'll still come visit. Louise said to say she's thinking about you and hopes you're considering her offer. Mrs. Wilson sends her condolences and hopes to see you soon."

And then, the one that blew his cover story completely.

"Marjorie says all the residents just love the new eggs, and she hopes you won't wait till egg delivery day to come see everyone."

That was the one that forced his hand, and made him realize he'd only been making excuses, and that the actual truth was simply that it would be very hard on him, emotionally, to go.

Still, egg day was coming up fast, and on egg day he knew he would have no choice. He was their egg supplier now. He had accepted that responsibility, it was not one to be taken lightly, and there was no part of Stewie that would consider letting them down.

———

The first person he saw was Joni, and he heard her before he saw her.

He had come in through the back way, just because it was a shorter route and the eggs were getting heavy. At least, he told himself that was why.

As he walked down the hall toward the reception area, he heard her lyrical accent.

"Hello, Stewie," it said.

He stopped. Turned around.

"Oh, hi, Joni."

"We thought maybe you didn't want to come visit us anymore."

"No, I do. Well. I do and I don't. I mean . . . I like you guys and all . . ." The eggs were simply too much of a burden, so he set the big packing carton down on the linoleum at his feet. "It's just hard. Now that . . . you know."

"Yes, I do know," she said. "We all know. We all understand your loss. But it's good to see you."

"Thank you."

"I was just thinking . . ."

"Yes?"

"If you're fresh out of grandmothers . . . well, it's only a crazy idea, but hear me out, please. I have two children. I have a son who is gay and a daughter who has no interest at all in having children of her own.

I always wanted to be a grandmother, and now it's looking like maybe I never will be."

"Oh, I'm sorry. Maybe your son'll get married to another man and they'll adopt. That happens."

"Yes," she said. "It happens. But I don't think it happens to my son. He's not a very fatherly sort. I suppose I could be proved wrong in the fullness of time."

Stewie waited, not sure what else to say. He shifted from foot to foot, waiting to see if there was more she wanted to tell him.

"But I think you're missing my point, Stewie."

"Oh. I'm sorry. What's your point?"

"You have no grandparents. I have no grandchildren. Maybe we could adopt each other."

Stewie felt his eyes go wide. He opened his mouth, but no words came out.

"Why do you look so surprised, Stewie?"

"I guess because I sort of thought you didn't like me."

"Now why would you think that? Just because I encourage you to keep your feet on the carpet and call people by their actual names?"

"I guess. I'm not sure."

"Anyway, it's not enough that *I* like *you*. We have to like each other."

"I like you!" he said. He pushed it out loud, and fast, because you should never keep a person waiting at a time like that. "I especially like your accent, even though I don't know what accent it is. Where are you from?"

"I am from Sierra Leone," she said.

"Ooh. That would be cool, to tell the kids at school I have a grand-mother from Sierra Leone. I think that makes you much cooler than everybody else's grandmothers, who are all just from boring old here. I really think you're too young to be a grandmother, though."

To his surprise, she responded with a shy smile.

"Well, if you're hoping to flatter me, Stewie, it's working very well. But I am plenty old enough. My daughter is thirty-seven and my son thirty-six. If they'd had children at the age I had *them*, my grandchildren would be older than you. They'd be graduating from high school by now."

Stewie stood in the hall without speaking for a few beats, his eyes wide, scratching that one spider bite on his hip that hadn't entirely stopped itching.

"I guess you just *look* like you're too young."

"That's a very kind thing to say to your grandmother," Joni said. "Now, come on. I'll help you get all these eggs into the kitchen."

———

"I still owe you for your last egg delivery," Marjorie said.

"Are you sure? I was thinking maybe I don't get paid for those because the deal is I was supposed to bring them into the kitchen."

Then he had to duck fast. A kitchen worker yelled, "Look alive, Stewie," and he jumped out of the way of a rolling rack of pies. Blueberry, he decided from the aroma.

"You thought we wouldn't *pay* you for those?" Marjorie asked. She sounded genuinely shocked. As if he'd just said he was born on some planet other than Earth.

"That was the deal, though. I'm supposed to deliver them to the kitchen."

"But we don't get them for free just because of where you leave them."

"If you're sure," Stewie said.

"I'll just go get the business checkbook. If a check is okay. Is a check okay? We're not allowed to keep much cash around, after . . . well, never mind after what, but anyway, we do most everything by check nowadays. Do you even have a checking account, Stewie? Can you cash it?"

"My sister, Stacey, can cash it for me."

"Good," she said. "Walk with me. We'll talk."

They set off down the hall together. He felt Marjorie's hand brush against his arm, and looked over to see that she was holding out her hand for him to take. He slipped his hand into hers, and they walked down the hall that way.

It reminded Stewie of the time he and Marilyn had walked hand in hand, and, because of that, it was a little sad even though it was also good.

"Know how many grandchildren I have?" she asked as they passed residents napping in wheelchairs.

"No I don't. We never talked about your grandchildren."

"Thirteen."

Stewie stopped dead in the hallway. A couple of steps later Marjorie stopped as well. She looked back and down at Stewie, probably trying to assess the holdup.

"Thirteen?"

"I wouldn't make a thing like that up."

"That's a lot!"

"Tell me about it."

They walked again, still holding hands.

"You're not superstitious," he said, "are you?"

"Not at all."

"Well, that's a relief."

"I was just thinking . . . what's the difference, really? Thirteen grandkids, or fourteen. I'd hardly notice the difference."

"You're about to have another one?"

"I meant you."

They had arrived at the office by the time she said it, and Boris let them in and handed Marjorie the checkbook. For a time, there was too much going on for Stewie to say what he thought about that. If he even knew.

She wrote out his name, and the amount, and signed it, and had Boris sign it. The checks had two signature lines, which Stewie had never seen before. It made them seem unusually official, and he found it slightly exciting.

"Here you go," she said.

He folded the check carefully and slipped it into his shirt pocket.

Then he took her hand again and they walked back toward the kitchen.

"What do you think of my idea?" Marjorie asked. "Six or seven of the ones I've already got are your age, or pretty close to it. You could come over to the house for family dinners, and maybe you all would get along."

"You're actually the second grandmother to adopt me just since I got here today," he said. "And I've only been here for, like, ten or fifteen minutes."

"Good."

"You don't think it's too many grandmothers?"

"How can it be too many? Most people start out with four grandparents."

"You don't think it's selfish to take two? Oh, wait, it's not two. It's three! Because Louise has been offering for a really long time."

"Here's what I think. Here's what I say. I say take what you can get in this life, Stewie. For a long time you had to get by on very little, so take what you can get."

"Okay, then," Stewie said. "All right. Then I guess I say yes."

———

He ran into Mrs. Wilson on his way to the stairs. On his way up to see Louise and arrange his third adoption of the day. Mrs. Wilson was sitting in the long hall in her wheelchair, looking in both directions as if about to cross a busy highway.

"Oh, Stewart," she said when she spotted him. "Thank goodness. I thought maybe I'd missed you. I've been asking everybody if they'd seen you. I was afraid you were already gone. Do you have a minute?"

"Sure," he said. "I guess so."

"Miss Jenna and I have something of a proposal for you. Give me a push, will you, and we'll see where she's gotten off to."

Stewie walked around behind her wheelchair and gave it a good push, but nothing happened. It refused to be pushed, and he nearly slammed right into the back of it.

"Oh, oh, wait, Stewart. I'm sorry. I have to take the brake off. I guess I forgot to take the brake off."

"Which way?" he asked when he could see she had released the brake.

"This way," she said, and pointed with one spotted hand. "I think she's in the activities room. At least, that's where I saw her last."

He pushed her down the empty hall, looking at the back of her head—at the way little tufts of her snow-white hair jutted out of its braid. He knew he was supposed to think of it as messy, but somehow it was beautiful to him, though he could never have explained how or why.

"I don't really know what a proposal is," he said as he pushed.

"Well, you will in a minute or two," she said.

They found Miss Jenna in the activities room, just as Mrs. Wilson predicted they would. There did not seem to be any activities going on. It must have been in between programs, time-wise. Miss Jenna was only sitting in a chair, talking to Mr. Watkins and Mr. Peterson. They all three looked up and said, "Stewie!" at almost exactly the same time.

"Oh, good, you found him," Miss Jenna said. "We were afraid he'd dropped the eggs and gone home."

"I never drop the eggs," Stewie said. "That's the worst thing you can do if you sell eggs. That's the first thing I learned not to do, and I never once forgot it."

Miss Jenna was on her feet now, moving in their direction as she spoke.

"I didn't mean drop them as in drop them on the floor. I meant drop them off."

"Oh," Stewie said. "Sorry. I guess I'm a little sensitive about the idea of dropping eggs."

"Let's go talk in the corner," Miss Jenna said. "Because it's a bit embarrassing what we have to say."

He wheeled Mrs. Wilson to the corner of the room, helped her put the wheelchair brake on, then stood with his back in the corner. He felt equal parts eagerness and dread, waiting to hear.

"So what's a proposal?" Stewie asked.

"It's just a general term," Miss Jenna said, "for anytime someone is proposing something to you. Anyway, this is what Emma and I are proposing . . ."

"Wait. Who's Emma?"

"I'm Emma," Mrs. Wilson said.

"Oh. Sorry, Mrs. Wilson. I just always call you Mrs. Wilson."

"Don't apologize, dear. You're very polite and that's nothing to feel bad about. Here's where we're going with this, Stewie." She paused briefly to look up at her friend. "Do you mind, Jenna?"

"Not at all," Miss Jenna said.

"Jenna and I have grandchildren. Quite a few between the two of us, but they never come to visit. Never. That's the part that we find a little embarrassing. Not that we think people haven't noticed anyway, but still. Our children come out on birthdays or major holidays, but less than they used to and not for all that long, and the grandchildren always seem to have something better to do than come along for the visit. It's really quite lonely, especially when you have to watch the other residents getting visitors while you never do."

After having said all that, Mrs. Wilson seemed to run into a wall of her own sadness and just stall there. Miss Jenna picked up the thread of the conversation and ran with it.

"And all this time you were so faithful and so dedicated about visiting Jean Clements, which we found a bit curious, since we were of a mind that there were kinder and nicer people in the world. I really don't mean to speak ill of the dead, and I hope I haven't offended you, Stewie. I'm sure she had her good qualities."

"It's okay, I guess. I sort of know what you mean. She was like my real grandmother was, so I guess I was just used to it. What's the proposal?"

"If you're fresh out of grandmothers, we were thinking of offering ourselves."

"Oh," Stewie said. He just stood a moment, his back to the wall, feeling his own surprise. It didn't make sense that he should have been surprised, given how all of the morning's conversations had gone, but maybe it was simply unlike him to assume that everybody wanted to adopt him, no matter how many times it happened. "Well, I'm not exactly fresh out. Both Joni and Marjorie offered to adopt me this morning. And Louise has been offering for a long time. I was just about to go upstairs and tell her I say yes to that."

"It's up to you," Mrs. Wilson said, still sounding sad. "We're here if you need us. That's mostly the point we wanted to make."

"I don't know," Stewie said. He was thinking out loud, which might have been rude. "Am I allowed to have five grandmothers?"

"Allowed by whom?" Miss Jenna asked. "Who's going to stop you?"

"I don't know. I guess . . . I don't know. But still, I mean . . . *five grandmothers!*"

He said the last two words much more loudly than he had intended, and Mr. Watkins and Mr. Peterson overheard him, and immediately rose and started moving in their direction. Mr. Watkins walked with a cane, Mr. Peterson with a walker. Still, they made good time.

"What's this I hear about five grandmothers?" Mr. Watkins called when he had reached about the halfway point.

Stewie's heart fell.

"See? I knew it. It's too much. It's too many grandmothers."

"I'll say it's too many grandmothers," Mr. Watkins said, stopping in front of Stewie and leaning both palms on his cane. "How do you have five grandmothers and no grandfathers? Doesn't that seem a little unbalanced to you?"

Stewie felt his head spinning with all the sudden changes to his situation.

"Grand*fathers*," he repeated. "I never even thought about grand*fathers*. I never even had one. Well, I had two, of course, like everybody else, but I didn't have any that I actually knew. So a grandfather never even occurred to me."

"Major oversight," Mr. Peterson said. "Very unfortunate oversight. But don't worry. Earl and I will fix it."

———

Stewie stuck his head into the old familiar room. The one that had been Marilyn and Louise's just a week ago, and now was Louise's alone.

She was sitting on her bed, staring out the window, but with her hands in rapid motion. She was crocheting something out of robin's-egg-blue yarn. Her normally wild mass of gray hair had been pulled back into a wild ponytail.

"Oh, Stewie," she said. "I wondered if I'd see you today."

He walked around and stood in her line of vision, between her bed and the window, so she didn't have to crane her neck around.

"Are you okay, Stewie? You look a little shell-shocked."

"I'm not sure what that means."

"Oh. Let's see. It's really originally about men who lived through a war, but in this case I guess it means . . . sort of . . . worn out by shocks or surprises."

"Oh. Okay. Yeah, that's me, I guess. I came to ask you a question. Remember when you said I could adopt you for a grandmother if I ever needed to? Well, I was on my way up here to say, 'Yes, please. I need to.' But then, on the way up here, the strangest things started happening. Everybody else started adopting me. Joni and Marjorie and Miss Jenna and Mrs. Wilson. And then Mr. Watkins and Mr. Peterson overheard, and they decided I shouldn't have all those grandmothers but no grandfathers, so then they adopted me, too." He watched her closely as he spoke, to see if he was disappointing her, but it seemed almost the opposite. A little smile seemed to be budding on her face. "Now I'm not sure if I should ask you, because I don't really *need* to adopt you, what with all those other grandparents, and maybe it's too many people. I guess my question is . . . is that offer still open?"

"Why, of course it is!" she said, unleashing the smile completely.

"But that would be five grandmothers and two grandfathers."

"So? Couldn't happen to a nicer young man, if you ask me."

"You don't think it's selfish?"

"How is it selfish? Who does it hurt? All those people offered because they wanted to. Because they enjoy your company. They probably wanted it as much for their sake as for yours."

"That's nice of you to say. But most people only get four."

"Stewie," she said. She reached out and took a gentle but firm grip on his forearm, pulled him over to the bed, and sat him down next to her. "Listen to me. All your life you've had less than everyone else, and it wasn't fair. But did anyone act like it was selfish of them to have more when you didn't? Did anybody ever give up a parent or a grandparent so you wouldn't feel so bad?"

"I guess not, no."

"Take what's offered to you, son. You had too little, less than everybody else gets, now you have more. Sounds like it evens out just right to me."

———

It was nearly dark by the time he came through his own kitchen door. Stacey and Theo were eating dinner at the kitchen table, and they looked up at him with mild surprise.

"Your plate is in the oven," Stacey said.

"Okay. Great. Thanks. I'm starved."

He opened the oven and touched the plate briefly to see how hot it was. But the oven was only on "Warm," so he could pick it up without a hot mitt. It was a ham steak with macaroni on the side, which struck Stewie as exciting. It meant that Stacey had just gotten paid.

He sat down at the table with it and dug in.

"We were surprised," Stacey said. "We thought you'd just deliver the eggs and come right home. Because of . . . you know. Things being what they are now. I even woke up around lunchtime and got a little worried and called over to Eastbridge, but they said everything was fine and that you were just there visiting."

Stewie set down his fork and spoke with his mouth rudely full of ham. It was unlike him, but he simply couldn't wait another minute to share the news. Only his hunger had delayed him this long.

"Ask me how many grandparents I have."

A few beats of silence fell.

"I don't get it," Stacey said.

"Just ask me."

"You don't have any grandparents. Or . . . I don't know. You have four but they're all gone? Oh, wait, I'm sorry. I forgot about Marilyn. You have five but they're all gone? Do they all count even though they're gone?"

"*Stacey!*" he said, unable to disguise his irritation. He shoveled another oversize piece of ham into his mouth and spoke while chewing. "You're not doing this right!"

"Well, I'm sorry, Stewie, but I guess I don't know what right is in this case."

Theo looked up from his single-pointed focus on his plate and chimed in.

"You do it like this, Stacey. Stewie. How many grandparents do you have?"

Stacey only looked confused for a moment.

"Was that right, what he just said?" she asked Stewie.

"Perfect," Stewie said.

"Theo, how did you know that?"

"Because I know Stewie. When he tells you to do something like that, you just take him very literally. Because he means it very literally."

Stacey blinked a few times and then set down her fork. She had just about cleaned her plate anyway.

"Stewie," she said. "How many grandparents do you have?"

"Jeez, it's about time. *Seven!* I have *seven* grandparents. Five grandmothers and two grandfathers."

"All adopted, I assume."

"Yeah, but I don't think that makes it any less good."

"I don't, either. I think it's great, hon. All from Eastbridge?"

"Yup."

"That's handy," Theo said. "Because that way you can visit them all in one place."

"Exactly! Only, I think I may be going over to family dinners sometimes at Marjorie's, so I can meet her other grandkids. There are *a lot.*"

"Oh, that reminds me," Stacey said. "I have a message for you from Janet at Eastbridge. She's the one I spoke to when I was worried about you earlier. She said she didn't get a chance to talk to you today because you were so busy with everybody else, but she wants you to call her or come visit. She has an idea she wants to run by you."

Stewie rolled his eyes expansively.

"Eight grandparents!" he shouted. "Six grandmothers and two grandfathers!"

"How do you know that was her idea?"

"Because that's *everybody's* idea!"

———

He was in bed but not asleep when Stacey came around and stood in his open bedroom doorway. The only light in the house was a glow that trickled down the hall from the kitchen, but it was enough to let him know that it was Stacey, and to make her look a little bit like a dream about an angel.

"You asleep?" she asked in a whisper.

"Nope. I was just lying here thinking about all those grandparents. How come you're not at work?"

"I have Sunday nights off this month. You knew that."

"Oh, that's right."

She came across the room to him and sat on the edge of his bed. He rolled onto his back so he could see her better in the darkness, and she brushed his tangled hair off his forehead with her fingers.

"I was just wondering if you're doing okay with all these changes," she said.

"You act like it's a bad thing."

"No, no. Not at all. Definitely a good thing. It's just that . . . I know you, Stewie, and I know you have trouble with new things and new people. And I just thought it might all be a little . . . overwhelming."

"I'm not sure about that last word."

"Just, like . . . too much all at once."

"Oh, that," he said. And sighed. She was still brushing his hair with her fingers, even though it had been properly removed from his forehead. It wasn't like her to be so physically affectionate with him. It felt nice. "Yeah, kind of. I was sort of just thinking about that right before you came in. It *is* an awful lot, especially for all in one day. Most of them I don't even really know all that well. I know Louise the best, but the others I just know a little. But then I thought, well . . . I'll *get* to know them. You know. When more time goes by it'll just happen, sort of all on its own. That's what happens with new people. Time goes by and then they don't feel so new anymore. It's like I was telling Marilyn about her roommate when her roommate was new. You feel like you can't settle and get used to it because it's so new, but if you can just open your eyes and look down the road and see that new things don't stay new forever, then it's not so hard."

"That's a very good way to look at the thing, Stewie. I wonder what Dr. Briggs will say about all this?"

"He'll probably say, 'Hmm. That's interesting.'"

"Interesting? Interesting how?"

"No, never mind. That's not really what he'll say. That was just kind of a joke I was telling myself. He'll say it's really good."

"Think so?"

"I know so."

"Okay, then," she said. "You get some sleep."

She kissed him on the forehead and then rose and let herself out of his room. He stopped her at the doorway, though, before she could get away.

"Hey, Stacey."

"Yeah, Stewie?"

"You think it's true that all those people asked to adopt me because they like my company?"

"I think it's indisputable."

He rolled his eyes, but of course in the dark he knew she wouldn't see.

"I have no idea what that means."

"It means yes."

"That's a pretty long, complicated way to say yes."

"Sorry. My bad. I forgot who I was talking to. It means they like you. Everybody likes you."

"Oh, no," Stewie said, and shook his head hard in the dark. "Everybody doesn't like me. Talk to the kids at school if you don't believe me."

"Okay, then. Smart people like you."

"Hmm. That's interesting."

"You can live with that, right?"

"Yeah. I guess I can. I can live with that."

"Now get some sleep," she said, and closed the door behind her.

And even though Stewie thought his mind was too full of thoughts and ideas for that, he was wrong about it in the end, and he slept.

—

He walked to school with Theo in the morning, matching his pace to his brother's uneven stride. Now and then he glanced over his shoulder for possible trouble, but there was never anybody there.

"I guess I'm just a little jealous," Theo said.

It seemed to Stewie to come out of nowhere. They hadn't been talking about anything that would make Theo jealous. They hadn't been talking much at all.

"Of what?"

"I'd like to have grandparents, too, you know."

"But you *do*, Theo! You already *do*."

"How do you figure? Are you saying you're going to share them with me?"

"I don't even *need* to share them. It's just the way it already is. They're my grandparents and you're my brother, so they're your grandparents."

He glanced over at his brother, who looked a little skeptical.

"They might not think so, though, Stewie. Because we're not all blood relations."

"Then I'll just have to explain it to them," Stewie said. "It's not even . . . I mean, there's nothing to argue. It just *is*. It's like math, except it's not math. But *like* math, sort of, because there's only one right answer. It's just . . . what's the word?"

"Genealogy?"

"I don't know that word."

"Like family tree stuff."

"Yeah. Like that. How do you feel about grandfathers?"

"I don't know. I never had one. But it sounds like a pretty good idea."

"Good. Because you've already got two. And that's just . . . what was that word again?"

"Genealogy."

"That's a hard word," Stewie said.

He glanced behind them again, but there was no one there.

"They're not back there," Theo said.

"How do you know?"

"Because they take the bus now."

"Oh," Stewie said. "Good!"

"Yeah, things are looking up all around," Theo said.

"I'm not sure I understood that sentence," Stewie said. "Does it have anything to do with looking up and around?"

"No, it just means everything is better."

"Oh," Stewie said. "Then that's good."

They walked the rest of the way without talking. Apparently, at least for the moment, nothing more needed to be said.

BOOK CLUB QUESTIONS

1. The main protagonist in the book, Stewie, takes his responsibility for caring for his grandmother's chickens and egg delivery business very seriously. When one of his favorite chickens, Mabel, is dying, Stewie tells his sister that he will stay at Mabel's side because "nobody should have to be alone at a time like that." What does this say about Stewie's values as a person? Do you think that some of his reaction to Mabel's illness comes from losing his grandmother?

2. Stewie insists that animals know when you care by your actions and your words. He believes they are much easier to connect with than others may think. Do you agree with him? Do you think his sister made the right decision letting him stay home from school to care for Mabel?

3. In an effort to comfort Stewie after Mabel's death, Marilyn makes the effort to visit Stewie for the first time. She tells him, "It's always 'something is lost, but something else is gained.'" What are some examples in the story that show this to be true?

4. The book deals in a sensitive way with the many layers and stages of grief. The author explores the concepts of deciding when the time is right to move on, and that

experiencing grief is not a straight line. How do Stewie and Marilyn differ in the way they experience grief?

5. Marilyn and Stewie have a very complicated yet deeply rooted relationship. How does their friendship ultimately help them get through difficult times?

6. When Stewie hopes to teach Elsie to fly, he soon comes to realize, to his disappointment, that it's inhumane and not fair to expect Elsie to do something she's not built to do. Why do you think he worked so hard to help Elsie feel that she is not to blame?

7. Stewie's sister worries that he feels responsible for fixing everyone around him. What are some of Stewie's biggest challenges he has to face to overcome this issue?

8. One of the many things Stewie takes away from his counseling sessions is that there are no wrong feelings. What do you think his counselor meant by this, and do you agree? Why do you think people tend to bury their emotions, and how does Stewie come to realize that may not be best?

9. A large part of Stewie's inner struggle and anger comes from the fact that he never got to say goodbye to his grandmother. Dr. Briggs tells Stewie that "anger is not without its purpose." He is trying to give Stewie a compass to help him find his own way. What are some of the main insights and healings that Stewie draws from these sessions?

10. After Marilyn's death, Stewie becomes despondent about starting to care deeply about people again when they're just going to die. He weighs out the concept that either you have no one at all in your life, or you have people you care about but risk losing. How does he come to resolve this dilemma and decide how to move forward?

ABOUT THE AUTHOR

Catherine Ryan Hyde is the *New York Times, Wall Street Journal,* and #1 Amazon Charts bestselling author of more than forty published and forthcoming books. An avid traveler, equestrian, and amateur photographer, she shares her astrophotography with readers on her website.

Her novel *Pay It Forward* was adapted into a major motion picture, chosen by the American Library Association (ALA) for its Best Books for Young Adults list, and translated into more than twenty-three languages for distribution in over thirty countries. Both *Becoming Chloe* and *Jumpstart the World* were included on the ALA's Rainbow list, and *Jumpstart the World* was a finalist for two Lambda Literary Awards. *Where We Belong* won two Rainbow Awards in 2013, and *The Language of Hoofbeats* won a Rainbow Award in 2015.

More than fifty of her short stories have been published in the *Antioch Review, Michigan Quarterly Review, Virginia Quarterly Review, Ploughshares, Glimmer Train,* and many other journals; in the anthologies *Santa Barbara Stories* and *California Shorts*; and in the bestselling anthology *Dog Is My Copilot.* Her stories have been honored by the Raymond Carver Short Story Contest and the Tobias Wolff Award and have been nominated for Best American Short Stories, the O. Henry

Award, and the Pushcart Prize. Three have been cited in the annual *Best American Short Stories* anthology.

She is founder and former president (2000–2009) of the Pay It Forward Foundation. As a professional public speaker, she has addressed the National Conference on Education, twice spoken at Cornell University, met with AmeriCorps members at the White House, and shared a dais with Bill Clinton.

For more information, please visit the author at www.catherineryanhyde.com.